Another Wolf's Mate

REBECCA PRATT

Another Wolf's Mate

Copyright © 2019 Rebecca Pratt

Cover credit to Miblart.

Editing by Lindsey - Liji Editing

Formatting by Rik – Wild Seas Formatting

ISBN: 978-0-6452207-4-2

To my army

PROLOGUE

In the werewolf world, from the moment you are born you are given a mate. One soul that is to be tied to yours for eternity.

Decided by the Moon Goddess herself, these unions are set in stone. The thought of a perfect match—your very own soul mate——is the stuff of dreams. To have a person created just for you and you for them.

My mind lately has been doubting the Moon Goddess' choice for me. I haven't met my mate yet. Although the thought has crossed my mind that she may have gotten it wrong for me. You see, my heart belongs to someone already. He is not my fated mate, but he is my best friend.

Cody and I have known each other since birth. Our mothers are best friends. We were born just three days apart. Cody is older than me, and he never lets me forget it either. Our lives have been entwined for a reason, I just know it.

Sunshine is glowing through my window, warming my bed. I lay here, pondering why mates are such an important thing. I wonder how many people decide to go against the Moon Goddess and choose their own destiny. Cody and I have spent almost every moment of our lives together. When I say he is my best friend, I truly mean it. We are inseparable. Others in the pack frown upon our relationship. But if I'm honest, I couldn't care less. He knows me like the back of his hand, and I know him just as well.

"Raven," I hear my mother calling me from downstairs. My Bambi-brown eyes lift and look over to my bedroom door, expecting to see my mother at any moment.

My body is heavy with all of the emotions and feelings that I have been holding in for weeks now. Cody has no idea that I have been in love with him for a while now. In fact, I have only just really admitted it to myself.

Shifting from my stomach, I slide off my bed ever so ungracefully, pushing my mahogany brown hair behind my ear. I decide to head downstairs before Mum chooses to come up looking for me. My mum is one of the most amazing people I know, but I don't ever want to be on her bad side. She is the Luna of our pack. As all great Lunas do, she cares for everyone as if they are her own children. I generally find her in the kitchen, but as I enter, I notice she isn't there.

"Mum?" I call, waiting for a response.

"In your father's office," she chimes back. Grabbing an apple from the kitchen counter, I saunter towards the office. Peeking inside, I notice my mum sitting in a chair beside my father's desk. My dad is pacing, which can only mean something bad is happening. My father is Alpha Damon. He is a courageous and fair alpha, but I would hate to get on the bad side of him. He is known for his strength and take-no-shit attitude.

My parents are mates, and they met when they were twenty years old. This is around the age when you find your mate. They can be from within your pack or even another pack. I am currently twenty—almost twenty-one—and still I have no mate. But that's okay right now because my heart isn't calling for my mate, it's calling for my best friend.

We are surrounded by many other packs. Each pack has an alpha and a certain amount of space called a pack land.

Occasionally, alphas can become a little hot-headed and battles can break out over territory. Thankfully, we haven't had that issue in a few years and my father has won every battle so far—if one has arisen.

It is rumoured that when you find your mate, your inner wolf senses them and calls out to you. I was always so excited for that moment, until recently. My inner wolf's name is Akira. She is just like that tiny voice in the back of your mind. She has her own personality though and is very stubborn. As wolf shifters we can transform into our wolves. The transformation is swift and happens in a matter of seconds. It is like a shiver when you walk into cold winter air.

Shifting becomes second nature as you grow older. We generally shift when we are around sixteen years old, but this can vary. We communicate through—what we call—a mind link. You focus really hard on the person you wish to contact and make a connection. Our inner wolves can communicate with each other, making the use of mobile phones almost obsolete. Mind link does have limitations though. You cannot communicate with others if you are a particular distance away from them, unless you are completely mated, then you can communicate no matter how far away you are.

"Your dad is having some issues this morning," my mum mentions in a whisper, gesturing to my pacing father. "So he's going to do some training with you and Cody later."

The mere mention of Cody's name makes my heart beat faster.

"You might be going with Dad to a meeting with the Stony Valley Pack later this week," she adds, giving me a wink. "Perhaps your mate will be there…”

The word 'mate' makes me intake a sharp breath. Recently, my feelings have been getting in the way of the idea of finding my mate. I just can't help it.

I don't know what to do about my feelings towards Cody.

Since I am not training now, I decide to go to the best place I know——to think.

The lake.

CHAPTER ONE

BEST FRIENDS

I have been sitting out by the lake for hours. I came here to think. About what, I wasn't overly sure, but it's like my mind is in overdrive. I shake my head, trying to empty it of all my wild thoughts, but I can't think clearly.

The cold wind whips against my face, making my nose turn a slight shade of red.

I'm sitting with my back against a tree, my eyes scanning my surroundings. The lake is beautiful and one of the places I love to be the most. The water and the forest surrounding the area makes me feel safe.

I pick up a nearby rock, turning it over in my palm a few times. I love how soft it feels in my hand. Suddenly, a small hint of frustration comes over me and I hurl it into the water. It makes a minor splash but has hardly any effect on the waters' surface, which pisses me off even more.

I pick up another rock, and just as I am about to throw it, my senses spike, feeling a presence coming closer to me. I listen carefully. Standing up, I push myself away from the tree, the bark leaving small indents on my hands. I brush them gently against my legs. I can feel Akira become more alert. A slow smile spreads across my face at the familiar sound of my best friend approaching.

Cody and I have been friends since birth. He is one of the best people I know. He's taller than me but only by a little bit, and he's well built, which isn't surprising since his dad is the beta of our pack. He has the most gorgeous blue eyes—you know, the ones that look like an ocean.

Ohh I could swim in that ocean, I think to myself.

Within seconds, Cody had popped out from behind the bushes on my right-hand side. His wolf is large, and he has dark grey fur and soft blue eyes. I smile happily at him and relax again, sitting back against the tree.

Cody pads over towards me, taking a seat next to me. I reach out, touching his soft fur. He lets out a low sound, like a moan, and I smile. Unexpectedly, he pulls away from me, and then, as quick as lightning, he licks my face.

"Eww, gross. What have I told you about licking my face, Cody?" I scream, jumping up from the ground in disgust and rubbing my sleeve across my cheek, trying to remove his slobber.

Cody spins around excitedly with his tongue hanging out of the side of his mouth, and I know he must be laughing at me.

"You love it…" Cody mind links to me.

"I do not," I yell loudly, watching him as he retreats behind a tree to shift back into his human form. He comes back a few seconds later with a pair of shorts on and no shirt.

Looking at me, he notices I have a grumpy look on my face. He laughs loudly before grabbing me in a headlock and running his knuckles over my head. "You know you love it!" He laughs before letting me go.

I give him my best grumpy pouty face and he smiles, bringing me in for a hug.

"Why are you out here all alone?" Cody asks, picking up a rock and throwing it into the lake. I watch as the waters' surface is broken with the rock, the ripples making circles that grow larger and larger.

"Just thinking," I respond quietly, looking down at the ground.

Cody moves in front of me and places his hand lightly under my chin, lifting my face to look up at him. I look into his eyes and just stand there, mesmerized. He is so beautiful and kind, and gosh, he looks so amazing without his shirt on. I blink quickly, pushing my thoughts away.

Tears threaten at the corners of my eyes.

"Hey, tell me what's wrong?" he asks, bringing me back into his chest and holding me tightly.

I try my best to hold my tears back. I try to slow my breathing, hoping that will keep my tears at bay. I lay my head against his chest, slowly breathing in and out, just drinking in his masculine scent.

I felt so safe here. He is my rock and the one person I can tell anything to.

Until recently, I have told him every single one of my problems. My newest problem, however, I can never tell him. He will look at me differently and I know it.

How could I have let this happen?

How could I have fallen in love with my best friend?

Realising that I haven't answered him, I tilt my head to look at him. Cody looks at me questioningly. I hastily wipe a stray tear that has slowly begun to make its way down my cheek with the sleeve of my top, and I walk out of his arms.

I can't tell him how I feel, it would ruin our friendship. Just let it go.

"I feel like a run, how about you?" I ask, trying to sound far more confident than I feel. Cody stares at me with a concerned look on his face.

I was stupid to think that he wouldn't notice something was up with me, but he did very well to humour me and ran behind a nearby tree to remove his clothes before shifting into his wolf.

I remove my clothes also. I don't want to ruin these clothes like I have many times before. My mum would murder me if she had to keep buying me new clothes. I remove my top and pants, looking over my shoulder to make sure no one is watching before removing my underwear.

The transformation from human to wolf is difficult on the body. Your bones stretch and rearrange, twisting and contorting until you land on all fours. The first time I shifted was quite painful, but now, it is merely uncomfortable. It feels like a cold wind gripping your body, sending shivers up your spine. I welcome the familiar shiver that comes over my body before letting my wolf, Akira, out.

It feels good to be in my wolf form, and Akira howls excitedly. She loves being let out and she knows a run is in store. Her competitive side is outrageous and gets me into trouble a lot of the time.

Akira is beautiful. She has amber eyes and white fur with brown smudges. Most of the females in my family line have been pure white, so when I shifted for the first time and I was white with brown, many people in the pack had questioned my mum. My dad, of course, was furious over the accusations that my mother had been unfaithful and no one ever questioned Akira's colouring again.

I listen to my surroundings. My senses are heightened. I can hear the birds in the trees. The cheeky wind whispering through the leaves. My eyes focus on the wolf standing across from me.

"Are you coming or what?" Cody asks through our mind.

CHAPTER TWO

THE RACE IS ON

Running out from behind the tree, I take off through the forest like a speeding bullet. The wind in my fur feels amazing. Akira is howling; she is so excited.

"I'll race you to the pack house," I call to Cody, even though he is now in front of me.

We run for a few moments and I slowly begin to overtake Cody. *Ha, you can't beat the daughter of an Alpha.*

Not happy with the fact that he is losing, Cody lets out a slow growl. I laugh to myself and try to make my legs move faster. We round out past some trees, and I can see the pack house far in the distance. I smile to myself; I am going to win.

All of a sudden, my legs go out from underneath me and I tumble, slamming into a rock and landing on my back with a large grey wolf leaning over me. I feel pain shooting through one of my back legs. Without meaning to, I let out a howl of pain and suddenly shift back into my human form.

Cody shifts back and leans over me, trying to work out what is wrong. His face shows how worried he is, and I feel a little bad for crying. I hold my knee and silent tears roll down my cheeks. Cody moves to hold onto my knee—to keep it from moving.

His hands feel hot against my skin, which lights my whole body on fire. I squeeze my eyes shut, partially from the pain and partially because I want him to take me right here in the middle of the path.

"What's wrong, Raven?" Cody asks me in a panic. He is being ever so gentle with me. "My knee hit a rock when you tripped me," I say through gritted teeth.

The pain is unbearable, and I'm sure I have broken something.

Suddenly, I realise that not only am I naked, but Cody is too—and he's leaning over me.

I try my best to cover myself, then I realise that I'm staring. I mean, come on, how was I not meant to look at Cody's gloriously naked body when it was right in front of me? Cody—on the other hand—doesn't seem to be phased by his or my nakedness. He is too busy trying to see what damage has been done from when he purposefully knocked me down. I was beating him, and he never has been one to enjoy losing.

"I'm naked," I say shyly.

I honestly have no idea why I'm suddenly so damn shy about being naked. I'm a damn wolf for crying out loud. Plus, Cody has seen me naked numerous times during my lifetime, just like anyone else in the pack. It's just the norm when you're a wolf.

"It's okay, I'll be right back," Cody says before running off.

I sit there alone, praying that none of the other pack members come by. A few minutes later, he returns with a large T-shirt. He helps me up from the ground and passes the shirt to me before turning away so that

I can put it on.

"Bit late now," I say to myself, under my breath. The shirt comes down to—just—cover my bottom. I pull the collar up to my face and breathe in. It smells like him, and I smile.

"Okay, I'm covered," I call out.

Cody turns and smiles at me, with a smile that could melt butter. He then lifts me into his arms and carries me the rest of the way to the main pack house. My knee is already starting to heal—one of the great perks of being a wolf. It must have been dislocated to cause me so much pain, but with my accelerated healing, there is no sign of injury at all by the time we reach the pack house.

When we reach the front door, I wait for Cody to put me down, but instead, he just stands there, holding me.

"Thanks for carrying me back," I say quietly.

"You know I would never hurt you, right?" Cody says, staring down at the ground.

"I know," I say shyly, before reaching out to touch Cody's cheek. He looks into my eyes and I can see that he is hurting.

I wrap my arms around his neck and just hold him. He still hasn't put me down. We stay like that for a while before I hear a commotion coming from inside the house. We break apart and he lowers me gently to the ground, holding onto my elbows to make sure that I can stand by myself.

"Thanks again," I say, smiling up at him.

My eyes lock onto his lips and my face suddenly begins heating at my wayward thoughts of pressing my lips against his. I need to stop looking at his lips, so I decide the best idea is to look down at the ground. I realise that my feelings are getting the better of me.

I need to stop thinking about Cody this way. I have a mate out there, somewhere. *Who cares about mates?* I finally thought. I love Cody. *But what if he doesn't love you?*

Not knowing what else to say, I begin to run my hands up and down my arms in an awkward motion.

"Better get inside," I finally say after a few moments of uncomfortable silence. I look back over my shoulder after hearing a loud bang coming from inside. Oh gosh, who knows what's going on in there?

I lean in and kiss Cody's cheek gently before breaking away from him and walking inside. I quickly close the front door, and I can feel Cody watching me until he makes sure I am safely inside.

Sighing heavily, I lean against the back of the door and slowly slide down to the ground.

Exhaling, I wrap my hands around my knees and fight my tears. *Now isn't the time to cry*, I think in anger. *Like seriously, Raven, stop being so damn emotional,* I scold myself.

Little did I know, someone was watching my tears begin to flow.

CHAPTER THREE

CROSSING A LINE

My mum suddenly appears from nowhere, looking flustered and hot like she had just run a mile. Her hair is a little dishevelled and she runs her sleeve over her brow, wiping away a line of sweat.

"What on earth are you wearing?" she asks, breathing heavily. Looking at me, she places her hands on her hips, waiting for an explanation. I smile shyly and wipe away a stray tear on my sleeve before standing up and pulling the shirt down over my body as much as possible, when a blur of blonde hair runs through the middle of us.

"I'll get you, you little devil," my mum shouts, running off after my brother.

I let out a laugh. My little brother, Max, is running around the house like a wild animal. That must have been the commotion I could hear outside. He loves to play chase inside and my parents love trying to catch him.

Max is only eight, so he hasn't shifted yet. Usually, we tend to shift at sixteen years of age, so he still has time. That didn't stop him from acting like a wolf when he was playing around the house though. So many lamps, vases and photo frames have had to be replaced due to his shenanigans. I assume this is why my mother is chasing him around, she's probably trying to avoid any more destruction.

I shake my head and begin heading towards my room. I barely have one foot on the stairs when I hear my dad come running down them towards me.

"Hey, kiddo," he says, ruffling my hair. "Have you seen your brother? It's bath time and he's hiding." I laugh loudly, pointing him in the direction I just saw my mother run. He heads off in the direction, calling my brother's name.

I make it to my room and throw my sore body onto my bed. I breathe in the scent of Cody from his shirt. I slowly drift off to sleep with a Cheshire cat-sized grin on my face. Cody is such an amazing guy… his eyes, his personality, his body…

'He's not your mate,' Akira growls angrily at me before disappearing and not waiting for my response.

Sunshine abruptly bursts through my bedroom windows without warning, blinding me. I pull the covers over my face, shielding my eyes. I hear a window being opened and I feel the cool breeze flowing into my room.

"What the hell?" I yell loudly, letting out a growl.

"Don't you growl at me, Raven," my mum's voice retorts.

So, this is the reason for my rude awakening. Mum has decided it is time for me to be awake. I slowly begin pulling the covers back down, away from my face, and let my eyes adjust to the bright light that has now spread throughout my entire bedroom. As I expected, I feel the edge of my bed move as my mum sits down.

"Okay, spill," she says, looking me straight in the face.

"What?" I say, trying to act nonchalant as I climb out of bed and walk into my walk-in wardrobe. I remove Cody's shirt and stash it in the back of my wardrobe, so Mum won't find it and wash away Cody's smell.

I search around and finally pick out a dress to wear. Turning, I notice that mum has walked over to the door to my wardrobe just as I'm pulling the summer dress over my head. As the dress comes down over my face, my eyes meet my mum's, and as I predicted, she is giving me her best ever 'mum stare.'

How does she always know something is wrong? I scrunch up my nose and stare down at the ground.

"I'm not stupid, Raven, I know something's wrong. You came home with Cody's shirt and nothing else on last night, so spill," she says, walking back over to my bed and patting it, asking me to sit.

Me and my mum are super close. I tell her everything. She is a strong Luna and I absolutely adore her—even when she tries to pry into my private life. I watch her face as I walk over towards the bed. I know she's concerned; I can tell by the look on her face. I gently sit on the bed, lowering my eyes to the floor.

I honestly don't even know where to start. Wolves have mates and they generally find them around the time they turned twenty-one. I am only twenty, so it is expected that I will find my mate sometime within the next year. My biggest issue is that I know that I'm not Cody's mate, but I have still fallen in love with him. We are destined to be with our mate right from the moment we are born.

My mum looks at me expectantly.

"I..." I start, but I can't keep my tears at bay, and all of the tears that I have been holding in—suddenly—burst forward.

My mum moves closer to me and holds me in a tight hug.

"It's okay, darling, you can tell me anything," she coos in my ear.

She sits back, wiping the tears from my cheeks with her thumb. I try my best to smile at her.

"I've fallen in love… with Cody," I burst out. I can't hold it in anymore.

Way to go, Raven, don't let it out slowly, just blurt it out. It feels so good just to say it out loud, but the look on my mum's face is another thing entirely.

"No," she says loudly, standing up from the bed and moving away and to my window, shaking her head and looking down over the grounds.

Slowly, she turns back to me, looking at my tear-stained face. "No, you can't love him… he isn't your mate," she says, as if that is the only option in this situation.

I begin to cry again, and my mum moves quickly back towards me and holds me. She slowly pats my hair and rocks me from side to side.

That certainly wasn't what I thought her response would be, and it has shocked me. At first, I feel sad because I know she's right. You should only have love for your mate when you find them.

But soon, anger starts to overtake my sadness. I don't understand why my mum isn't happy that I have found someone special to me— and that I love.

Some people go their whole lives and don't find love. Feeling another surge of anger, I push away from my mum's hold and growl loudly. I stand up from the bed, moving as far away from her as possible.

"Why can't I love him?" I cry at her. She doesn't understand. I know I'm acting like a complete brat, but my feelings are my own, and no one will ever understand how I can love someone who isn't destined for me.

CHAPTER FOUR

HEARTBREAK

My mum stands, and I can tell she wants to say something. I thought for sure that—out of everyone—it would be my mum who would understand how I was feeling.

I don't want to hear it. I twist angrily and quickly shift into my wolf, tearing my clothes. Looking around my room, my eyes meet hers and I can see the hurt in them. I run and jump straight through my open bedroom window. Running across the roof, I jump down onto the back decking. It's quite high up, seeing as I was on the second floor, but I'm so angry that I didn't even notice.

I just run and run. I don't even know where I'm going until I realise I'm at the lake. I pace up and down the edge of the water, kicking large pebbles with my paws as I go.

How could she tell me who to love? I'm so angry.

I have been pacing for what feels like hours when I decide to shift back. I sigh, looking down at my naked body, realising much too late that—in my rush—I didn't bring any clothes with me. Then I remember the clothes that I left behind yesterday. It's handy to leave clothes lying around the pack lands, in case of instances like this.

I begin walking to where I left my clothes, when I suddenly stop and look around. The sun is warm and heating my bare skin. Smiling to myself, I begin walking back towards the water and slowly wade in. The sunshine has warmed the—usually—cool water. It feels so good against my skin.

I swim around a little before just floating.

"Wow, two times seeing you naked in two days," Cody calls from the banks.

I was so lost in my thoughts that I hadn't even heard him arrive. I quickly duck underneath the water so that only my head and shoulders are showing. He's seen me naked way more times than I can count.

"Perve," I answer back smartly, smiling at him.

He begins to remove his clothes, out in the open, and I turn away, embarrassed. I can hear Cody walking across the pebbles and then slowly into the water. "You can look now," he says in such a way that I can tell he has a smirk on his face.

I turn towards him. He is standing a few meters away from me, just staring at me. He makes his way slowly over to where I'm standing. I suddenly feel very small in this big lake.

When Cody reaches where I'm standing, I notice that his eyes have changed, and they have a look about them. He reaches out towards me, touching my cheek softly. I lean into his hand, accidently letting a moan escape my lips.

I look up into his eyes, embarrassed. His eyes bore into mine as he leans into me. I hold my breath as Cody gets closer to me. I don't know what he's doing, but my heart is beating a million miles an hour. Swiftly, he swishes his hand through the water and splashes me.

In shock, I fling myself backward, landing underwater. My arms and legs are flailing around, and finally, I push myself back up to the surface. I gasp for air and try to pry my wet hair away from my face.

"What the hell, Cody? I thought you were going to kiss me!" I say angrily before realising what I have said. My hands fly up to cover my mouth. *I can't believe I just said that out loud.* Embarrassed, I cover my face with both of my hands, peeking out through my fingers.

Cody had been laughing and holding onto his stomach, but now he's stopped, and his eyes snapped up to mine as soon as he heard what I said. He stares at me intently for a few moments before slowly walking closer to me. I instinctively take two steps back. Cody stops and continues to stare at me.

"You wanted me to kiss you?" Cody asks so quietly that if I didn't have wolf hearing, I wouldn't have been able to hear him.

I stare at the water that is so still now that we aren't moving. I don't know how to respond. After a few moments of silence, Cody takes another step towards me and tries to reach out to me.

I look up at him and our eyes lock.

"Yes," I say, almost inaudibly before looking back down to the water. I notice the water moving as Cody takes another step towards me, grasping onto both sides of my face. He lifts my face to look at his and begins to open his mouth as if to speak.

Oh God, this is it. This is where I learn if he feels the same way or not. My heart is beating so fast in my chest, I feel like it might actually break through my skin.

Finally, he softly replies, "But you're not my mate."

It is like all of the air has been sucked out of my body in this moment. I hastily push his hands down from my face and quickly wade as fast as I can out of the water. As soon as I am back on land, I shift into my wolf and begin to run. I can hear Cody calling my name but I don't even look back. I just need to get away from him. My heart feels like it is going to split in two.

I run for what feels like hours around the pack lands, before deciding that I should go home. I'm not really excited about being there either. I pad around to the back of the house and shift back into my human form. I quietly open the back door, hoping to sneak upstairs and avoid my parents. I make it half-way up the staircase when a soft knock comes at the front door. I just stand there, frozen. I hear one of the chairs in the dining room scrape across the floor. It is now or never. I take two steps at a time until I reach the top. Then I quickly run into my room, locking the door behind me.

I notice a cool summer breeze drifting through my room, and I see that my window is still open. I begin looking around my room for something to put on. After all the running I have done for the day, the breeze is welcome. I notice my torn dress is missing from when I shifted this morning. I pick up some shorts and a singlet from the chair next to my bed. Looking down at my naked body, I note how dirty I am from running through the underbrush and I decide to go and take a shower.

One of the great perks of being the alpha's daughter is that you get the biggest house, meaning I not only had a walk-in robe but also an ensuite bathroom all to myself. With a little brother, that is one of the things I am most thankful for.

I turn on the water in the shower and hold my hand under, waiting for the water to become warm. Stepping into the steaming water, I let it cascade down my body. It feels so good. I take deep breaths and wish that things could be different.

Of course, Cody was right. I couldn't be with him. I have a mate out there somewhere and so does he, but I just can't help the feelings that have begun to stem over our twenty years of friendship. I feel stupid. I feel hurt, but I know that I just have to let this all go.

After a while, the water begins to turn cold, so I decide to get out of the shower. I walk slowly towards my walk-in robe. Pulling at each one of my sets of pyjamas hanging on the hangers, I think to myself, *nope, nope, nope.* I finally decide to grab the shirt that I stashed in the back of my wardrobe earlier today. I know it is a bad idea but my heart is still aching and my feelings won't just disappear straight away, it will take time. Tugging Cody's shirt over my head, I lift the front up over my nose with both hands and breathe in his scent. Tears begin to spill from the corners of my eyes, and I rub the back of my hands over my them harshly, willing my tears to stop. I walk out of my wardrobe and towards my bed.

I'm so distracted by my disappointment and broken heart that I didn't notice that I'm not alone. Someone is in my bedroom.

CHAPTER FIVE

THAT KISS

I growl loudly, warning the intruder.

"It's just me," Cody announces, walking towards me from the dark corner of my bedroom, holding his hands out in front of him as if trying not to scare me.

I stare at him, wanting to run into his arms, but I still feel the sting in my heart from his earlier comment, so I stay where I am.

What he said earlier keeps replaying over and over in my mind, tormenting me.

"But you're not my mate." That's what he said to me. Even though I know it's true, it still makes my heart feel broken.

Cody walks over to me, and as he gets closer, I know that he can see that I have been crying. He grabs me by my shoulders and pulls me into a hug.

I go willingly, knowing that I want to be in his warm embrace.

"I'm so sorry," he whispers in my ear. "I didn't mean to say what I said. I was shocked that you wanted me to kiss you."

"It's okay," I say with a whimper. There is no way that I can stay mad at him. He is right after all, even though I wish he wasn't.

Why did I have to fall for him?

"It's not okay," Cody says, pushing me back and holding me at arms-length. I look up at him, his glorious eyes boring into mine. "Because I wanted to kiss you."

I try to speak but no words will come. Unexpectedly, Cody crushes his lips to mine. At first, I'm shocked, but as he kisses me, I begin to slowly move my lips against his. It feels amazing, and my whole body lights up. I push my hands into his hair and pull him even closer to me. A low moan escapes his lips as the kiss deepens.

I open my mouth just a little and Cody presses his tongue inside and begins to massage my tongue with his. *This is amazing.*

After a moment or two, Cody slowly pulls his lips away from mine. Our foreheads are still together, and our breathing is erratic.

"Wow," I say without realizing.

Cody has a cocky look on his face, and a sly smile spreads over his face. "Wow yourself," he says, quickly pecking my lips again.

I don't trust my legs, so I quickly move to my bed, sitting down. Folding my legs neatly to the side so as not to expose my underwear under the T-shirt I'm wearing, I stare up at Cody, speechless. Not that it matters, I guess he has seen me naked twice this week. When we were younger and shifted, it didn't seem to matter as much, but since these feelings have surfaced, I feel a lot more conscious of it.

"You're wearing my shirt," Cody notes, pointing at me before sitting down in front of me on my bed.

"Yeah," I say, looking down at the ground, embarrassed.

Cody places his hands softly under my chin and lifts my head to look into my eyes. I smile slightly at him.

"How long?" he asks quietly.

"How long, what?" I ask, looking at him quizzically.

"How long have you liked me?" he asks with a smile on his face.

I roll my eyes and smile, unsure of how to respond.

"I don't know," I reply. "I think it's been a while, but I've only just admitted it to myself."

Cody shifts closer to me, resting his hand on my bare leg. I look down at his hand, noticing how nice it feels against my skin. He leans in again and presses his lips softly to mine. This time, I'm ready, and I happily welcome his kiss.

Suddenly, he leans back. "I came to the front door to ask for you earlier but your Dad said you weren't home, so I shifted and went looking for you."

"I came in through the back door," I say quietly. "Actually, how did you get in here?" I ask with a surprised look on my face.

"I came in through your window," he says, smiling. "I followed your scent up here." I smile at him and a yawn escapes my mouth.

"You're tired," he says, standing. "I should go."

I sit up quickly. "Please don't go," I say, my eyes pleading with him.

Cody moves back over to my bed and lays down next to me. I lay down and he pulls me towards him. I can feel his body heat against mine and I easily drift off to sleep.

All of a sudden, I'm shocked awake to the sound of someone grabbing and shaking my door handle. "Raven," my mum calls from the hall. It's morning, and I look over my shoulder, expecting to find Cody, but he's gone and my window is closed.

Maybe I dreamt it all?

I get up to open my bedroom door before my mum knocks it down.

"Oh, you are here." She smiles at me. "I didn't hear you get in," she says, walking into my room and looking around.

"Looking for something?" I ask, walking after her tiredly.

"Oh, no, honey," she says, acting strangely. "You never lock your door, that's all," she says, smiling.

I watch as my mum walks around my room as if she's trying to search for something—or someone. She seriously must have the keenest senses. As much as I love this woman, I must admit that I'm still a little pissed off at her after yesterday. She picks up some dirty washing from my floor and walks out of the room, not even mentioning what happened yesterday.

After my mum finally leaves, I find some clothes in my wardrobe, getting dressed before heading downstairs for breakfast. Today is a training day. When I was younger, I was home-schooled for the most part. Some of the other members from the pack went to our local high school but my mum and dad decided it was safer for me to be home-schooled. Now that I am old enough, I don't attend school anymore, which leaves loads of time for training.

I like to train a few days a week to keep myself fit and healthy, and also so that I will be prepared in case of an attack from another pack or any rogues that may happen to pass through our territory. I know if it came to a war, my dad would never let me fight. He has already told me so, but he lets me train anyway.

There aren't many she-wolves that come to training. They mostly keep the homes, raise their pups and do the office work for the pack— which I think is absolutely ludicrous. Why shouldn't a female be able to defend herself? Whilst we are one of the largest packs in Australia, there are still other packs out there that love to cause trouble over land wars. Also, many rogue wolves that have been driven out of their pack because they have broken pack rules. Rogues are dangerous. They have no alpha, which means that they answer to no one.

I run to the training grounds and find a few wolves already training. Some are in human form, whilst others have shifted. I decide that today I will train in human form. I walk slowly over to the weights station and begin choosing and preparing the weights that I want to use.

"Raven," my dad calls to me as he notices me getting ready to train. I wander over to him, giving him a quick hug.

"Hey, Dad," I say, stepping back from him.

"We didn't hear you get in last night, your mother was worried," he says, raising his eyebrow at me. "Cody came by looking for you."

I know that look. It's my dad's roundabout way of asking what I was up to last night. By telling me that my mum was worried, he thinks I will just up and tell him anything.

"I went for a run," I tell him, shrugging my shoulders and walking back to the weights station.

He nods silently, but I notice a worried look flash briefly over his face. I can't help but wonder whether my mum has told him about what we talked about. Surely not, otherwise he wouldn't be so calm right now. I watch him out of the corner of my eye as I lift my weights and begin doing a round of curls. He looks over at me like he wants to say something, but he decides not to say anything and returns to his rounds of training.

I look around, noticing that Cody isn't at training. *That's strange.* He never misses training. I push the thought aside and continue with my weights.

After training, I decide to go for a walk down to the lake. When I arrive, I find Cody leaning against a tree. I stand silently and watch him for a moment. I can tell he's deep in thought, otherwise he would have noticed me coming. I watch as he throws pebbles into the lake.

His concentration breaks when I step on a twig, causing a snapping sound to fill the silence. Cody notices me and quickly pushes himself away from the tree, rushing towards me. He quickly hugs me to his chest and presses his lips against mine roughly.

He kisses me without reservations, pressing his tongue greedily into my mouth. I hungrily accept it and massage it with my own.

When we break apart, he grins at me before whispering, "Hey."

Taking my hand, Cody leads me over and we both sit down by the tree. Cody sits down first, bringing me in to lean my back against his front.

After a few minutes, Cody leans down to my ear and whispers, "You have no idea how long I've wanted to kiss you."

I smile and turn my head to the side to kiss him. So many thoughts are running through my head. "Me too." I sigh, closing my eyes and leaning back against him. His chest rises slowly each time he takes in a breath. He is my safe place.

Inside my brain a battle of wits is haunting me.

"My parents won't allow this," I say, finally pulling away. I stand and walk towards the water, thinking about my mum's reaction and wishing that it had been different. I wish that she could understand how I feel about Cody.

Cody follows behind me and wraps his arms around me. His smell of vanilla and honeycomb surrounds me. I silently wish that we could stay this way forever.

"I know," he says sadly. "I hate all this hype about mates," he says, sounding angry. He releases me and walks away from me. "Why can't we choose our own mate?" He speaks almost angrily.

I turn from the lake to watch Cody standing with his back turned to me. He has his hands resting against the tree, as if he is trying to hold himself up. I walk to him and touch his back lightly.

"We could always keep it a secret?" I say quietly, looking into his beautiful eyes.

CHAPTER SIX

THE SECRET

He stares down at me and nods happily before grabbing me. He lifts me into the air, spinning me around. I watch the smile spread across his face. He gets little crinkles next to his eyes and the most beautiful dimples. Placing my feet gently back onto the ground, he walks me backwards, quickly pushing me against the tree before kissing me passionately. When the kiss ends, I can barely breathe. I have never kissed anyone before, and it is even better than I had imagined. After sitting and talking for a while by the lake, we decide to head home for lunch.

Once we make it back to the main path, we go our separate ways. Cody kisses me quickly, his eyes scanning the immediate area. If we are going to keep our relationship a secret, we can't be caught kissing by anyone, because they would mind link my dad immediately.

I wander home, daydreaming about kissing Cody, thinking about the way his lips met mine. They were firm yet soft, and he tasted so amazing.

Akira protested constantly in the back of my mind every time I even thought about Cody, clearly unhappy with my choices, but I don't care. I am in love. She and I are destined for a mate that is nowhere to be seen right now. I'm not even sure that I want a mate. Surely, I couldn't love anyone more than I love someone I have known my entire life?

The rest of the day goes by without anything exciting happening, which is the usual around here. I'm surprised when I arrive home. I had expected to hear Max running around, destroying the house. Mum is in the lounge folding washing when I got home but I ignore her and run upstairs to my room. Dad must still be out on the training field as I didn't see him anywhere.

Later that night, I'm getting ready for bed. I have showered and put on some super cute pink pyjamas with love hearts on them. I sit down at my mirror to brush my hair, when I hear a small tap on my window. Turning sharply, I notice Cody waving at me to be let in. I quickly run to the window and open it up, helping him to climb in. Once he is upright, he quickly holds the sides of my face and kisses me deeply.

"Gosh I missed you," he says, taking a deep breath as our kiss ends. I smile coyly. "I missed you too."

Climbing into my bed, he holds me in his arms and we talk for hours about all kinds of things. I'm just so comfortable with him. He knows everything about me; my likes, my dislikes, my favourite colour, how I like my coffee and my favourite food, amongst other things. I couldn't imagine that having a mate could be any better than finding my own person to love. After a while, I begin to feel tired. We fall asleep in each other's arms. It is a restful, wonderful sleep, but the morning—as always—comes way too quickly.

Waking up abruptly to a loud banging noise, I notice that my mum has burst into my room, making the door slam against my wall. I sit up, still half asleep. "Where's the fire?" I ask, looking around. My mum smiles at me before picking up my washing and exiting my room. I slump back down onto my pillow. My God, that woman is great at waking me up. All of a sudden, I remember Cody. I look down next to me, but he's gone.

I get up and ready myself for training and run downstairs, scooping up a couple of pancakes on my way through the kitchen and shove them into my mouth before running down to the training area. I can hear my mum yelling after me for not sitting and eating, but I don't really care.

When I get to the arena, I notice that Cody is already training. He looks up at me and smiles widely. He comes over and pulls me into a hug. It doesn't last long as my dad interrupts us, telling Cody to continue his training.

"Yes, Alpha Damon," Cody replies hurriedly before heading back to his training.

"You and that boy spend too much time together," my dad's voice booms at me. "It's not right, he isn't your mate," he says dismissively before walking away with a stern look on his face.

I look away from my dad and notice that Cody has heard what my dad said. He is staring down at the ground with a sad look on his face. His eyebrows scrunch as if he is in pain. My heart screams out to him. I know my family will never understand the way that we feel about each other.

For weeks, Cody would come over at night and we would fall asleep in each other's arms. I couldn't believe how amazing it felt just to be near him. We had—so far—kept the secret going. At times, Cody would come through the front door and then pretend to leave again by saying goodbye to my parents and Max and then sneak around the back of the house and come in through my window. I was so in love, and I couldn't imagine that things could get any better than this. I woke every morning to an empty bed. Cody always left before sunrise, which was a really good thing because my mum burst into my bedroom every morning. I swear she knows something is going on, but she's never said anything, and Cody's scent is already over my bedroom—since he always comes to visit me. Today, however, no one came bursting into my room to rudely wake me.

Realising that Mum must be out for the day, I head downstairs and help myself to some cereal before heading down to training. I decide to train in my wolf form today. It is so different from training as a human. I shift before leaving home and leave my clothes out by the back patio, just in case. Sneaking inside naked is getting a bit difficult.

Training is the same old, same old. Once I am finished, I decide that I want to go for a run. I run around the very outskirts of our land before heading home. My body is definitely tired and I need a shower desperately.

Cody is waiting in my room when I get home, which surprises me. I slump down onto my bed, absolutely drained, and my legs are on fire.

"Hey," he says, staring down at me before kissing me gently.

He then throws himself down and we lay next to each other. I am tired from my run, but I know I have to have a shower. Cody leans down over me again and begins kissing me lightly, but soon, it becomes more urgent. I gasp suddenly as I feel his excitement against my leg.

He pulls away and stands up from the bed. "I'm sorry," he says, looking down at the ground. I sit up on my bed and smile to myself.

I made him excited... Me!

Akira isn't very happy with me. *"It's not right, he's not our mate."* I push her thoughts aside and stand up from the bed, walking over to Cody.

I grab his shoulders and turn him around to face me. He looks deep into my eyes. "I... I haven't done anything like that," I say shyly, looking anywhere but his face.

Cody lifts my chin. "I know, me neither."

I wrap my arms around his neck and pull him in to kiss me.

So many thoughts begin racing through my head. Am I ready to take the next step? Perhaps this is a bad idea? My body wants him, but my wolf is strongly insisting against it.

CHAPTER SEVEN

WILL YOU?

Looking into my eyes, Cody sighs, "I will wait until you are ready, Raven," Cody says softly before pressing a gentle kiss on my forehead. We have been seeing each other for seven weeks now—in secret—both here at night and during the day at the lake. My parents seem none the wiser. I'm not sure that I'm ready to take the next step in our relationship yet, but I know that I am so happy with Cody. I wouldn't ever want my mate if he did show up. Cody is my destiny now.

We lay in bed, watching a movie. Before I know it, my bedroom door swings open, loudly. Keeping my eyes closed, my hands slowly move over the smooth cotton sheets to the other side of the bed. Feeling it is cold, I know Cody has left already. He always manages to sneak out without me noticing.

"Mum says to come downstairs," comes a small voice from the door. My eyes open lazily and I see Max standing in my bedroom doorway. I watch him roll his eyes before walking off. Getting up, I slip into my dressing gown before wandering down the stairs. Mum is waiting for me at the kitchen table. My eyes search the table and I note that no one else is around and that she has made me breakfast.

"Sit," she says in a demanding tone. Wide eyed, I sit down, a million thoughts rushing through my head. *Does she know?*

"Raven, your father spoke with me about how much time you're spending with Cody…" She sighs, placing her hand gently on the table and pushing the plate of toast towards me.

"So? He's my best friend." I shrug, taking a bite out of the warm strawberry jam toast in my hand.

"We think you need to branch out and meet up with a few other friends, you know, girlfriends," she says pointedly.

"I'll see," I answer, standing and turning to walk away from the table, leaving the food she has made—mostly—untouched.

"Don't think that I don't know that he sneaks back in through your window at night, Raven," she calls. I turn back to her, shocked. I thought that I had been getting away with it. But apparently, I was so very wrong about that. "You are lucky your dad is so busy that he hasn't noticed. Stop it now before people get hurt."

I walk away, rubbing my temples. I decide not to say anything back and I make my way back into my bedroom. Showering and getting dressed, I decide to head out for a walk.

"Girls don't like me," I speak out loud to myself. They never have. Being the alpha's daughter—as well as being home schooled—pretty much makes it impossible to make friends. I have Cody and he has me. I never even tried to mix with any other friendship groups. They were all scared of what my dad would do if we had a disagreement. Being the children of the alpha and beta makes us outsiders from the rest of the pack.

"Where are you?" comes an unexpected mind link from Cody.

"Out for a walk," I reply, smiling.

"Meet me at the lake in ten minutes," comes his response. I can sense his excitement through our link before he closes it off.

It will take me ten minutes to get there if I walk fast enough. I want to rush to him and feel his strong, warm arms around me. I turn from my current course and make my way towards him. As I walk briskly, I wonder why he wants to meet. We haven't been meeting as often during the day as my father has been keeping Cody busy with tasks and training.

Cody is standing by a rug laid out by the lake, and I spot a picnic-style lunch. Tilting my head to the side, I smile warmly. Cody looks up from what he's doing, finally spotting me. Running to him, I launch myself into his embrace and push my lips against his. My speed and pressure knock Cody from his feet, sending him backwards. We land on the ground roughly, chest to chest, our lips inches apart and I look down into his eyes, worried that I hurt him. We stare at each other, our eyes speaking volumes about how much love we share. Cody reaches up, brushing my hair behind my ear. I watch as his hand skims the side of my cheek and I close my eyes, enjoying his touch.

"I've made you a picnic," he says shyly. I finally sit up and push myself up into a sitting position.

"This looks beautiful." I sigh, looking around at the beautiful scene in front of me. He has set up a beautiful plaid blanket with navy blue and emerald-green woven strands that make an intricate pattern. A basket sits, overflowing with luscious looking fruits, dips and other antipasto staples. Two tall glasses stand, like a pair of towers, both filled to the brim with bubbling liquid.

I look back up at Cody, noting that he is standing, watching me admire the beautiful date he has prepared for me. I stand and walk into Cody's arms, pressing my ear to his chest. His heart is beating quickly. Kissing my forehead, Cody grasps my hand and brings me over to sit on the blanket.

We sit and eat whilst chatting about our days. "Your dad's been keeping me so busy I haven't been able to see you very much," he says, pouting.

"My mum knows about you sneaking in at night," I quietly say, watching his face for his reaction.

"Yeah, she saw me yesterday sneaking out," he says, sounding annoyed with himself.

I shuffle myself over to him and lay between his open legs, leaning against his chest. His arms rest back behind him, holding him upright. The sun is slowly sinking lower in the sky, and I know we will have to go our separate ways soon.

I can feel Cody's warmth seeping into my back. We sit in silence, happy to just be in each other's presence.

"Raven, I need to ask you something…" Cody finally announces, a slight tinge of nervousness in his voice.

"Mmm?" I reply, not moving.

"Uh, i don't know how to say this but… Will you…" .

CHAPTER EIGHT

IT'S OFICCIAL

I turn, facing him when he seems to stop talking—as if he isn't sure what he's saying. I don't think I have ever seen him so nervous. "Ahhh, just say it, you coward."

He sighs, standing up abruptly, leaving me sitting on the mat—a little confused.

I stand and watch him cautiously.

He sees the look on my face and moves forward to grasp both of my hands.

"Will you be my girlfriend?" he asks in a strong voice, but I can see him wince as if he's waiting for me to laugh and decline him.

The silence is spreading between us. I'm still in so much shock.

"Forget I said anything, I knew it was a bad idea," he says suddenly, running his hands through his hair in frustration. He begins to collect the food and place it back into the picnic basket.

I grab his arm and watch the hurt spread across his face.

"Nothing would make me happier." I beam, smiling up at him.

His face changes as a huge smile spreads across his face. He pulls me to his chest and crushes me to him before pulling me back slightly and pressing a soft kiss on my lips.

Five weeks have gone by, and Cody hasn't been able to stay with me at night. We've been official for five weeks, but I guess, really, we've been unofficially together for just over three months now. I miss him being with me whilst I go to sleep. His warm arms make me feel so safe. We still meet when we can, stealing kisses when no one's watching.

The sexual tension between us has been growing quickly, and I am starting to think that I may actually be ready to have sex for the first time. I lay back in my bed with my hands above my head, thinking about all of the times I have felt his dick up against me when we kiss. The heat spreading down below is becoming ever so hard to ignore. My body wants him; I want him. My core begins throbbing at the thought of him invading my body with his hard dick. My hands slowly trail down from behind my head. My legs squeeze together, trying to create even the smallest amount of friction to ease my neediness. I breathe out a shaky breath as my hands trail down over my stomach. It is bare, due to my shirt riding up, and goosebumps rise on my skin against my gentle touch. I finally reach the top of my pants, when suddenly, I can hear a commotion downstairs. I let out the breath I had been holding in and decide to head down to investigate.

My dad is walking around his office—and by walking around, I mean pacing backwards and forwards in a huff. He is practically yelling down the phone, and his alpha tone scares me. I decide to leave him be. Wandering into the kitchen, I see my mum washing up some dishes. We haven't been close lately and I know that she knows Cody and I have been seeing each other behind her back. She is way too in tune with me.

"Your dad is in a right mood this morning, keep clear of him," she mumbles, not looking up at me. "Some alpha off to the far east has been making threats." She sighs, scrubbing a pot a little harder than it actually needs.

"I heard," I reply quickly before snatching the first thing I can grab from the bench. I run out the door with a slice of toast in my hand, biting into it quickly as my stomach rumbles.

I head straight over to Cody's house; I need to see him. His dad will be out conducting the training today because my dad is still at home. Knocking on the door, I take a look around to see if anyone notices I'm here. Cody opens the door and quickly whips me through his house, down the hall and into his bedroom.

"Mum and dad are out." He smiles at me before kissing me. His tongue invades my mouth hungrily. His hands slide down my waist and grasp my ass. I groan into his mouth and my body pushes against him, relishing in this feeling.

I can hear Akira trying to protest in the back of my mind, but I push her aside. We break apart, and I take a few unsteady steps backwards. Cody holds his hand out to me, and I walk slowly forward, placing my hand in his. He grasps my hand firmly, pulling me quickly against him again.

His eyes are burning into mine. I can hear his heavy breaths leave his mouth. His chest heaves. I am affecting him just as much as he is me. My mind begins racing and I pull Cody backwards to his bed. The backs of my knees hit the edge of the bed and we fall together. Cody presses himself against me and my body squirms underneath him. I can feel his dick pressing against my core. His eyes devour me, and he leans in quickly, kissing my lips with abandon. I hungrily pull at the hem of his shirt and awkwardly pull it up over his head, trying not to break our kiss for too long. His hands slide up my shirt and grasp onto the top of my bra, pulling it down sharply before palming my breasts. It feels so good, and his hands on my body make me feel like I am going to combust right then and there.

Our kissing is urgent. I trail my hands down over his stomach and towards the hem of his pants.

"Are you sure?" Cody asks, sounding breathless.

"Yes," I say breathlessly, bringing his lips back to mine.

CHAPTER NINE

MATE

He slowly moves his hand down under the hem of my pants and into my underwear. I push myself into his hand and moan into his mouth as his fingers slowly begin to circle around my needing nub.

Unexpectedly, Cody's bedroom door bangs open loudly and my dad storms in. Cody flies back off me and stands staring at my father.

"Leave. Now," my dad's alpha voice booms through the room.

Cody quickly scoops up his shirt and runs out of his own house. I hear the door shut and I wince at the loud noise it makes. My dad stands in the doorway, and I can feel the anger emanating from his body. I don't know what to say, so I stay quiet, embarrassed that my dad has just caught me about to have sex.

I mean, seriously, that has got to be the worst possible thing to ever happen to a person—other than walking in on your own parents having sex. I shudder at the thought.

"How could you, Raven? He's not your mate," my dad growls at me.

"You can't see him anymore," he declares before slamming the door shut and leaving. I throw myself down onto Cody's bed, crying for what feels like forever.

So now I am on house arrest. My mum and dad have decided that the only way to keep me from seeing Cody is to keep me locked up at home. So far, I haven't seen him in three weeks. He contacts me by mind link every single day, but it just makes me more upset. I just want to hold him. I feel so awful. It is my fault he isn't allowed to see me.

Over the coming weeks, Cody has begun to speak to me less and less, and by the fourth week, I haven't heard from him in days. I have tried to contact him, but he never answers. I miss him so much. I want to hold him in my arms, and I want to kiss his soft, full lips again.

After four weeks on house arrest, my parents finally allow me to go out for a run. I am honestly surprised that they didn't follow me, but I took the longest way to the lake, stopping every few meters to check if I was being followed. They must honestly be okay with me being out alone because after a few detours, I can tell no one is following me.

Once I reach the lake, I smell around to see if Cody is nearby. His scent is everywhere, but it is weak—meaning that he has been here previously but he isn't nearby right now. I sit down in my wolf form and sigh heavily. I guess I will just wait here and hope that he comes soon.

I lay there for a while; the sun is high in the sky by now. It must be about one in the afternoon. Still no sign of Cody. Suddenly, I hear a twig snap from the far side of the lake, and I sit up excitedly, thinking that it is Cody.

A light brown she-wolf stands there, staring back at me. When I realise it isn't anyone I know, I lower myself into an attack position and growl loudly. The other wolf lowers herself also and glares at me.

"You are trespassing, she-wolf," I say aggressively.

The she-wolf lifts her head and laughs loudly, as if mocking me.

"I'm waiting for my mate," she announces before sitting down.

I don't move from my spot; I just stand there, waiting, in case this is a trick and she is waiting for me to lower my guard.

"Who is your mate? I ask.

I wait for her answer, but none comes. Surprisingly, a wolf bounds through the bushes and runs straight towards the stranger. Cody's wolf. My eyes follow him as they both shift and he embraces the stranger, lifting her off her feet and swinging her around before placing her down and kissing her wildly.

I feel the air suck out of my lungs—and the pain—as I try to draw in a breath that is burning me from the inside out.

"I'm waiting for my mate," the stranger had said.

Cody has a mate. The thought rebounds through my mind until I shift involuntarily and fall backwards, holding my chest. The two of them notice me falling, and suddenly, Cody is by my side, leaning over me.

"Raven, are you okay?" he asks, sounding worried.

The she-wolf has followed him and is growling at me from behind.

"Mate," I say weakly, staring up into his eyes.

He casts his eyes down and then looks back at me. "I wanted to tell you," he says gently, pulling me to my feet and resting his hand on my arm to make sure I am steady enough to stand alone.

"Raven, this is Ava, my mate," he announces proudly.

I look over at Ava and notice she has beautiful blonde hair and hazel eyes. She is slim and gorgeous. My chest is burning in pain. How could this have happened? Cody wasn't meant to find his mate, and yet, here she stands in front of me. She is both striking and enchanting.

Ava begins to growl at me, and I notice it's due to Cody still touching my arm. All three of us stand naked, staring at each other.

I can't take it anymore. I shift and run as fast as I can. Cody tries calling me through mind link, but I block him out.

My heart feels like it is being pulled from my chest. I always knew this could happen but I thought we would have a few years together before it happened, and that when it did, we would reject our mates and be together. Now I know why my parents had been so keen on me going for a run, and also why Cody has been ignoring me for the last few days.

It is a while before I stop running. My chest heaves as I try to get some air into my lungs. I look around, not noticing anything familiar, which quickly makes me realise that I have run so far that I have accidently left our pack lands. I can hear howls coming at me from all different angles, and I don't know what to do. I try to turn around and head back, but I'm stopped by three wolves who are much bigger and stronger than me.

"You're trespassing, she-wolf," one of them says.

Ironic. I was just in this situation.

CHAPTER TEN

TRESSPASSING

I look up at each of the wolves. None of them are alphas, so that makes me feel a little better.

"State your name, stranger," the wolf to my left demands loudly.

Hearing his voice in my mind. I stand my ground. It was uncommon for other wolf packs to communicate via mind link with a stranger.

"I am Raven, daughter of Alpha Damon of the Silver Creek Pack," I state proudly. The three males look at each other as if asking each other what they should do. "Shift," the centre male demands.

"No way, buddy. I will be exposed and naked." I laugh.

The larger of the three males takes a step towards me. I hold my position and he laughs loudly.

"She's feisty." He smirks. "I like that."

"Let's take her to the alpha," the wolf to the left announces.

"Wait," I say, lifting one of my paws up and placing it back down. "Can't I just go back? I didn't mean to trespass."

"Sorry, Miss, but all trespassers must be taken to the alpha," the largest wolf announces. "Fine," I say, walking forwards and through the centre of them all, smiling to myself.

They all turn quickly, moving to my side. One to my left, one to my right, and one in front of me. No one speaks as we walk. It feels like forever before we reach the pack housing, and the moon is starting to come up. *My parents are so going to kill me*, I think sadly. I let out a low whimper. No one has tried to contact me since I left, so maybe they aren't worried at all.

Suddenly, I realise why no one has contacted me, and I start to panic. I am too far from the pack. No one will be able to mind link me because I am so far away. I think about being at home and then realise that is the last place that I want to be anyway.

Cody. No. I shake my head. He isn't mine anymore. I let out a quiet whimper and a tear escapes my eye and rolls down over my fur. The larger wolf—who was to my right—looks over at me and stares at me. I look up at him but he doesn't say anything. I look back down, but I can see out of the corner of my eye that he is still watching me.

After what feels like a lifetime, we reach the door to a large house. I wait, and suddenly, the front door opens and a tall, intimidating man exits the house, staring down at me with angry dark eyes that almost look black.

"Shift," he demands with his alpha tone before throwing a robe at the ground in front of my feet.

Everyone has turned around, including the alpha. I shift and quickly wrap the robe around my cold and naked body.

Everyone turns back and looks at me. "So, Raven," the Alpha says, looking at me whilst tilting his head to the side. "I am Alpha Nicholas, come inside."

I follow him inside to a seating area. A euphoric smell fills my senses. But I have no second thought as there is a large fire roaring, dancing in a huge open fireplace. I rush forward and try to warm my freezing hands. Alpha Nicholas walks away to a different area of the house but later appears and takes a seat at a nearby desk. He places some reading glasses onto his face and looks at me—over the top of his glasses—and smiles.

"So, I bet your dad will be missing you," he says with a slight angry tone to his voice. "If my son did what you did, I would be very worried."

"I was just running, and I didn't realise I had crossed into your land until it was too late," I say, looking up at him apologetically.

"No stress, child," he says, laughing now. "Your father and I are old friends."

He looks deep in thought for a moment, and I realise he must have mind linked with a member of his pack. I wonder who he has been talking to as I haven't seen any other wolves since I arrived at the house. His eyes eventually drift back over to me.

"What were you running from, child?" he asks in a calm tone.

I look down at the ground, trying to think of something to say. Alpha Nicholas clears his throat. It makes me stumble with my words, knowing that he wants an answer—and promptly.

"I fell in love with another wolf's mate," I say quickly. Tears start streaming down my face and I throw my hands up to cover myself.

Alpha Nicholas stands up from his desk and makes his way towards where I am sitting. He takes a seat on the nearby lounge and places his hand on his chin, as if he were in deep thought.

"I see," he finally replies after a few minutes.

"You fell in love with another, but you haven't yet found your mate," he says, not really asking a question but stating a fact.

I don't respond. I just continue to cry silently, nodding my head.

"I will contact your father to come and collect you tomorrow, it's far too late to collect you now," he finally states after a few moments. He seems lost in thought. I look up at the clock, noting that it is now almost midnight. The time has gone so fast since I began running. He moves to me and holds his hand out to me. I look up at him and grasp his hand.

He is a nice alpha. I'm very lucky. Usually, when you trespass into another pack's territory, you are sentenced to death. Luckily, I have picked a neighbour that is in an alliance with my father. Talk about luck.

Alpha Nicholas leads me upstairs to a luxurious room. He has a maid bring me a nightgown, and I shower. As I walk back into the large room, I pull the nightgown over my head. My nose catches the smell of food and I notice a small tray sitting on the dresser, just inside the door. Moving over to it, I find a steaming bowl of soup and some crusty bread. After eating, I silently climb into the large king bed and sleep takes me swiftly.

After a sleep filled with nightmares and horrors, a light knock on the door wakes me. I stretch out and call, "Come in," to whomever it is. After a few seconds, a maid enters and announces that my father has arrived. I jump out of bed as fast as I can and dress quickly. Moving swiftly down the stairs, I go back into the lounge where I had been the night before. Just before I reach the doorway, I can hear my dad and Alpha Nicholas talking. I stop and listen.

"It was wrong of her to cross into your land, and I am in your debt to you for not harming her," my dad's voice sounded.

"Damon, it was no issue, she was safe here. Now, if she had crossed into Rhys' land, things may have been very different," Alpha Nicholas responds in a warning-like tone.

I remember my father talking about Rhys once before. He is the Alpha that lives to the north of our pack. His land also goes alongside ours, with a small patch of unowned territory in-between. I have heard many bad stories about Alpha Rhys, and I think to myself that I am definitely lucky that I ended up here and not there. I notice that they have stopped talking, so I continue into the room.

As soon as I enter, my dad rushes over to me and grasps me in a warm enveloping hug. "Hey, Dad," I whisper into his chest as he holds me tightly.

He pulls me away from his chest, holding me at an arm's length and looks deep into my eyes. I can't tell if he is mad or just happy to see me.

"It's time to go," he says finally, looking away from me.

I thank Alpha Nicholas for all that he has done and then begin to leave with my father. We shift into our wolf forms and begin the run back home. The three wolves from the night before escort us back to the border. They don't speak for the whole run. My dad gives them a nod once we reach the edge of their territory, and then they turn to return home themselves.

Now that we are back on our own land, we slow from running. I have a million thoughts running through my head, and being back here just makes me want to bury my head and never leave the house again.

"Why didn't you tell me?" I link to my dad. I stop walking and wait for my dad to respond.

He turns back to me and looks down at the ground. He knows exactly what I am asking.

CHAPTER ELEVEN

THAT FEELING OF BETRAYAL

My dad's eyes look away. *"I knew you loved him, Raven. I didn't want to be the one to break your heart."* He can't even look at me when he says it. He straightens himself up and looks me in the eye. *"We knew this day would come, and admittedly, it happened a lot sooner than we thought, but we knew it was coming."*

Tears start forming in my eyes. My dad pads over to me and nuzzles his big head against mine.

"She was a rouge," my dad says suddenly.

My eyes snap up to meet his.

"She crossed into our land and we sent a team out to kill her, but then it turned out that she was Cody's mate. He turned on all our men to protect her. You know our laws, Raven, we cannot kill another wolves mate," my dad states, staring into my eyes.

No words come, and I stand there shocked for a few moments.

"Let's go home," he says softly before starting to walk away. I follow behind him despondently. I feel as though my essence and love for life

has been sucked from my body.

When we reach the house, I go straight to my room and take a bath. I lower myself completely into the water, and for a few seconds, there is no sound other than my own heartbeat in my ears. It makes me feel safe.

After a while, my lungs start to strain, so I come up for air and just lay there in the deliciously warm water. The water soon begins to turn cold and my body starts to turn all prune-like, so I decide to hop out.

Walking into my bedroom in just a towel, I know before he speaks that Cody is in my bedroom.

I don't speak to him, I just continue to walk into my robe and get dressed. "I'm sorry," he finally says as I walk out of the robe.

I look over at him and feel the urge to run into his arms, but I know his feelings for me are gone. When you find your mate, your whole world literally revolves around them. You can sense their feelings, hear their thoughts and feel their pain.

I honestly don't know what to say, so I just stand there, staring at him. Then suddenly, I notice something different about him.

"You mated with her," I tell him—rather than asking. I can easily smell it on him. "Of course I did," he says, looking shocked. "Ava is my mate."

I stumble backwards at his words. It is like they have pierced through me like a sharp sword.

Cody walks toward me and holds onto my arms. "I know you still love me, Raven, but you can't anymore."

I pull away from him and push him backwards.

"Stay away from me," I scream at him.

I'm hurting. He has pulled my heart from my chest and I feel so stupid that I gave it to him so willingly. I was stupid. I knew this would happen, yet I still wanted him.

Cody stands, staring at me in shock, and it's like he doesn't know what to do, so he just walks away. I throw myself onto my bed as I hear the front door close, and I cry until I can't cry any more.

I wish so many hurtful things in the next few moments of my life. Things that I would never have wanted to wish on anyone that I love. When I stop crying, I'm glad that I don't verbalize the horrible things that I had been thinking.

My life goes by in a blur for the next few months. It is the same thing over and over, like Groundhog Day. I feel numb. Everyone around me has slowly separated themselves from me. Which is totally fine by me.

My days start with breakfast, then training, then a run, and then I generally spend the rest of my day crying in my bed. I know my parents are starting to worry, but I shut them out. They don't understand. I know they are happy that Cody has found his mate, so that he won't love me anymore, but that doesn't stop me from loving him.

One day, whilst I was out on my daily run, I ran into Cody and Ava, kissing. I literally walked around a corner of one of our pack buildings and walked straight into them. Cody had Ava pinned up against the weatherboards and was kissing her ferociously. When I made contact, they pulled apart.

"What the hell, bitch?" Ava asks, pushing my shoulder. Cody doesn't say anything, he won't even look at me. I just run. I don't know what else to do.

I decide to visit the lake. I have been avoiding it at all costs, knowing that this was the place that used to be special to Cody and me. When I arrive, there are a myriad of different pack smells. *So many wolves have been here.* But the one smell that I was hoping to smell is barely there. I can tell that Cody hasn't been here in quite some time.

I have seen Cody and Ava around the pack grounds. They are all over each other. Seeing them together makes me want to be sick. I know that it has been months since they found each other but my hurt is still as real as ever. Cody hasn't even spoken to me since then, which is killing me. We had literally spoken every day of our lives, and I knew falling in love with him was such a bad idea, but I did it anyway, and now look at me.

I shift and change into a dress that I have been carrying with me. Sitting down, I lean my back up against the tree and sigh deeply. Closing my eyes briefly, I soon fall asleep. At home, my—once lovely—dreams have turned into terrifying nightmares. I barely sleep anymore.

I am shocked awake to the feeling of someone grabbing me roughly. I try to swing my arms around and kick my legs as I feel them pull a bag over my face. I try to shift but before I can, something hard strikes me over the head and I black out.

CHAPTER TWELVE

KIDNAPPED

I open my eyes but quickly close them again. My head feels like it is going to explode. I touch my hand to my forehead. It feels wet and crusty. Pulling my hand away, I can smell blood. My blood. Then I connect the blood and my headache. Someone knocked me out. I squint, looking around, trying to see where I am. I'm in an unfamiliar room. Slowly, my eyes adjust and I can open them fully, and that's when I realize that I'm not in just any old room... I'm in a prison cell.

The bed is hard, and the room is dirty. I sit up slowly and my head begins to spin. "Hello?" I call quietly. My voice echoes around the room.

Suddenly, someone moves into my view and stares down at me.

"Call the alpha," he demands. I realize that he has said it to someone who is out of sight.

I sniff and soon realize that I have to be in someone else's territory as none of the smells are familiar to me. I don't even know the man who is stood in front of me.

After a few moments, I hear a small commotion coming from—

what I assume—is down a long hallway of cells. A man opens the door to the cell I'm in and another man steps in. He stares down at me with deep eyes. I pull myself into a ball on the bed. I can tell right away that this man is no friend of mine.

He has a sly smile on his face and watches me cower before him.

"I am Alpha Rhys," he announces piercingly.

I stare up at him, realizing my worst nightmare is coming true, right at this very moment. I have been stolen by another pack, and not just any random pack, but one that I know will hurt me.

"You are Raven," he tells me. "Daughter of Alpha Damon," he sneers, taking a step towards me.

I don't know what to say, so I decide it would be best if I don't respond. Instead, I move further onto the bed and try my best to get myself right against the wall. Alpha Rhys stalks towards me, like a lion on his prey before sitting down on the bed.

"Your pack stole one of our females, so I have decided to steal one back," he announces, sounding proud of himself.

I stare up at him, shocked. I haven't heard anything about a stolen female. It doesn't really surprise me, as I haven't really been interested in anything to do with the pack since Cody has found his mate. I haven't spoken to anyone for weeks now.

"I don't know what you're talking about," I say quickly, looking him straight in the face.

"Her name is Ava," he says back, smirking at me.

My wolf lets out an involuntary growl, low in my throat.

Alpha Rhys sits up a little straighter and hearing my growl means that he knows I know about Ava.

He smiles cunningly at me before reaching over and stroking the backs of his cold, unwanted hands up my leg. I try to push his hand away but he moves quickly, using his forearm to push against my throat, shoving my head against the brick wall of the cell.

"I will touch you whenever and wherever I feel like, got it?" he spits at me whilst slowly sliding his hand up my leg and towards my groin.

Akira growls loudly and I pull away from his touch as best as I can, considering I'm trapped beneath his forearm. He releases me suddenly before bringing the back of his hand down across my face in a hard slap. I fall sideways onto the bed, nursing my face with both hands.

I hold onto my face, just waiting for him to try something else. I feel him move away from the bed, hearing the door to the cell open and close again. I overhear voices but I can't hear what they are saying. Tears begin to well up in my eyes. I do my best to hold them at bay as I don't want to appear as a weakling, but with everything that has happened today, all I can do is cry.

I curl myself up into a ball and cry until I fall asleep. There is no sense of time down here in this cell. I have no windows, and I can't seem to find a clock anywhere. I feel like I have been gone for at least a full day. I wish my mind link would work, but again, I am too far from my pack to get anything through.

Food had been brought into my cell earlier, but I refuse to eat it. I don't know if it has been poisoned. I give it a sniff but I don't trust it, so I shove it away. The guards change regularly but never speak to me. I try to check each one for a watch, but so far I haven't been able to see anything.

The alpha doesn't return for what felt like a few days, perhaps three or four. I haven't eaten and I am beginning to feel weak. I decide to try some food the next time it is brought for me. If I am going to try and stand up against Alpha Rhys and his unwanted advances, I will need my strength.

The food tastes so good when I finally decide to eat, and it isn't poison. After a few days, I have finally worked out that I am brought one meal each day, so I begin to use this as my clock. I use one of the utensils from my meal each day to make a small mark on the floor near my bed. So far, I have counted twelve days that have gone past. I have been missing for over two weeks, surely someone will be looking for me.

Laying on the bed, I suddenly hear the door to my cell open. Sitting up, I notice Alpha Rhys advance towards me. He places his hand roughly against my throat and pushes me down until I am lying flat on the bed. I struggle against him, but it is useless. He is far too strong for me. He then lowers himself over me and pins my legs down under his weight. Realizing what he is going to do, I try my best to scream and buck him off me.

He presses his crotch down onto me and I can feel his hardness against my private area. He grabs at my breasts roughly and squeezes them hard. I squeeze my eyes shut as hard as I can, not seeing him move closer but feeling his harsh breath on my face. Suddenly, he presses his lips against mine unforgivingly and kisses me. He begins to grind himself against me, hard, and it hurts. I can't move, so I close my eyes and scream internally. This shouldn't be happening. I'm still a virgin. He is being brutally rough with me and I can't do a thing to stop him.

He pushes his tongue into my mouth. I try to stay as still and emotionless as possible. I try to shut my mind down so that I feel nothing. Soon, his hand wanders down and pulls the edge of my dress up as he goes for my underwear. I try my hardest to buck him off me again. He removes his hands and again brings the back of his hand down over my face. It stings and I wince, trying to move away.

All at once, his movements cease and he jumps up from the bed and flies out of the cell, slamming the door closed. I can hear yelling and wolves growling. Standing, I quickly move over towards the bars of my cell. I can't see anything but I try my hardest to hear anything that I can.

"Raven?" my dad's worried voice calls through mind-link.

CHAPTER THIRTEEN

THE RESCUE

I slide to the ground. *"Dad,"* I call back as I fall to the ground, relief washing over me like a wave on a surf beach.

I can hear wolves howling, the sound growing louder the closer my pack moves into Alpha Rhys' territory. The sounds of a fierce battle can be heard. I stand behind the bars, helpless. The guards left the minute they heard what was happening above ground. I look around for anything that I can use to possibly unlock the cell door.

A piercing howl rips through the air and I can tell something has happened. I call for help until my throat hurts. I slowly sink to the ground. No one can hear me, and my dad hasn't called out to me again.

Suddenly, I hear footsteps coming closer to my cell. Looking up from the ground, my eyes meet Cody's. His face looks sad and shocked to see me this way. He looks down at my bare legs, covered in bruises from Alpha Rhys' rough hands. I can see him breathe in deeply, as if trying to restrain his wolf from turning.

He begins looking around for something to open the cell.

Unexpectedly, a wolf enters the hallway. I can smell it before I can see it. It's grey fur is matted, and it steps forward, hackles raised, mouth dripping with saliva and blood. Cody shifts quickly, abandoning his efforts of looking for the key.

The matted wolf lunges at Cody, snapping at him, trying to catch any part of his body in its jaws. They spin around wildly, each trying to cause harm to the other. The dark wolf moves quickly and almost grabs Cody's back leg. I watch as they fight furiously, unable to do anything but stand and stare.

Cody suddenly grasps the wolf's front paw in his jaws, and I hear a cracking of bones. The wolf calls out in pain before slashing his chest angrily. I can see blood start to wet Cody's fur. I whimper softly and see Cody's eyes snap to mine, hearing me. Distracted, the wolf knocks Cody to the ground. Leaning over him, the wolf goes for Cody's throat.

"No," I yell desperately. Thankfully, right at that moment, more of my father's pack members appear and overwhelm the lone wolf. Soon, his body lays limp on the ground.

Cody shifts quickly and runs over to me, his hands holding onto both sides of my face. His eyes search mine. It's like he is silently checking over me. My eyes drop from his. My heart is screaming at me.

"I got the keys," calls one of my father's pack members.

Cody holds up a set of keys that he had been holding in his hands and begins trying to find the key that belongs to the cell I'm in. The lock clicks open. The second the door swings open, I fling myself into Cody's arms. His warmth envelops me. I gently touch the shallow cut on his chest. He winces slightly. My body feels weak. Cody is holding me up. He grasps my arm and I call out in pain. Cody looks down at the dark bruises on my arm.

"Raven, did he hurt you?" His eyes snap back up to mine and I can see him hardly controlling his wolf. Not wanting to say anything, I just close my eyes and lay my head against his chest.

"Please get me out of here," I beg.

He lifts me into his arms and carries me out of the hell hole that I have been held in. Once we are outside the dungeon, I notice a wolf lying dead on the ground underneath a very familiar wolf. My dad. He stands over the dead body of Alpha Rhys. My father has a large gash in his side. I am surprised to see him still standing. The wound looks quite nasty.

Nearby, I notice that Alpha Nicolas also stands, waiting. I recall the smell that I smelt the first time I met him. It smelt so nice, but I couldn't put my finger on it. My father stands proud. His body is bruised, and he has some small cuts on his back.

All of Rhys' pack have moved away and stopped fighting as soon as they realized their Alpha was dead. There are a few other bodies lying around on the ground but I don't know which pack they belong to.

Rhys' beta, Sam, steps forward, offering a hand of peace to my father, stating that he never agreed with Rhys and his ways and that the pack was now under his control. Sam is very apologetic and tells us that Rhys had used his alpha control on everyone, so that they couldn't refuse him even if they wanted to.

I don't know what my father is going to do, but he slowly places his hand in Sam's. He seems a little sceptical but agrees that as long as no harm comes in the future to any member of our pack or Nicholas' pack. Sam agrees and then my father announces that everyone is to leave and head home.

Cody carries me over to my father, where he sets me down on the ground. My father's wolf stares into my eyes and I can tell he is relieved to see me, but I can also see the hurt in his eyes. My face must look a mess and I haven't showered in over two weeks. I'm sure that I look absolutely horrible.

Cody decides that I am too weak to walk or run home in wolf form. I'm not sure that I even have enough strength to shift. He carries me the entire way back to our pack lands before setting me down by the lake. My father stops and stares at me.

"I'm fine," I say, trying to reassure him.

He huffs at me and slowly begins to walk away. Everyone that had come along to fight against Alpha Rhys' pack have all returned home. Either nursing wounds or to brag about their win and rescuing me.

I wade slowly into the water, fully dressed, and submerge myself. It is so nice to be in the cool water. There are no sounds other than the sound of my own beating heart. Feeling like I have been down forever, my lungs start screaming for air. For just a minute, I think about giving into the darkness at the bottom of the lake. The one person in the whole entire world that I want doesn't want me in return. My survival kicks in and I rush to the surface, coming up for air. As my face hits the cold air, shivers cover my entire body. Tears begin flowing from my eyes, and sobs wrack my body.

Cody has been standing on the bank, watching me carefully. As soon as he notices I'm crying, he quickly walks to me and pulls me to his chest. I don't embrace him, I let my hands fall to my sides and just stand there, numb.

Cody doesn't seem to mind. We both just stand there in the water and he holds me whilst I cry. I begin shivering uncontrollably. Turning out of Cody's embrace, I begin to walk out of the water. He follows me, passing me a towel. I look up at him with an enquiring look on my face.

"I had someone bring them down for us," he responds to my unasked question.

I pull the towel around my shoulders and sit down, leaning against the tree. Cody places himself next to me and pulls me into his lap. I lean my head on his shoulder and sigh loudly. The silence between us is absolutely deafening.

"You know I still love you, right?" Cody asks after a few minutes. I look up at him, shocked. Our eyes meet and my eyes wander to Cody's lips and snap back to his eyes. Cody begins looking from my eyes to my lips and back again, like he's conflicted. I lean in and kiss him lightly. It isn't the same anymore. His love for me now is completely different since he has found his mate.

"What the fuck are you doing?" I hear a female voice yelling. Both Cody and I turn suddenly to see Ava storming towards us. Ava pulls me from Cody's lap by my hair. I scream and pull myself free.

"What the hell?" I scream at her, holding onto my hair, hoping that she hasn't removed a huge patch.

Cody looks shocked but also like he doesn't know what to do. He has been caught red handed being kissed by another female, by his mate no less.

"Why were you kissing my mate?" Ava spits at me like a poisonous snake.

"It was a thankyou kiss; he just saved my life from your rapist alpha. Rhys said he did this to me because *you* ran away, this is all your fault," I scream back at her. Even though that is only half the reason I kissed him.

I needed to see if my feelings were still there, but they weren't, and I could tell his weren't either.

She stands there, shocked, and Cody rounds in front of me saying, "What?"

I look down at the ground before saying, "Alpha Rhys said that Ava used to be in his pack but she ran away. He said we stole her, so that's why he stole and tortured me," I add with a sob, remembering the past two horrible weeks.

Cody looks up at Ava, staring at her for what felt like the longest time.

"You lied to me," he says before shifting into his wolf and running away through the woods, howling loudly as he goes.

"This is all your fault," Ava says, pushing me harshly before running off after Cody.

CHAPTER FOURTEEN

IT'S PARTY TIME

I have no idea how any of this is my fault, but I know Cody well, and I know he absolutely hates being lied to. I let them go and walk home, wrapped in my towel. Once inside, I'm grabbed swiftly by a very short person. Looking down, I found Max. I smile and ruffle his hair. "Hey, little man, what have you been up to?"

"I missed you," he says, wrapping his arms around my waist. I smile softly. "I missed you too, buddy."

Out of nowhere, I'm suddenly clobbered by one very hysterical Mother.

"What happened? Why didn't you come straight home? Why are you all wet? Oh, look at your poor face. Oh, my baby, I'm so sorry, are you okay?" she says in a single breath.

I just smile and hug her. Max is squished in-between us and begins complaining. Squeezing out from between us, he runs off. I hold onto my mum and rest my face into the crook of her neck. Soon, tears begin to spill down my cheeks. Mum doesn't move, she just holds me.

After my return to the pack, I've pretty much been house-bound. I don't really want to go outside, except for training and the occasional run. I have barely seen Cody or Ava. As much as I know it was partially my fault for their current issues, I miss Cody's friendship.

I miss the times where we would sit and talk for hours, and all the amazing times at the lake. But I know things will never be the same. Ava hates me being anywhere near Cody.

I even missed his twenty-first birthday party. I sent over a small gift and a card, but that night I came home from shopping and found them on my bed unopened. I decide it is best for my mental state to just let it go, so I put the gift and card away and go on with my life.

Before I know it, it is my birthday. I'm turning twenty-one. My mum and dad have planned a huge party and have even invited Alpha Nicholas' pack to join us. I went shopping a few days before with my mum to find a beautiful party dress. I had wandered into a total of ten different stores, trying on a multitude of different dresses. Nothing was feeling right and I began to feel a little disheartened. We tried the eleventh shop and right there, in the window, was the most exquisite gown I had ever seen. It was love at first sight. I pulled my mum into the store and excitedly asked the sales lady if I could try the dress on.

It was a beautiful deep blue silk dress that clung tight to my hips and sat low over my chest. It hugged me in all the right places and flowed effortlessly to the floor in a trumpet style. It also had some lovely gathering near my left hip area.

My mum and dad were seriously going all out. I had always wanted my twenty-first birthday to be magical, and I felt like I had been planning it my whole life. I knew exactly what I wanted and how I wanted it. We decided to do it on our back patio. I wanted festoon lights all around. It was going to look amazing.

Today is my birthday, and I can hear everyone busily setting up downstairs. I begin doing my hair and makeup. With the hairbrush in my hand, I walk over to my window and look down to see how everything is going. It looks beautiful. I can't wait to see all of the lights lit up when it gets dark out. There are lanterns all around the edge of the pool, and they look amazing. I can see in the distance that Dad has even put up some twinkle lights on the trees in the grassed area that flows from the back side of the patio, next to the pool. They look absolutely beautiful. *This is going to be an amazing night,* I think to myself before returning to the mirror to complete my hair and makeup.

As I begin to finish off my hair, I hear my mum come into my room. She smiles at me and walks behind me, placing her hands on my shoulders. "It's go time, baby girl," she says quietly. I can tell she is trying not to cry.

"I just need to put my dress on," I reply, standing and walking into my closet. I place my dress on and my mum helps me to zip it up. I have my hair in a low ponytail with loose parts around my face. My makeup is natural but still flawless. I feel so beautiful.

Once my dress is on, I walk over to my full-size mirror and stand in front of it. I take a deep breath in and breathe it out slowly. Today, I am becoming an adult. I hope that now I am twenty-one that I will find my mate. I turn to face my mum who is silently crying behind me.

"You… look… so… beautiful," she says between sobs. I smile at her and hold my hand out to her. She grasps my hand, and we walk together downstairs. Guests have already started to arrive and I soon lose my mum as she gets grabbed by some of her friends to discuss how wonderful everything looks. I smile and continue walking, and I am about to step out onto the back patio when I feel hands grab my waist and pull me off to the side. It all happens so quickly, I didn't even get to see who had grabbed me.

Finally, we come to a stop just near the laundry, in a little hidden alcove, and I look up at who is holding me. "Cody?" I say, holding my hand up against his chest. "What on earth are you doing?" I ask, realizing he is far too close. I push him away from me.

"I need you to know something," he finally says, looking down at the floor. I'm not sure that I want to be alone with him right now, so I huff and turn to walk away. He grabs my wrist and turns me back around roughly. "Don't walk away from me, you have to listen," he says hastily. I look from my wrist where he is holding me and up to his eyes. I can tell something is wrong.

"What is it?" I say softly.

Cody reaches up, holding the bridge of his nose, as if what he is trying to say is really hard. He begins to speak, when my dad suddenly appears.

"What's happening here?" he asks in a booming voice, looking at Cody's hand holding my wrist. Cody cowers and keeps his eyes to the floor. "Speak," my father's voice thunders.

"I was coming to warn Raven, Alpha Damon," Cody finally says.

"Warn her about what?" my father says with a worried look on his face.

"I overheard Ava last night on the phone. She thought I was sleeping," he adds. "She was sent here as a spy," he says, almost choking on his words. "She didn't know she would find her mate here. It turns out that Alpha Rhys had some followers that agreed with the way he did things," he finally gets out with a disgusted look on his face. "They have turned rogue and will be coming to attack the pack. They know Raven is your daughter, and they want you to pay for killing their alpha. They are coming to get Raven," he says despondently.

CHAPTER FIFTEEN

THE PARTY MUST GO ON

My hands fly up to my mouth as I let out a choking, shocked noise. My father seems to grow a whole foot taller before mind linking some members of the pack to keep an eye out for any unwanted guests. My dad then turns to me and Cody and announces that my birthday isn't going to be ruined and that everything will go ahead as planned. He then walks away in a hurry, leaving us alone.

"Raven, I rejected her," Cody says, turning to me and grasping both of my hands. "We can be together now."

I don't know what to say. I'm being hunted by a pack of angry rogues, Cody has rejected his mate and is now single again, and I'm meant to go out and have fun at my birthday party.

I silently pull away from Cody and begin walking back to my bedroom. He makes no move to follow me. Suddenly, I bump into my mum. "Where are you going, darling? The party is that way," she says, pointing in the opposite direction to where I'm walking.

"Ask Dad," is all I manage to say.

My mum grabs my hand and pats the top of it lightly. "I know, darling, but you can't let this ruin your night, sweetheart. We are all well protected and Alpha Nicholas has most of his pack here also. They would be very stupid to attack tonight."

I sigh, looking down at the floor and then back up at my mum. "Okay, I'm just going to re-check my makeup and freshen up and I'll be right back down," I say with the best smile I can put on. Mum pats the back of my hand again and walks out to the patio, smiling widely at my guests.

I quickly make my way back upstairs to my room and sit down at my vanity. My makeup is still flawless but I pop on a little bit more lip gloss before heading to the toilet. After about ten minutes, I decide that I shouldn't wait anymore, and I listen to my mum's advice. Standing, I make my way downstairs. I can hear everyone talking. The music playing loudly outside calls me. I take a deep breath and step outside onto the patio.

I am instantly greeted by many members of the pack, who all congratulate me and want to give me a hug. After what feels like a million hugs, I finally make it to the bar section where I order myself a drink. I think I deserve one after everything that went down earlier. I turn from the bar with the drink in my hand and watch everyone. The dance floor is full of people boogying away to some awesome eighties music. Everyone looks like they are having a blast.

My dad finds me soon after and hugs me tightly. "You look beautiful," he says proudly. "Is this what you imagined?"

I looked up at him, smiling. "It's better."

My dad lets a huge smile fill his face before kissing my forehead and walking away into the crowd. I slowly finish off my drink and place the empty glass onto a tray of a waiter that is walking by and then I make my way to the dance floor. More and more guests arrive over the next half an hour. There has to be close to three hundred people. The yard and patio are filling up quickly.

I dance with my mum for a while before I can hear someone calling my name. I turn to look around and notice that my dad is calling me over to him. I laugh at my mum's dance moves, kissing her on the cheek and waving to her as I begin to walk over to my dad. As I get closer, I notice that he is talking with Alpha Nicholas.

I smile to myself and continue through the crowd. Finally, I make it over to them and hug my dad tightly. I shake Alpha Nicholas' hand and he bends down politely, kissing my hand.

"Happy Birthday, Raven," Alpha Nicholas says as he stands back up straight. "I was going to introduce you to my son," he says, turning to find no one behind him. "Oh, there he is coming back from the bar," he says, looking around.

I nod politely, looking around. Suddenly, my eyes connect with a really handsome young man who is walking towards us. I feel a pull inside my body like I have never felt before. Akira is scratching at me to come forward, but I push her back. Her voice rings out through my head.

"Mate," she whimpers.

"Raven, this is my son, Chase," Nicholas announces as his son reaches his side.

"Mate," Chase says breathlessly as he reaches me.

My dad and Nicholas look at each other, shocked. Soon, they begin slapping each other's shoulders and smiling wildly. "This is fantastic, Raven," my dad says proudly before dragging Alpha Nicholas off to tell everyone.

I'm still unsure of what just happened, and I stand there, stunned. Chase reaches his hands out and grasps mine.

"Hello, Raven," he says smoothly. I feel as if I may just melt right here. Everything about him is amazing. The sound of his voice, his touch, and just being near him. He lights me up from inside. No words come out of my mouth, but I manage to smile shyly.

Suddenly, I'm nearly knocked sideways as my mum hugs me excitedly. "Oh, my baby, you found your mate," she squeals before letting me go. She grabs Chase and hugs him eagerly. Chase looks a little shocked, but he smiles down at me, holding onto my mum. It seems like forever that my mum has been hugging Chase. My dad has returned and asks her to actually let him go. *How embarrassing, Mum.* I roll my eyes.

"Let's leave these two to get better acquainted," my dad says, winking at me before steering my overly excited mother away and through the crowd.

I throw my hands up to my face in embarrassment as Chase moves closer to me. "Well, they seem fun," he says with a slight laugh. He holds his hand out to me. "Would you like to go for a walk?"

Nodding, I place my hand gently into his and immediately my whole body is surrounded by tingles. I gasp and my eyes shoot up to meet his. He smiles, and I know he can feel it too.

CHAPTER SIXTEEN

LIKE LIGHTNING

We wander off into a quieter zone of the garden and sit on a stone park bench. When we sit down our hands separate. Although, I don't want them to be. I sit quietly, listening to my own deep breaths. I am super nervous but so happy all at the same time.

I steal a glance and notice his incredibly carved jaw. His skin has a glow about it. He is just perfect.

His eyes turn to look deeply into mine and my breath catches in my throat. His eyes are grey with specks of gold scattered through them. I take in a breath, realizing my lungs are screaming at me.

"So, how old are you?" I finally ask when the silence is getting to be too much to handle. "I'm twenty-one, just like you," he answers, smiling.

He slowly reaches out and grasps my hand again, and I gladly give it to him. It doesn't even feel weird just sitting with him. After all, we have only just met. Soon, I feel him close the gap between us as he slides closer to me. I lay my head on his shoulder and I hear a satisfied noise come from deep within his throat. I can tell Akira is very excited as she is screaming, "*Mate,*" in my head over and over again.

"I'm so happy I found you," Chase finally says, breaking our silence. I turn my face up to look into his eyes and melt slowly into his arms. If he weren't holding me, I swear I would have fallen off the seat.

"I can't wait to get you back to my pack and live a long and happy life together," he breathes into my hair. Hearing these words leave his mouth makes my soul sing.

When you find your mate, you move in with them almost immediately. It is tradition. My father found my mum whilst visiting another pack. Mum always told me the story of how she moved in with dad and his house was a complete shambles. I can't help but think about what Chase's house will look like.

The connection between us is indescribable. The pull is so strong. It's like Chase just became my favourite person in the whole entire world. I watch his eyes move from mine, down to my lips and back again. I can tell he wants to kiss me, and boy do I want him to. I tilt my chin slightly upwards, inviting his lips closer to mine. He leans down and I can feel his warm breath fan across my face. Goosebumps spread across my skin like wildfire. We are lost in each other's presence. Nothing can ruin this moment.

Unexpectedly, I feel a force pull us apart. I am thrown to the ground harshly, and when I look up, Chase is lying flat on the ground, not far from me, looking shocked. That's when my eyes follow legs upwards, and I notice Cody in his wolf form, standing in-between us.

"What are you doing, Cody?" I ask with a shocked sound to my voice.

Cody looks back at me and whimpers loudly.

Chase is already back on his feet and looking between us cautiously. His stance is solid, as if he is ready to shift right then and there.

"Shift," I demand, staring angrily at Cody.

Cody looks deeply into my eyes before shifting into his human form, standing naked between us. I try to move to Chase but Cody moves in front of me.

"You're mine," Cody says demandingly.

I stare up at him, shocked, trying not to look down at his naked body. No words come out of my mouth. I don't know what to do but I begin to laugh.

Is this guy serious?

"Raven is *my* mate!" Chase announces loudly. Being a future alpha, Chase has a certain sense of authority in his voice, and Akira purrs loudly in my mind, proud of her mate.

Cody rounds and turns from me to look at Chase. Chase doesn't look intimidated by Cody's nakedness, but I'm starting to feel a little uncomfortable standing here with them both.

Cody's body begins to shake in anger. "She belongs with me," he screams at Chase before running at him. Cody shifts back into wolf form just before he reaches Chase. I rush forward,

screaming out to Chase before stopping in my tracks as I realize Chase has shifted also. His wolf is tall and strong. He is solid black and absolutely gorgeous.

Akira is doing an incredibly loud happy dance in my mind, but I am too stressed about what is happening in front of me to be happy about seeing my mate shift for the first time.

Watching Chase move is just awe-inspiring. My body reacts to seeing my mate in his wolf form and I can feel myself becoming excited at the sight of him. I move back slightly as the boys circle each other, growling and snapping their jaws together. The sound so loud that it echoes across the garden. I don't want to get in-between them if they are to fight. That would just be stupid. Chase is a soon-to-be alpha and Cody has a beta for a father. They are both strong. Chase, of course, more so.

Cody strikes first, launching at Chase. Chase is much quicker and moves out of the way before Cody can land on him. Cody turns and strikes Chase with his front paw, pushing Chase backwards. Chase rounds back and looks at Cody with anger emanating from his body.

Cody calls out to me through mind link.

"We are supposed to be together, Raven." His voice sounds sad. I stumble backwards at his words as all of my feelings for Cody suddenly rush to the surface. I loved him, but then he found his mate and forgot all about me.

"I've found my mate now, Cody," I send back to him.

Distracted, Cody doesn't notice Chase running for him. Chase collides with him at full pace, and they both wind around each other, clawing and biting each other.

Suddenly, there comes a sound of rustling in the garden that makes each of us turn around. My father and Alpha Nicholas are standing there, looking over the scene in front of them.

"Shift," my father orders Cody. He has no choice but to shift back.

Chase shifts back and begins walking towards me. I can't help but glance at his naked body before he reaches me. His body is like nothing I have ever seen before. He is a God. I squeeze my legs together, hoping that he doesn't notice how aroused I am just looking at his amazing body. Reaching me, Chase wraps his arms protectively around my waist, shooting a growl towards Cody.

He leans into me and whispers seductively into my ear, "I can smell how much you want me." I look up at him, shocked, and hope that no one else has noticed. He has a smirk on his face, clearly proud that he has turned me on.

The sound of his voice and his warm breath on my neck doesn't make things any easier on me, and without realizing I'm doing it, I press my behind against his naked body. Chase's hands hold me tighter as I feel him growing harder behind me.

My dad's voice brings me back to the present as he demands to know what is going on.

Chase speaks up first. "He wants my mate for himself." He turns his head pointedly towards Cody.

My father's eyes become angry. Alpha Nicholas steps forward but decides to stop. Cody casts his eyes down at the ground, knowing that he doesn't stand a chance against my father, Chase, or Alpha Nicholas for that matter.

"Leave," my father orders. I watch silently as Cody walks away with his head down. He shifts into his wolf form and begins running through the woods.

I would usually feel the need to follow him, he was my best friend after all, but now that feeling has gone and I know it is because I have found my mate. Now I completely understand why Cody came to me that night to tell me that I couldn't love him anymore. Because he couldn't love me in the way that I wanted.

My dad nods at Chase and then he and Alpha Nicholas walk away, leaving Chase and myself standing in the garden, alone. I turn to face Chase and wrap my arms around his neck.

"That was so scary," I say, sounding worried.

"It's all okay now," Chase says, running the back of his hand down my cheek ever so gently. He slowly leans in and stops just before our lips meet, as if silently asking for permission to kiss me. I come in the rest of the way and our lips meet softly. The touch of his lips on mine sets off fireworks in my body. It feels like tingles are running through me from head to toe. My body heats and it is like lightning has scorched through me.

Our kiss deepens and I feel myself leaning into him and melting against his body. Suddenly, I can feel his arousal pressing into my thigh. My thoughts begin to run wild and I wish he would just take me right here in the garden.

I giggle against his lips and step back, turning around and facing away from him. I press both of my hands against my face, embarrassed at my wayward thoughts.

"I'm so sorry, Raven," he calls to me. I feel him move behind me and place his hands around my waist. "Let's go find me some clothes." I feel him smiling against my neck. It is as if he also finds the situation funny.

We can't exactly walk back through the middle of the party to get Chase some clothes, so I run back to the house to find him something to wear. I make it all the way up to my bedroom without being stopped, which is surprising. I expected everyone to stop me and congratulate me on my twenty-first birthday and finding my mate.

As soon as I set foot into my room, I can feel him there. I can smell him. His sweat and cologne is a familiar smell to me.

"What are you doing here?" I ask in an aggravated tone.

CHAPTER SEVENTEEN

MOVING ON

He stands in the dark shadows of my room, staring at me. The only light in the room comes from my walk-in wardrobe. I must have forgotten to turn the light off after leaving my room earlier. He begins to move towards me, and I take a step back. His eyes bore into mine and I can just make out the hurt expression on his face.

"We were meant to be together, Raven. I rejected my mate for you," he says, taking another small step forward.

I hold my ground; my eyes suddenly gaze over his body. He is naked. He must have come straight here after he left us in the garden. He doesn't even try to cover himself.

"We can't be together, Cody," I say sympathetically, looking down at the ground. "I never asked you to reject your mate."

I don't know what else to say. Now that I have found Chase, I don't want to be with anyone else. Just the thought of being with anyone else makes me feel sick.

Cody suddenly moves forward, grabbing me, pressing his lips to mine and pressing his tongue into my mouth without warning.

I am shocked, and I try my best to push him away from me. He holds me tightly, hurting my arms as he forces me against him. He pulls away from my mouth and suddenly pushes me down onto my bed. I look up at him, shocked. He moves towards me and leans down over the top of me.

"So, help me, Cody, if you try anything, I will never speak to you again," I scream in his face, thrashing my hands and hitting him in the chest. He leans back, sitting next to me and starts laughing.

I look up at him, shocked.

"You honestly think I would rape you?" he asks, shocked.

"You just kissed me without my permission, so, yes, I do think you would rape me," I spit back at him, sitting up and pushing him aside. I stand up from my bed and storm out of my room. I go into my parents' wardrobe and collect some pants and a shirt for Chase before heading back outside.

Cody never followed, he just sat on my bed with a shocked look on his face.

Poor Chase must think I got lost. I run back to the garden as quickly as I can and find Chase sitting on the bench, waiting for me. I pause and watch him. His body is to die for. His abs, his arms… Gosh, I am the luckiest wolf alive.

Noticing me, he moves to me, quickly grabbing onto my hands and looking me over.

"Are you okay? I sensed you were upset and that something happened," he asks, sounding worried.

"I'm fine," I reply, smiling and handing him the pants and shirt. He quickly puts them on before pulling me into a hug.

Unexpectedly, he pushes me back, holding me at arm's length.

"Why do you smell like him?" he asks, his eyes turning black.

I look up into Chase's eyes, unsure of what to say, but finally, I get out, "He was in my bedroom when I went to find you something to wear." I have no idea why I feel so bad, but I don't want to go into details as I can feel Chase becoming angrier. I run my hands down his beautifully sculpted arms and I feel him becoming calmer under my touch.

"Why does he think you're his?" Chase asks, trying to keep the anger out of his voice. I know he isn't angry with me, but with Cody for wanting me.

"You have to understand that before I found you"—I pause—"I did love Cody," I say delicately. "We both loved each other but my father forbid us to be together. My parents had me on house arrest, and during that time, Cody found his mate."

I feel him tense under my hands when I mention loving Cody. I move my hands over his skin, it is so soft and warm. He takes a deep breath and then pulls me to his chest. He kisses the top of my head and I breathe in his amazing scent.

"I've kept you from your party for long enough, let's head back," he says, grabbing my hand and pulling me gently back towards the party area.

When we arrive back at my party, it is in full swing. Everyone seems to be having a really great time, dancing, eating and drinking.

"Are you thirsty?" Chase asks.

I nod coyly, smiling at him as he walks away to get me a drink. He returns a few minutes later with a drink for me and one for himself.

We sit down by the pool and talk quietly, learning about each other. Suddenly, the music seems to become quiet and my dad's voice booms through a microphone.

"Where is our birthday girl?" he calls into the crowd and starts looking around for me.

Chase helps me up and walks with me, holding my hand up to where my dad is standing. He releases my hand, and suddenly, I feel like part of me is missing. I look back down at my empty hand and Akira lets out a small whimper.

"Won't be for long love," Chase says to me through our mind link. I look up to meet his eyes and he gives me a reassuring smile.

I step up next to my dad and smile widely out at all of my guests. My dad begins talking about how proud of me he is and how excited he is that I have found my mate. Then he mentions something that has never occurred to me.

"We always knew you were destined to become a Luna." He beams proudly.

Chase is next in line to be Alpha of his pack, which means I'm going to be a Luna, or alpha female, if you prefer.

My brain is spinning at a million miles per hour, and I don't even notice my dad trying to pass me the microphone.

Finally, I'm shaken out of my daydream and realize that I'm meant to make a speech myself.

Embarrassed, I make a small giggle noise before I grab hold of the microphone. Looking around the patio filled with people, I thank everyone for coming. I search the crowd again, looking for my mum. Our eyes meet and I notice my dad standing behind my mum, holding her waist. I thank both of my parents and all those who helped to set up such an amazing party for me, and finally I hold my hand out to Chase. He smiles, stepping forward and taking my hand.

"I never thought I could be so happy," I start. "To find my mate who has completed me," I finish, looking deeply into Chase's eyes. He smiles widely at me and leans in to kiss my cheek.

I pass the microphone back to my dad—who starts telling a really embarrassing story about me when I was six. I slowly move us away and lean into Chase's chest, wanting to be as close as possible to him.

We continue on with the party, walking around, talking with everyone. At one point, I lost Chase to my mum, who stole him and pulled him onto the dance floor. I watched from the side lines as he whirled my mum around the dance floor like a professional dancer.

Everyone sang happy birthday; I blew out the candles and cut the cake. I hit the bottom, naturally, and Chase was standing the closest, so he got the kiss.

We are sitting, talking with Chase's dad and a few other members of the pack, when Chase leans into me.

"I'm sick of sharing you," he whispers into my ear. "Can we go somewhere private?" he asks.

CHAPTER EIGHTEEN

TEMPTATION

Looking up at his beautiful face, my words can't get out fast enough.

"Sure," I say, smiling up at him.

I grab his hand and we sneak away from my party. I take him upstairs to my bedroom. Cody has gone, but I can still smell him in my room. Chase must notice also, as I feel his grip tighten on my hand.

"You really look beautiful," Chase says, pulling me back into his arms. "I am the luckiest wolf on the planet," he whispers in my ear before moving his lips down to the very top of my collarbone. I moan and lean into him more.

He moves his lips down to the special spot on a wolves neck where your mate marks you and leaves tiny kisses all around the area.

"I.... won't.... mark.... you.... now," he says between kisses. "Even though I want to."

I look up at him questioningly, asking "why not" with my eyes. He looks down at me and smiles.

"I want it to be memorable," he answers my silent question.

This makes me feel so special. I wanted it to be special but most male wolves marked their partners right away and didn't really give it a second thought.

I yawn involuntarily.

"Am I boring you, Miss. Raven," Chase asks mockingly, holding his hand up to his chest, acting as if he is wounded.

I shake my head, giggling. "I'm sorry, I'm just so tired."

"Come, love, let's sleep," Chase says, pulling me towards my bed.

I sit on the edge of my bed and watch as he removes the shirt that I gave him earlier. He walks into my walk-in robe, and I can hear him ruffling around. He soon returns wearing one of my loose fitting pyjama bottoms. His torso bare. His abs are magnificent.

I giggle and throw myself backward onto my bed, throwing my hands over my face, before leaning up on my elbows and smiling at him.

"You like what you see?" Chase says, wiggling his eyebrows and walking over to me.

I sit up and smile widely at him. "Yes, you look great in my pooh bear silky shorts," I say, covering my mouth, trying not to laugh any harder. I make my way into my wardrobe and find some pyjamas to wear. Realizing that I need help to get out of my dress, I come back out of the wardrobe to find Chase staring out of my bedroom window.

He turns as soon as I touch his amazingly chiselled back. "Everything okay, love?" he asks when he notices that I haven't changed.

"Uh, I need help unzipping my dress," I ask bashfully.

Chase moves towards me, and I turn so that my back is to him. He places his hand gently at the top of my dress and the other moves to the zip. He pulls it down slowly, opening up the back of my dress. I can hear his breathing change—as does my own. I feel the slightest touch of his hand against my skin.

I feel him move closer to me as soon as he has undone my zip. He kisses the very back of my neck, right in the centre. It sends shivers down my spine. My skin lights up with goosebumps. My dress releases and pools down my body, landing on the floor in a mass of fabric.

Chase suddenly turns me around and presses his lips urgently against mine. I move my hands up into his hair and pull lightly. A deep moan escapes his lips and his kisses become more intense. He bites down on my lower lip, causing my mouth to open. Without a second thought, he presses his tongue into my mouth and begins massaging my tongue gently.

Suddenly, we're moving, and he navigates me towards the bed without once breaking our kiss. My knees hit the back of my bed and I fall gently with Chase landing on top of me. He holds himself up on his elbows and breaks away from our kiss. He stares into my eyes, and it feels like he is looking right down into my soul.

I can't take it anymore. I wrap my hands around his neck and pull him back to me. His lips are so soft and warm, and the feeling of his tongue against mine is heaven.

Suddenly, he jumps back off me and moves away, shaking his head. He stands with his back to me, one hand pressed against my wall and the other over his eyes.

Feeling a little rejected, I pull a pillow over my front, hiding my underwear. Looking down at the ground, silence fills the room.

"What's wrong?" I finally ask. "Don... don't you want me?"

"Oh, Raven..." He turns back around, coming to sit next to me, "Of course I want you, you have no idea how much I want you."

He runs his hands through his hair in a frustrated way. Moving back towards me, he pulls me into his lap.

I can feel his erection against my underwear, so I know that he wants me as much as I want him.

"We can't do this here," he finally says. "I want everything for us to be special and memorable, not just driven by hormones and lust."

I kiss his lips quickly and pull him against me. His head rests on my breast and I can tell he is listening to my steady breathing and heartbeat that is now slowing down.

After a few moments, I climb off his lap and walk into my robe to get some pyjamas. After popping on some shorts and a singlet, I climb into bed. Chase has already laid down with his hands up behind his head. When I get into bed, he pulls me against him. Within minutes, he has fallen asleep.

I lay listening to the steady rhythm of his breathing. Feeling safely wrapped up in his arms, I eventually drift off into wonderful sleep. Having my mate here with me is absolute bliss.

CHAPTER NINETEEN

BEST GIFT EVER

When I wake in the morning, Chase is wrapped around me. I smile as I remember the events that occurred the day before. I try my best not to move as I don't want to wake him. I just lay there in complete harmony.

"Good morning, beautiful," Chase says suddenly, snapping me out of my daydream with a kiss on my neck.

I roll towards him and smile widely. "Good morning."

"What would you like to do today?" he asks, pushing a loose strand of hair out of my face and behind my ear.

Unexpectedly, my mum comes walking through my door for her usual morning wakeup schedule.

"Oh, I'm so sorry," she yelps, covering her eyes.

"It's okay, Mum, we're not doing anything, we just woke up," I say as I climb out of bed, trying to show her that I am completely dressed.

"When you're ready, come downstairs. You have many gifts to open," she says smiling and turning to leave. Before she is completely out the door she turns, smiling, and says, "Good morning, Chase, dear." Then she turns and disappears.

Chase sits up, smiling widely. "I think she likes me," he says, slowly getting up out of bed.

We both get dressed and make our way downstairs. There are a mountain of gifts on the dining room table.

Mum and dad are sitting at the island bench in the kitchen, talking quietly. When they spott us, they jump up and move towards us.

"Good morning you two," my dad says, embracing me. When he lets me go, he turns to Chase and shakes his hand.

"Look how many gifts you received," mum says excitedly, clapping her hands together.

"Open ours first," my mum almost squeals, pulling me over to the couch before passing me a small pearl coloured box with a large navy-blue bow pinned on top. I slowly open the box. My dad joins my mum, wrapping his hand around her waist from the side, as if waiting for my reaction.

The box has rose petals all inside it. I dig my fingers into the box and find something small and cold inside. Picking it up, I scream, jumping up from the couch.

"You got me a car!"

I scream so loud that my dad puts his hands over his ears. I almost fly across the lounge room and hug my mum and dad together.

"Now you can come and see us after you move in with Chase," my dad says—almost sadly.

"Thank you, thank you, thank you," I say whilst still holding onto them. I look back at Chase who is sitting on the couch.

"Let's go see," I say excitedly before moving back to him, grabbing his hand and dragging him towards the front door.

The moment I step out the front door and see my new car, I scream again. Chase covers his ears this time and laughs loudly.

We both walked over to my amazing BMW M3. It is the most beautiful colour, almost like a brushed, blue metal. I press the unlock button on the remote and sit down in the driver's seat. Chase is looking over the car and running his hands over the amazing paintwork.

"She's nice," he says finally, sliding into the passenger seat.

He runs his hand over the dashboard before reaching out and taking my hand from the steering wheel.

"You do want to live with me, don't you?" he asks, sounding worried.

"Of course. I want to be everywhere you are," I respond, turning my body towards him.

"Oh good," he responds, letting out a breath that he had clearly been holding in. I lean in and kiss him softly.

We get out of the car and wander hand-in-hand back inside to open the remainder of my gifts. I am very spoilt and receive many beautiful gifts. Mum did the good old mum thing and sat by me, writing down all of the gifts I received so as to remember who to send thank you messages to, whilst Dad disappeared after the third gift—clearly he was getting bored.

"I'm sorry I didn't get you something more special," Chase says, finally handing me a small rectangular box. "It's from my family," he says, smiling.

I open the box to see a small delicate white-gold bracelet with a small wolf charm hanging from it.

"It's beautiful," I say, holding it out for him to put onto my wrist.

There is a knock on the door and I look up, wondering who it was. My mum answers the door and greets Alpha Nicholas and a beautiful lady—who I assume is his Luna. I watch her with curiosity as they walk into the lounge room.

Unexpectedly, the mysterious Luna throws herself at me, almost crying with happiness.

"Oh." She sighs. "You truly are as beautiful as my husband told me. I'm sincerely sorry that I missed your birthday, I was away visiting my family and only returned this morning," she says rather quickly.

"Umm, hi," I finally manage to say, feeling a little flustered. I can feel the amusement on Chase's face even though he is standing behind me.

"Please excuse my wife, Raven, this is Alexandria, Chase's mum," he announces, leaning over and giving me a kiss on the cheek.

"Oh, I'm so sorry, dear," she says, holding onto my hand and patting it. "I'm just so thrilled that my baby has found his mate," she squeaks excitedly.

"Let's not scare her away," Chase says, wrapping his hands protectively around my waist and resting his chin on my shoulder.

My dad appears in the lounge, and he moves forward, greeting our guests. He shakes Alpha Nicholas' hand and kisses Luna Alexandria on the cheek. Then he announces that he has made lunch outside on the patio. We all go outside and eat a delicious lunch together. We talk and laugh and get to know each other a little better.

Once lunch is finished, I help my mum carry everything back into the kitchen. She suddenly grabs me, hugs me to her and begins to softly cry.

"We're going to miss you being here," she says in-between sobs.

"Max is away at camp and now you're leaving. The house just won't be the same."

"I'm not going that far, Mum, and besides, we still have tonight," I say, rubbing her back, "Max is already three weeks into his camp, it's only a four-week camp," I say, trying not to laugh.

I hold onto her for a little longer, understanding how she is feeling. I'm so excited to be with Chase, but at the same time, I'm sad to be moving away from my parents. Thankfully, our lands join, and I can hopefully get away and visit regularly.

Stepping away from my mum, I go back out to the patio to find that my dad has taken Chase's parents for a tour of the yard. My dad loves his gardens. Chase is sitting at the table alone, staring out over the pool. As soon as he notices me, he stands and quickly moves towards me.

"Hey," he says, lightly kissing me.

"It feels weird that I'm not going to live here anymore," I say whilst Chase moves and hugs me from behind.

"I have to go back to my pack and make preparations for you to come and live with me. Will you be okay here tonight?" Chase asks against my neck before kissing it softly.

I turn to face him and pout. I don't want him to go, but I know that he has to. The mate bond forms a strong spiritual connection between mates. You want to be with them at all times and being separated makes you feel like a part of you is missing. Chase lifts my chin, staring into my eyes, waiting for an answer.

"I don't want you to go, but I know you have to," I finally get out in a sulky voice.

He pulls me into a hug and kisses the top of my head. "It won't be long, love. I'll be back to get you tomorrow."

CHAPTER TWENTY

THE BOND

My mum returns from the kitchen a few moments later and asks where Dad has gone. I point silently out into the garden, and she giggles before walking out into the garden to find him. He is very proud of his garden, and I really can't blame him. It really is lovely. The other members of the pack have their houses spread across our territory, just beyond the edges of our garden.

"You want to go for a walk?" Chase asks.

I nod up at him and he releases me from our hug and takes my hand in his. When our skin touches, it feels like lightning running over my whole body. I look up and meet his eyes. I know he can feel it too. He smiles at me and squeezes my hand.

We walk around the gardens, hand-in-hand for what feels like such a short time before we bump into our parents. Alpha Nicholas announces that it is time to leave as he swings his car keys around his finger.

My parents bid everyone a goodbye at the front door and Chase's parents go to get into their car. Chase waits with me on the front doorstep. My mum pulls him into a tight hug and then holds his face in both of her hands. When she begins to ramble on about coming to visit all the time, my dad pulls her away and quickly shakes Chase's hand before disappearing inside and closing the door.

My eyes are cast down to the ground. I have only known Chase for a day but the connection between us is so strong. The mate bond is like adding food colouring to some water. Once joined, it is like a collision where they can never be separated again. It makes me think of Cody. No wonder he didn't want me anymore. This feeling is just too right.

Looking back up at Chase, my future alpha, I see that he is kind and strong, and so handsome. My mind is racing when he places his hand gently under my chin and lifts my head. My eyes look into his and I can tell he is trying to be calm about leaving me behind.

"Tomorrow," is all he says before crushing his lips down onto mine. The kiss is way too short and leaves me wanting more. He breaks away from me before I'm ready and runs over to his parent's car. A small sob comes from my mouth, but I put my hand up to hold it in. *It is only one night, Raven, get a hold of yourself.* I watch as their car drives away. Once it is out of sight, I turn and go inside.

My parents are in the lounge, watching a movie together, so I decide to go up to my bedroom and begin to pack away everything that I want to bring with me to my new home.

I know I can come back and get anything that I want, so I'm not too picky about packing everything. I have one large suitcase with clothes and a small washing basket filled with personal items from around my room, along with my toiletries. I walk back into my wardrobe and look down at all my shoes. Wow, talk about a hard choice. I'm not sure about my wardrobe space in my new home so I decide to only pack five pairs.

After packing for a couple of hours, I go downstairs and say goodnight to my parents. Of course, my mum holds onto me in a tight gorilla-style hug and cries continuously until my dad drags her away and swiftly kisses my forehead before suddenly going stiff. I watch his face and realize he is being mind-linked by someone. Shrugging, I walk back up to my room. It is only early, but I decide to get an early night, so I go to bed.

That night, I try my best to sleep, but I just keep tossing and turning. I guess it is all the excitement of moving to a new house tomorrow. I have been trying to sleep for three hours, so eventually, I decide to give up and try to relax by taking a bath. I go in and run the warm water, filling up the tub. I add some beautiful essential oils that smell like those yummy pink musk lollies. I'm going to smell good tomorrow.

Once the bath is full, I sink down into the warm water and soak away my stress. I lay there for what feels like a short time but it is more like twenty-five minutes. The water begins to turn cold, so I decide to hop out.

I wrap the towel around myself and walk out into my bedroom. As I walk out of my bathroom, someone grabs me unexpectedly, covering my mouth with their large warm hand. I try my best to scream but my mouth is completely covered. It is large, so I assume it is a man's hand. He eventually lets me go and I realize who it is.

"What are you doing here?" I ask harshly, pushing him away from me.

"I need to talk to you before you leave tomorrow," he says with a sad note in his voice.

Cody walks over and sits on the edge of my bed whilst I get dressed in my walk-in robe. When I come out, he looks up from the floor and smiles at me.

I stare at him and smile back. *Why is it so hard to hate this guy?* He broke my heart when he accepted his mate, I remind myself. But then, I also remember that we were never destined to be together and that I do still love him in my own special way.

"We didn't want him anyway, we wanted mate," Akira says in a snarky voice in my head. I chuckle a little, covering my mouth.

"What are you laughing at?" Cody asks with a questioning look on his face.

I just shake my head. I don't want him to know. Even though he broke my heart, he was still my best friend and I don't want to intentionally hurt him.

The silence suddenly fills my bedroom, and I don't know how to break it. "Ava tried to come back into our territory tonight," he finally says, breaking the silence.

"Why would she come back? I thought you rejected her?" I ask, looking shocked.

Then I suddenly remember my dad being pack linked when I went down to say goodnight. *I wonder if that is what was happening?*

"I did. Well, I didn't do it the proper way, but I told her to leave the pack and she went back to Sam's Pack as far as I know," he replies quickly. "I think she was coming here looking for you."

When you reject your mate, you have to look into their eyes, say their full name and say 'I reject you.' I note to myself silently that Cody never mentioned to me that he had never really rejected her properly.

I looked up at him, shocked. "What happened to her?"

"Your dad's warriors caught her, and she's down in the prison cells," he says, watching me carefully.

CHAPTER TWENTY- ONE

THE PRISONER

I quickly stand up and move to leave my room. Cody moves to me and grabs my hand. I turn back to him, not knowing what he is going to do.

I ready my hand to slap him if he tries to kiss me again.

"I'm not going to kiss you again unless you ask me to," he says, watching my palm. "I just want you to know that I love you and I always have. I really wish you would stay here and be with me."

I stare at him in shock and lower my hand. I'm stunned into silence.

"I want you to reject Chase and be with me," he says, realizing I'm not going to answer anytime soon.

Akira scoffs in my head and laughs loudly. I shush her and walk back over to my bed, slumping down onto it and covering my face with my forearm. My brain is running at a million miles an hour.

I'm not going to reject my mate. Is he crazy?

I feel my bed dip and I know Cody has sat down next to me.

He softly lays his hand over mine and pulls my hand away from my face. I look up into his eyes and notice he is crying.

My body takes over and I slowly move to him and wrap my arms around his waist. He sits still and sighs.

"I've made such a huge mess, Raven," he finally gets out. "I found Ava that day down by the lake and my heart just knew I was meant to be with her, but then I thought of you and I was so confused."

I sit silently whilst he lets it all out.

"She told me that she was a rogue and that she was just passing through. I never thought I would even find a mate, Raven, let alone that she would betray me and try to hurt you. You have to believe me, I truly do love you," he says, suddenly turning, looking deeply into my eyes.

"But I love her as well. I don't think she meant to hurt you, Raven, I think she was just scared of what Rhys would do to her if she failed."

I push Cody away from me, shocked. "She was a spy for her pack," I spit angrily. "Rhys abducted me because she was feeding him information about me." I watch as his face runs through a myriad of emotions.

"That day you found me," I speak quietly. "He was going to rape me."

I suddenly begin to sob. "How can you defend her?"

Cody suddenly stands up from the bed and begins pacing around my room. I can tell he is frustrated.

"I don't know what's happening to me, Raven. I feel like I'm being pulled apart from the inside," he whines. "My wolf is scratching at me to get back to Ava, but my heart wants to be here with you."

I sigh, staring up at him. I don't know what to say. My heart is screaming out in pain. How dare he do this to me now. If I hadn't met Chase, I would have run to him. But things are different now.

"I'm going to see her," I say, suddenly standing up from my bed.

Cody follows behind me, not saying a word. Not even trying to stop me. I don't know why I want to see her, but something inside me feels that I need to confront her about what happened to me. I'm going to be forever scared after what Rhys has done to me.

I grab a jumper from the chair in my bedroom and pull on a pair of shoes. Walking downstairs and out the front door, I go straight down to the cells which are not too far from the pack house. Once I arrive, I find a guard standing in my path.

"Let me through, Leon," I say in a demanding tone.

Leon steps aside. Cody walks ahead of me and finds the cell that Ava is being kept in.

I note how different our cells are compared to Rhys'. They aren't filthy and at least show some human compassion. Ava looks up from the bed, spotting Cody. I can see that she has been crying.

"Cody," she calls, rushing over to the bars.

Noticing me standing right next to Cody, her face transforms immediately.

"What is she doing here?" she asks with malice in her voice.

"You are on my land, rogue, you should have been murdered for what you have done," I spit back at her.

Cody puts up his hands in defeat and turns to me. "Please, Raven, don't."

I look deep into his eyes and can see the pain slowly spreading across his face.

"Fine," I say, throwing my hands in the air and turning, ready to walk away. I can see that I'm not going to be able to get anything out of her and decide that it was pointless even wanting to speak to her.

"I never wanted to hurt you, Raven," Ava calls loudly to me. "Rhys was a horrible alpha. He used to rape some of the younger women of our pack, he used to... rape me..." She pauses as if the memories are smothering her. "He picked the ones who didn't have mates," she adds. "One night, I ran away, but some of the warriors caught me before I made it to the border, and they took me back to Rhys."

Cody is now holding Ava's hand through the bars. I can see by the look on his face that he has never heard any of this from Ava.

"I had to do it, Raven," she pleads. "He told me that I had to come here and be your friend and get you to cross into his pack land so that he could do what he wanted with you, to repay your father for killing half of his pack a few years back."

My head snaps up and I look straight into her eyes. I remember a few years ago that a feud broke out between the two packs. Our pack was strong and—of course—came out on top. So, this plan of Rhys' was to steal me and torture me to get back at my father. And thanks to Ava, he almost succeeded.

"What about the rogues?" I ask, remembering what Cody said to me before my party.

"I don't know what you mean," Ava says, looking down at the ground.

"Don't play dumb, Ava, it doesn't suit you," I snap. "Cody told me that he overheard you on the phone to some rogues, and that they are coming for me." I start stepping towards the cell in anger. I want to reach through the bars and throttle her.

"I wanted to get back at you for kissing my mate," Ava retorts angrily, clearly not thinking about her words before speaking. "You were trying to take him away from me."

Cody lets go of Ava's hands and looks at her, shocked.

"She's my best friend, Ava. How could you?" Cody says angrily.

"She was trying to steal you from me," Ava says, desperately trying to reach out to Cody through the bars.

Cody shakes his head, his face unreadable, but I know deep down that he is hurting and confused. I know each of his facial expressions off by heart. Part of me wants to comfort him, and the other part knows it isn't my place anymore.

The silence is deafening, so I decide to retort. "I've found my own mate now, Ava, so you don't have to worry about Cody and me."

Cody's eyes snap up to mine. I can almost hear his heart breaking from where I'm standing. I don't know what he wants. One second, he is telling me to reject Chase and be with him, and the next, he tells me that he loves her. And just now, he was holding her hands through the bars like he wanted her and only her.

I shake my head and storm out of the cell block and begin making my way back to my house.

Cody follows me, grabbing my elbow, spinning me around to face him.

"What do you want, Cody?" I scream at him. "You're the one who found their mate and didn't want me anymore."

CHAPTER TWENTY-TWO

THE BIG MOVE

My words shock Cody into complete silence.

"Is that what you think?" he says after a few moments. He speaks so softly I barely hear him.

"What else can I think?" I reply, staring down at the ground.

"I wanted you so badly I was willing to send Ava away, Raven. I was willing to do that for you," he says, moving towards me and holding my face in-between his hands.

"Things are different now, Cody, we both have our mates now," I reply, pulling away and turning around. "I know you love Ava, Cody, and that's okay. I'm leaving tomorrow and you can be happy with her here, and I will be with Chase."

"I don't want you to go, Raven, stay with me," Cody says as he hurries towards me, hugging me from behind.

I turned in Cody's arms and kiss him lightly on the cheek. There are a million things I want to say in this moment. A part of me still loves being in his arms… I think it will always be there. Looking up into his eyes, I try to hold back my tears. "I will always be your best friend, Cody."

Then I slowly walk away from him, knowing that my feelings for him now had to be purely those of a best friend and nothing more. It hurts me to see his face as I walk away. I had given him my heart and he smashed it. Like dropping a crystal ball on concrete. Meeting Chase has changed all that. I finally feel whole again. As I walk away, I know that in my own special way, I will always love Cody.

I wake before my alarm. Something I'm not usually in the habit of doing, but today is a special day. Today, I'm going to live with my mate. I shower, dress quickly and rush downstairs. My mum rubs her eyes dramatically before asking me if I'm feeling okay. I look at her questioningly and she begins to laugh loudly, pointing out that I'm up before she has managed to come into my room and wake me herself.

Rolling my eyes, I grab a bowl and pour myself some cereal. Mum and I chat for a while before the doorbell rings. I squeal loudly, causing Mum to cover her ears.

I quickly jump down from my stool at the bench and run to open the front door. Of course, I know it is Chase on the other side of the door, I can feel it in my bones. Akira whines loudly in my mind, just wanting to be near Chase. I fling the door open and leap into his arms. I hug him tightly to me and breathe in his amazing scent.

"Hey, you," Chase purrs, picking me up by my waist and spinning me around before kissing me passionately.

When my feet finally touch back on the ground, I stumble forward a little, landing in Chase's arms again. I giggle and look up into his eyes.

"You make me so giddy," I say shyly, pushing my hair back behind my ear. Chase touches my cheek sweetly, leans in and kisses my forehead.

"Are you all ready to go?" Chase asks whilst leading me back inside, holding onto my hand.

I'm so excited for this day, but suddenly, looking around, I realize just how much I'm going to miss home.

"Oh, Chase, dear, good morning," my mum says cheerily, hugging him as we walk into the kitchen.

After my mum finally lets Chase go, we go upstairs to my bedroom to grab my suitcase. I open my bedroom door, walking in, holding Chase's hand as he follows in behind me. Pulling me to his chest, he presses his lips against mine. I lean into him and slowly move my lips against his. All too soon, he breaks away and smiles down at me. I want to stay in his arms forever.

"Ready?" he asks, looking around my room.

"As I'll ever be," I say, sighing and looking around.

Chase grabs my suitcase, and we make our way back downstairs. I know that my dad will be bringing over some of my other items in the next few days, so for now, all I need are my clothes.

As soon as my mum sees my suitcase, she bursts into tears and grabs hold of me. Chase reluctantly let's go of my hand as my mum seems to be holding me for longer than expected.

"I'll just pop this in the car," Chase says as he quickly makes his way outside.

I am so beyond excited to be moving into Chase's house. I can't wait to wake up next to him every day for the rest of my life.

Chase appears back in the kitchen and clears his throat in a bid to get my mum to let me go.

"Ohh okay," Mum says, finally releasing me and brushing tears away from her eyes, and smoothing her clothes as if something is out of place.

I smile at her, reminding her that I'm only a little while away and that I will be visiting all the time.

Chase smiles and holds his hand out to me. I take it willingly and begin walking out to the car. Once outside, I notice my dad leaning against my new car.

"I'll bring it over during the week," he says, wrapping me up in a big warm hug.

I nod into his chest. If I speak, I might just cry.

Soon, I am climbing in Chase's car and waving wildly at my parents. As we make our way down my driveway, tears begin to silently spill down my cheeks. Chase reaches across to me and takes my hand in his. He doesn't say anything, but this single gesture calms me immediately. It truly is amazing the way that the mate bond works.

The car ride takes about forty minutes or so, and as we come closer, I begin to feel a little nervous. Sensing this, Chase rubs his thumb over the back of my hand.

"It's okay, baby," he says, shooting me one of his glorious smiles.

When we pull into the driveway, I see some of the houses and notice that members of the pack are all busy. Some of the pups run after the car, yelling out to Chase. He beeps the horn a few times and they all stop and high five each other. I smile to myself and think of how sweet my mate is.

We pull up outside the main pack house and Chase parks his car. Getting out, he comes around to my door and opens it for me. I remember this house from my trip here earlier in the year. Alpha Nicholas and Alexandria have appeared on the front doorstep and seem to be beaming with pride. Walking over to them, they both envelope me in big hugs and invite me inside.

We go in and have some lunch. It's nice to sit around and chat with them for a while. I find out that Chase is an only child and doesn't live in the main pack house anymore. I'm a little shocked, but I guess he's going to be alpha soon and needs his privacy. Honestly, I'm a little relieved as it kind of felt weird knowing that I was going to be living with Alpha Nicholas and Luna Alexandria.

After lunch, we head out before hugging and waving goodbye to my new family. We get back in the car and drive for around five minutes—down to a more secluded part of the pack's territory. When we arrive at Chase's house, I'm blown away. It is a beautiful double storey villa.

Once again, he opens the car door for me. *Such a gentleman.*

Making his way towards the door, Chase looks back at me still standing beside the car.

"You coming?" he asks, flashing me his gorgeous smile and reaching out to me.

I move forwards slowly and take his outstretched hand. Once inside, he shows me around the lower floor, which has a lounge area, kitchen, bathroom, study and rumpus room. The house is beautiful. Chase heads over to the fridge, asking if I want something to drink, and I nod.

Unexpectedly, an unfamiliar guy comes jogging down the stairs, half naked.

CHAPTER TWENTY-THREE

ROOM MATE

I watch as he moves towards us. "Hey, man," he calls to Chase. "Sorry, I didn't know you were bringing her today or I would have dressed nicer." He laughs, looking me up and down and giving me a wink.

I move closer to Chase, taking note that this unfamiliar guy is shirtless. Chase looks up from the fridge and a wide smile spreads across his face.

"Hey, man," he says, walking over and giving this stranger a side hug. I watch them together and decide that they are clearly friends and that I haven't got anything to worry about.

Chase steps back and holds his hand out to me. I smile shyly and take it, and he pulls me forward and in front of him, leaning his chin on my shoulder.

"Raven, this is Mark. He's my best friend and for all intents and purposes, soon to be my beta," Chase announces proudly.

Mark holds his hand out, smiling, and I lean forward, shaking it.

"Hey."

Mark then turns and heads for the fridge whilst Chase hands me a can of soft drink.

Mark grabs a drink and walks back towards us. "She's cute," Mark notes, nodding and winking at me.

A sharp growl erupts from Chase and Mark laughs loudly. "Man, I love messing with you, the look on your face just makes it worthwhile." He laughs loudly, holding onto his stomach.

Chase's face changes, realizing his friend is taking the piss out of him. "Ha-ha, very funny, dude," Chase says back sarcastically before wrapping his arms protectively around my waist.

"So, you live here too?" I ask quietly, looking up at Mark.

"Oh, yes, sorry, I forgot to tell you," Chase answers quickly, looking deeply into my eyes as if worrying what I'm thinking.

"I hope that won't be an issue?" Mark asks, looking at me expectedly.

Grabbing a bottle of water from the fridge, Mark watches me carefully.

"I'm heading out to see Ally," he finally says, taking a quick swig from his drink.

"Who is Ally?" I ask, looking back at Chase.

"This douchebag's mate," Chase answers with a smirk on his face.

Chase then reaches for my hand and begins pulling me towards the stairs.

"Uh, bye," I call back to Mark, who smiles and uses two fingers against his forehead to salute me silently before heading out the front door.

We make our way upstairs and Chase shows me where Mark's room is, the main bathroom, the spare room, and then lastly, he brings me to the master suite—which is now to be our shared room. It is absolutely beautiful. I can't believe how big it was.

I walk around the room, looking out at the beautiful view. I turn to see Chase sitting on the edge of his bed. Walking over to him, I stand between his legs and smile down at him. He slowly places his hands on my hips and pulls me forward, causing me to lose my balance and fall forwards on top of him.

I look deep into his eyes and smile to myself. Akira is going crazy in my head, screaming for Chase to mark us as his own. He places his hands on either side of my face and smiles at me. Leaning forward, I press my lips to his; they are warm and so soft. He kisses me back with such fervour. Our kiss suddenly becomes more urgent, and I feel his hands slide down my back to my ass. He grasps it gently, and I can hear a small moans escape his mouth into mine.

My hands rest on Chase's chest. I can feel how firm his body is, and I have to admit, I'm starting to become very turned on. Not only from the feel of his body against mine, but also by the amazing kiss that we are sharing. It is like my body takes over and I press myself into his body. Suddenly, I become very aware of his erection pressing into my lower body.

I pull away and stand up, embarrassed.

"Shit, I'm sorry, Raven," Chase says, sitting up.

"It's okay," I say, moving back towards him. "It's just, I've never..."

The thought of Rhys hands roughly touching me flash through my mind.

"It's okay," he says, grabbing my hand and placing a soft kiss on my palm. "We will wait until you're ready."

I feel really bad for a moment, the poor guy. This is the second time this has happened; I slowly smile and kiss his lips lightly before sitting down on the bed next to him.

"How about we watch a movie?" Chase offers, standing up from the bed and opening up his bedroom door. Nodding my head, I stand and follow him from our bedroom and back downstairs to the lounge room.

"You pick out a movie and I'll grab us some snacks," Chase calls over his shoulder as he walks towards the kitchen.

Running my fingers over the spines of each of the DVD's in the collection, I finally decide on The Fast and the Furious. I pull it from the cabinet and place it into the DVD player and take a seat on the couch, waiting for Chase to return from the kitchen.

A few minutes later, Chase comes back into the lounge with his arms overflowing with snacks. He drops them carelessly onto the table and slides down onto the couch next to me.

"Oh, my God," he says excitedly.

"What?" I reply, a little puzzled.

"I have the best freaking mate ever," he says, laughing and pointing at the TV screen. "I freaking love this movie." He quickly leans down and places a soft kiss on my forehead before grabbing a bag of chips. He opens them up and offers some to me before pressing play on the movie.

I must drift off part way through the movie because when I reopen my eyes, the end credits are playing. I look over to see Chase has disappeared. The spot where he was sitting is still warm, so I know that he hasn't been gone for long.

Standing from the couch, I set off to look for him. As I reach the kitchen, I can hear voices coming from the front door. Curious, I walk towards the sound. As I get closer, I note that one of the voices is Chase's and the other belongs to a female.

CHAPTER TWENTY-FOUR

THE GREEN-EYED MONSTER

I'm not sure whether to stop and listen or to make my presence known. I decide to stand back for a moment and listen in.

"She doesn't have to know, babe," comes the female voice. My ears perk and a flush of anger flows through my body. Who the hell is this chick calling my mate 'babe'? Akira perks up from the back of my mind and lets forth a low, grumbly growl inside my head.

I want to know exactly what this female wolf wants. I listen for a few moments more, just in case I am mistaken. Akira is ready to burst forth and tear the she-wolf's head off.

"Sarah, I have my mate now, it's not going to happen," Chase responds. My heart beams, but then my face falls. Something has been happening with this she-wolf... before he met me. I know deep in my heart that what happened before he met me isn't something that I can control or hold against him, but at the same time, my heart aches just a little.

"It can be our little secret. Come on, babe, I miss you and your amazing dick," the she-wolf purrs. It takes all of my will to stop Akira from bursting out. I stomp around the corner, towards the door, and a guttural snarl rips from my mouth.

"Back the fuck away from my mate, slut," I spit, putting myself between Chase and the she-wolf. The she-wolf doesn't back away, but rather smirks at me.

Chase lays his hands on my shoulders. Without looking at him, I speak through gritted teeth. "Chase, don't touch me right now, I don't want to hurt you, I'm only just holding my wolf back." Chase removes his hands from my shoulders before speaking firmly.

"You need to leave, Sarah," Chase says calmly as he steps up beside me before grasping my hand and pulling me back inside.

"I know you will come crawling back, Chase," Sarah finally says, tossing her blonde hair over her shoulder before sneering at me and walking away.

As soon as Sarah is far enough away, I spin around sharply, ripping my hand out of Chase's grasp and make my way back to the couch before throwing myself down onto it, face first into some pillows.

I want to cry or maybe even scream, but all I can do is stare into oblivion.

Chase moves towards me slowly and kneels down beside the couch. He runs his hands through his hair and then places them roughly on his thighs, clearly unsure whether or not to touch me.

"I'm so sorry," Chase finally announces after what feels like forever. Slowly, he sits down beside me and places his hand on the middle of my back and begins rubbing small circles. This small gesture immediately calms me down. It's amazing how the touch of your mate can help to calm any emotion you are having.

Chase looks deeply into my eyes before a small smile comes across his beautiful lips.

I try being cross, but after seeing his smile, I just can't hold it in anymore. Sitting up, I smile shyly and reach my hand out to his.

"I'm sorry that I reacted that way. It's just... I could have ripped her pretty blonde hair off her head," I say, looking down towards the floor.

Chase moves up from the floor and sits down next to me, pulling me into his lap. "I'm sorry she came here. We were never in a relationship, it was just a casual thing, nothing more," he says quietly. I feel his hand tighten around me slightly, as if he is expecting me to run away from him. I can't be mad at him for having sex before we met... I almost did the same thing with Cody.

"It's okay, I should have guessed that you would have had sex before," I say, almost squeaking on the word 'sex' as it comes out of my mouth.

"How many were there?" I ask quietly.

Chase stalls for a little, running his hand backwards and forwards over my leg. "Two," he finally answers, looking away from me as if he is ashamed.

A million thoughts run through my mind. At first, I want to move away from him. I feel like I have been betrayed, but then I realize that I can't be mad at him for something that happened before we met.

"Please say something," Chase pleads.

"It's in the past." I finally sigh. "If she comes back here again, I will rip her face off though," I add. "Akira is not happy," I add, smiling as she huffs loudly in my mind.

"Akira?" Chase asks, looking at me sideways.

"Oh, my wolf, her name is Akira," I answer, smiling. Akira prances around in my mind, wagging her tail wildly. "What's your wolf's name?" I ask, touching Chase's face softly with my hand.

"Quinn," Chase answers, smiling. "He's very excited to meet Akira," he adds, leaning forward and planting a soft kiss on my lips.

"Well, Akira wouldn't mind a run," I answer, smiling.

Chase grabs my hand and pulls me from the couch. We walk just outside the backdoor when Chase begins removing his clothes excitedly. He is almost tripping over his own pant legs, trying to get them off so fast.

I stand back, watching my mate undress. He is just gorgeous. *How did I get so lucky?* Within seconds, Chase stands in front of me with nothing but his underwear on. My eyes graze over his body as I chew on the edge of my thumb nail. My eyes soon meet his, and I blush at having been caught ogling him.

A cheeky grin spreads across Chase's face before he moves closer to me. He leans in close to me and whispers in my ear, "I can hear how fast your heart is beating, my mate."

My breathing hitches and I almost forgot to take another breath in. How he affects me so much after knowing him for such a small time, I will never know.

"So, am I the only one getting naked over here?" Chase asks, smirking.

CHAPTER TWENTY-FIVE

LIFE IS GOOD

My eyes scan the ground. "Oh, uh, right, one second," I say, holding up my hand.

I kicked off my shoes and begin to undress. Suddenly, I become really self-conscious. I can feel Chase's eyes raking over my soon-to-be naked body. I remove my T-shirt and stand in just my underwear. My face is growing hot under his gaze. Realizing I am a little uncomfortable, he turns around whilst I remove my bra and underwear.

I let Akira take control and feel the smooth shiver of my shift come over me. Feeling myself change, I drop calmly onto all fours. My shimmering white and grey fur feels amazing in the breeze. As soon as the change is complete, I begin to run. I can hear Chase shift quickly and run after me, the gravel ground giving away his position. Soon, we enter the trees. Stripes of green and brown pass my vision like a speeding train flying down the tracks. The wind flying through my fur feels amazing. Akira loves being chased. Especially now that we have Chase.

"Hey, wait for me," he calls through our mind link.

I giggle to myself and continue to run. Chase catches me in no time, swiftly running past me. I follow behind him and eventually we come to a stop at an old ruin site. The remains of quite a few buildings are scattered around. Chase comes to a stop and sits down, waiting for me.

Taking a deep breath, I stand watching him for a moment. His black fur is just beautiful. Like a midnight sky, with no need for stars. He looks back at me over his shoulder, a small smirk on his face.

I sit down beside him and lay my head against his side. A low, happy grumble escapes Chase's throat. I reply in kind and lick the side of his face. Chase looks over at me and suddenly moves, causing me to fall sideways.

He makes a snorting sound, and I can tell that he is laughing.

I lunge towards him, and he swiftly moves out of the way. Chase then begins to run in and around the rubble of the ruins. I follow him promptly but soon find that I have lost him. I lower my nose to the ground to sniff him out, but his scent is everywhere. I make my way around, looking behind some of the larger walls that still stand, when suddenly, he jumps out from behind me, almost scaring me to death.

I love this side to him. The playful side. It reminds me of Cody.

My mind strays, thinking back to all those times Cody and I used to race each other. My eyes pan to the ground and I sigh deeply. Feeling the need to run, I stand swiftly and move away from the ruins. Chase follows me willingly. I am loving this moment with my mate, and I'm not going to let my memories of Cody ruin our fun. I look back over my shoulder to see Chase getting closer to me. He playfully grabs my tail, making me slow down slightly. He then manoeuvres himself so that he is beside me. Knocking me slightly, I fall and roll over a couple of times. We are now in a field with small tufts of grass filled with purple flowers.

Standing over me, Chase leans forward and nudges my ear with his snout.

Feigning injury, I can tell that he is worried as a small whimper leaves his mouth. Unexpectedly, I lick his face and stand from underneath him, causing him to stumble backwards, shocked. I run again, letting out a soft howl sound. Realizing I tricked him, he begins chasing after me again. We spend a couple of hours like this. Playing like two pups in a field full of wildflowers.

The sun is sinking in the sky, casting a beautiful copper glow. We finally lay down together and Chase lays his head on my back.

The earlier problems are forgotten. My mate is wonderful. I don't think I could be any happier if I tried.

The sun sets and the sky fills with beautifully bright stars. They appear sparingly at first, but soon the sky sparkles like a diamond necklace. After sitting together just chatting for hours through our mind link, Chase and I decide to finally head home.

Once we arrived back at the house, I notice two robes sitting on the front step. Chase shifts back and places the robe on before holding the other one open and waiting for me to shift. He is such a gentleman. I know how much he wants to look, but he doesn't. I'm not sure where my sudden shyness has come from, but I'm hoping that it will go away soon.

We decide that we aren't really feeling hungry, so Chase grabs a bag of chips and we go upstairs to our bedroom.

My suitcases lay open on the floor. I pick through, finding some comfortable pyjamas to put on. Once we are settled into bed, I lay against Chase's side as we watch another movie together.

I fall asleep easily in my mate's arms. It is just pure bliss. Just being near him makes my heart beat faster, my breath hitch in my throat, and the hairs on my skin stand on end.

In the morning, the sound of a knock comes from the front door, waking us. Chase hurries down, just wearing his boxers. I pull on the robe from the day before and make my way downstairs.

As I'm walking past the lounge, I'm hoping that it isn't that skank Sarah coming to call again. I will rip her face off. I don't even feel bad for the possessiveness over Chase.

Chase opens the door, and I recognise the person right away. It is my dad. I remember that he was bringing my car. I watch as his eyes roam up and down Chase, clearly noticing the lack of clothing. He eyes him sceptically.

"Hey, Dad." I smile, hugging him. I notice him take a sniff of my hair and I step back, scrunching my face up at him.

"What are you doing?" I ask, staring at my dad.

"He's checking if we are mated," Chase answers with a serious look on his face.

I stare at my dad, and he smiles. "Sorry, baby, your mum was bugging me to check. She keeps going on about grandbabies." He smiles shyly.

I slap my hand against my face and sigh. "It's been one day, Dad."

"I know, I know," he says, holding his hands up in a defensive way.

My dad soon leaves, leaving behind the keys to my car. I place them gently on the bench and turn to see Chase watching me.

"What?" I ask, looking down at my front, expecting to see something on me.

My eyes look back up at him and I notice his posture has changed.

"Grandbabies, hey?" He smirks.

I smile as he walks towards me and hugs me to his chest.

"At least your dad didn't mention that he would murder me for deflowering his daughter." I can feel his smile against my hair.

Slapping his chest, I wander into the kitchen to make breakfast.

We spend the day together, wandering around the pack lands, and Chase proudly introduced me to many of the packs people. They all seemed so welcoming. This pack is around the same size as my father's. They have many wonderful amenities including a wonderful hospital. I enjoyed just being near my mate.

That night, whilst Chase is having a shower, I sit on the phone to my mum, chatting about how wonderful my life is going to be now that I have found my mate. She continually asks me about when she can expect grandbabies, and I giggle, shaking my head. She isn't going to give up on the topic. After hanging up, I place my phone back down onto the side table and grab the remote, flicking on the tele. There is nothing on. I surf through the channels, when suddenly, I hear my phone ding from the bedside table.

The screen lights up and I notice a text message from Cody. At first, I want to ignore it, but the friend part of me is worried. Surely, he wouldn't message me unless it was urgent.

Grabbing the phone from the nightstand, I open the message.

CHAPTER TWENTY-SIX

LOOSING SOMEONE YOU LOVE

The message is plain, and I can't help but feel a little pang of guilt.

I wish you had stayed, is all that it read.

After staring at the message for a few minutes, I decide that replying wouldn't be in my best interests. I delete the message and sit back against the bed. I want to cry. No matter what has happened between us, he was still my best friend. I know how Chase feels about Cody, and I don't want it getting in the way of our newly formed bond, so I decide that I need to move forward, and that means forgetting about Cody.

My phone dings again, and I pick it up. This time it is my mum. The message reads, *'come over tomorrow for lunch'.* I reply quickly that I will. I have been gone only two days, but I already miss my mum so much.

Chase comes out of the bathroom with his towel wrapped around him before getting changed quickly into some shorts and climbing into bed with me. He smells divine. Falling asleep with your mate wrapped around you is beyond words. I drift to sleep easily, listening to the soft sounds of our breathing. My dreams are filled with Cody's message.

When I wake, I notice that Chase is gone. I remember that he mentioned going to do some training yesterday when we went for our walk around the pack lands. I stand from the bed and decide to head into the shower. The steam fills the bathroom as I step into the shower. The heat of the water warms me instantly. I sigh, just out of pure happiness. After showering and dressing, I decide to head downstairs. Walking past Mark's room, I notice that something sexy is definitely happening in there. I haven't met Mark's mate, Ally, yet. I hope that she's not a huge skank like Sarah and that I actually like her.

Grabbing an apple from the fruit basket, I see that Chase left me a note on the counter, letting me know to come down when I woke. Taking a bite from my apple, I begin making my way to the training field.

A constant stream of "Hello" and "Good morning" fills my ears the whole way there. Everyone is just so kind and welcoming in this pack.

Setting foot in the training field, I note that there are many strong men and women training—both in human and wolf form. Chase sees me and runs to me immediately, swooping me up off my feet, landing a soft kiss on my lips. I can hear a small myriad of "Aww" coming from those around me.

Chase slowly places me back on the ground and clasps my hand in his. His eyes scan my face, landing back on my own. I almost melt into a puddle. His eyes can practically see into my soul. When I breathe, I feel like I am just breathing for him.

"You want to have a go?" Chase asks, gesturing at a couple who are sparing in human form.

I nod and instantly drop into a defensive position. Chase's face quickly changes from a shocked look to a smile, almost instantly.

I guess he didn't know about me training back at my pack. It never came up in our conversations. This is going to be fun.

He changes his stance and waits. We both wait to see which one of us will make a move first.

I quickly move forward, ducking as Chase goes to grab me. I duck under his arms, kicking his left leg, causing him to stumble back a little. I continue forward, making him spin around to see me standing behind him with a smile on my face.

Many of the others' who had been training have stopped to watch us.

Smirking, I place my hand up in front of me and made a 'come here' motion with my hand.

Chase makes his way towards me. I quickly grasp his arm, swinging myself around him so that his arm lands behind his back. I can tell he is going easy on me, and I hate it. I want him to push my limits and see that I can fight just like anyone else.

Pulling on his arm sharply, I hear him take in a breath.

"Don't think that I can't take you, baby," I breathe in his ear.

Chase manoeuvres himself into a crouching position before twisting. He makes it out of my grip and swings his leg out, trying to trip me up. I jump quickly, stepping back. I watch as he smiles at me and makes the same 'come here' motion that I just made at him. Without hesitation, I run towards him.

Chase mimics my move from before, but feigns right, knocking me off balance, and I land heavily on my side.

Seeing me hit the ground, Chase's demeanour changes instantly and he moves to me quickly, holding his hand out to help me up.

"Are you okay?" he asks, his words dripping with concern.

I grasp his hand, pulling him forward harshly and manoeuvring myself on top of him, pinning his arms beside his head.

"I'm perfectly fine." I laugh, leaning forward to give him a cheeky kiss.

Unexpectedly, Chase flips us over and I'm lying on the ground with my hands pinned.

Chase leans forward, his lips hovering just over mine. He kisses me deeply before standing up and pulling him with me.

"I'm glad," he admits.

Chase continues to train whilst I walk around greeting people and watching their technique.

Training soon comes to a close and Chase grabs his bag. We make our way home but before we go inside, Chase grabs me and pulls me to his chest.

The sun has moved across the sky and my stomach grumbles, signalling that it is lunch time.

"Let's go for a run?" he asks. His eyes are hopeful.

How could I refuse him? Nodding, I think to myself, *I will go for a run now and then head over to visit my mum.*

We shift after removing our clothes and setting them on the front doorstep. Chase is ever the gentleman and turns away as I shift.

We make our way around the pack lands and soon come to rest together. We stay sitting together for quite some time. Quinn rests his head on the ground and Akira rests hers on the scruffy part of his neck.

Unexpectedly, Quinn sits up sharply, and instantly I know that he is being mind linked by someone.

"We have to go back," he says in a rushed tone before standing and beginning to move back the way we came. He looks back at me to make sure I'm following.

I'm not sure what has happened, but his reaction has me intrigued, so I follow him.

Instead of going home, he goes straight towards the main pack house. His father is on the front doorstep, waiting for us to arrive. Alexandria comes out of the house, holding two robes. I stand, waiting, showing that I'm clearly uncomfortable about shifting in front of my future mother and father-in-law. Sensing this, Alpha Nicholas moves inside and Alexandria lays the robes on the front step before following him. Chase looks around to make sure that no one is watching and he holds up a robe for me.

I shift and quickly pull the robe around myself. Kissing my lips quickly before grasping my hand, he pulls me inside his parents house.

Once inside the house, I follow behind Chase, still wondering what on earth has happened.

Chase leads me over towards his father's office. I know it well, seeing as I have been here before. Taking a seat by the large open fire, I note that Chase stands in front of his father—who is now seated at his desk.

"Raven," Nicholas speaks strongly. "Your father called just now." My body suddenly goes stiff, and I watch him with wary eyes. "There was an attack on your parent's house." I stand suddenly and rush towards Alpha Nicholas' desk.

"What happened?" I ask quickly, the air leaving my body, and I seem unable to draw more breath in. Chase wraps his hands around my shoulders.

It feels like an oblivion of time has flown by before he speaks again. "Your mother was badly injured"—he pauses—"she didn't make it."

My body seems to give up hearing these words, and I slide to the ground. The breath that I seemed to be unable to take suddenly races through my mouth and a large sob breaks forward through my parted lips.

Chase kneels next to me and pulls me into his lap. It is like time suddenly stands still, and all I can do is try to focus on the words that Alpha Nicholas just said to me.

There is no way that my mum can be gone. He's wrong, he has to be wrong.

I need to get out of here, I need to go and see for myself.

I climb out of Chase's lap and shift right there in the middle of the study. I run through the front part of the house and push past someone coming in through the front door.

I feel Akira sob sadly in my mind. My legs are carrying me as fast as they can go, but I push them harder. Soon, I feel a presence beside me and note that Chase has easily caught me. I know we are nearing the edge of Alpha Nicholas' territory, when suddenly, a sound stops me in my tracks. I skid to a stop and my ears prick. Again, my breathing seems to falter as I listen to the haunting sound.

The whole of my father's pack. I can hear them. A long drawn-out group of solemn howls can be heard. The sound of sorrow at the loss of their Luna. The wind carries their sadness to my ears, and my legs—once again—give out on me, causing me to sit involuntarily. Chase nudges me and I stand, my legs shaking but I move forward again.

Sooner than expected, I am outside my father's house. I shift, not caring about who will see me naked. I barge through the front door and make my way towards the lounge room, where I can hear voices.

When I finally make it into the room, I note a body on the couch, surrounded by my father, our beta and his wife and the pack doctor. My mother's body lays, unmoving. She is almost unrecognizable. A small sob escaped my lips, and my hand flies up to my mouth to stop any more from escaping. At the sound of my sob, my father's head shoots up and he quickly moves towards me, enveloping me into a bear-like hug. I feel his chest heaving up and down as he cries into my hair.

My tears begin to flow silently.

I can't believe that my mum is gone.

CHAPTER TWENTY-SEVEN

SAYING GOOD-BYE

Suddenly, something soft touches my back. I note that Chase is behind me. Taking the robe he is holding out to me, I pull it numbly over my naked body as I walk towards my mother. She is merely ten steps away from me, but as I walk, I feel like I'm in slow motion.

Each step brings me closer to one of the people that I love most in this world.

I sink down next to the couch and a small sound falls from my mouth without me even knowing it has. My hand moves up to my mouth, as if trying to stop any further noises from unexpectedly escaping. My hand is shaking. I tenderly reach up and grasp her hand. The second my skin touches hers, tears began to stream down my face. I feel someone lean down beside me. The person envelopes me in their arms, and I instantly recognize it is my dad.

I don't know how long I sit beside her. My tears ran out hours ago. My body is wracked with tiredness, and I begin to fall asleep sitting up.

I suddenly feel Chase's hands wrap around me as he lifts me from the floor and begins carrying me somewhere.

I look up into his eyes and I can feel his arms tighten around me as he looks down at me. We make our way upstairs to my bedroom and he lays me softly onto my bed before he pulls the covers up over me. My eyelids are heavy and close the moment my head hits the pillow.

Walking around to the other side of the bed, I feel him climb in beside me. Pulling me close to him, he places his chin on my head and speaks softly. "Raven, I'm so sorry." No words will form themselves in my mind, so I just nod sadly and soon drifted off into a troubled sleep.

I wake the next day, wrapped tightly in Chase's arms. My head rests on his chest, and I move my head up to look at him and smile softly as I watch him sleep. I climb out of bed as gently as I can and head into my bathroom. I turn on the shower and remove the robe I had been wearing all night. My whole body is sore from running my heart out to get here, as well as from all the crying that I did yesterday.

I climb in under the steaming water and begin to quietly sob again. I don't even hear Chase come into the bathroom, but as soon he has stepped into the shower, I turn to face him, looking deeply into his eyes. He watches me, his eyes intensely staring into mine. After a few seconds, he tilts his head to the side as if asking silently if it is okay for him to come into the shower with me. I nod softly and he walks towards me and brings me to his chest under the stream of fiery water.

We stand together under the water for a while before Chase lets me go and reaches for the shampoo bottle, squirting some into his hands. My eyes move from his hand to his eyes, his eyes searching mine for the answer to a silent question. I turn away from him and he begins to wash my hair. It feels so nice. My arms are so heavy and I doubt I would even have been able to wash my own hair anyway.

After the shower, we both sit on the edge of my bed. I'm wrapped up in a plush towel whilst Chase has his wrapped around his waist. We sit in a comfortable silence with my head resting on his shoulder and his arm wrapped around me. Chase finally pats my leg, as if telling me we have to get ready. I go into my wardrobe and pick out something to wear. I haven't left behind much but I manage to come up with a simple outfit.

Chase doesn't have any clothing, so he pops the robe back on and follows me downstairs. My dad is sitting at the kitchen bench, staring deeply at the pattern in the marble bench top. Hearing us enter the kitchen, his head snaps up and a ferocious growl breaks free from his throat before he realizes who it is. His eyes soften immediately before he greets us.

"I'm sorry, sweetheart. It's just... I keep expecting those mutts to try and come back," he speaks angrily.

"What happened?" asks Chase from behind me.

My dad shifts in his seat before launching into the horrible tale of how my mum was murdered.

"I was out at a meeting..." He almost chokes trying to not burst into tears. I move to him quickly and cuddle into him. He wraps his arms around me and kisses the top of my head lightly before trying to speak again.

"I was out at a meeting with our beta, when suddenly, I could hear your mum screaming out to me through our mind link. The rogues were here for Raven," he answers, looking into my eyes.

"I got here as soon as I could, but I was too late," he speaks sadly.

"I have no idea how they even made it into our territory, we had so many wolves out on patrol. Someone has to have helped them in. When we all got back to the house, I found her in the lounge. She was barely able to speak to me, and I lifted her onto the couch and held her hand. She was trying to tell me something, but I couldn't understand."

I watch as a tear escapes his eye and rolls silently down his cheek.

"She kept repeating the same sound, she wasn't making any sense and she wasn't able to speak properly before she slipped away from me. I assumed she was calling for you, Raven, but I knew you wouldn't be able to get here in time," he chokes.

I begin to sob, and my dad rubs my arm softly.

"We will have her funeral in two days, under the full moon," my dad announces. I look up at him and try my best not to cry again.

The next two days are absolute torture. I barely leave my bedroom. Max has returned from a friends' sleepover—the night that mum was found. He has barely spoken a word. I sat with him whilst Dad explained to him what happened. It was like hearing it for the first time. My heart broke all over again. I held Max whilst he cried loudly. My dad withdrew into his office and buried himself under a mountain of paperwork, just to keep himself from breaking down. He is working around the clock, trying to find out who committed this horrible act. He questioned each of the guards on duty. No one knew anything. There wasn't even a trace of scent. His anguish is growing. He already looks ten years older.

We eat dinner in silence. No one has the heart to talk. As night falls, I yawn loudly and begin walking up to my bedroom. As I'm walking past Max's bedroom door, I overhear him talking to Mum, wishing that she would come back. That night, I go in and lay with him until he falls asleep. When I arrive back into my room, Chase lays, waiting for me in bed. I manage a small smile and climb in next to him. He is so thoughtful to stay with me during this time. I really appreciate him.

"Thank you for being here with me," I say, placing my head on his bare chest.

"I wouldn't be anywhere else," he says, placing his hand on my back and making small circles. Soon, I drift off into a restless sleep.

The next day is to be my mother's funeral. I have organised a black dress for myself and a suit for Chase, along with a small black suit for Max.

I help him to dress in the afternoon when the sun is beginning to hang low in the sky. We make our way towards the open field to the west of our territory. The whole pack begins to gather. We stand in a large circle around a pyre that has been built especially for my mother's cremation. Wolves don't have cemeteries; they burn their loved ones to send their spirits back to the Moon Goddess to be reborn.

My father begins the ceremony by standing beside my mother's casket and speaking some beautiful words about her. My mother was an amazing Luna. She was always someone that I looked up to and someone who I hoped to follow in her footsteps when I became a Luna in the future.

After my father finishes speaking, he moves along with our beta and two others—who I know to be my father's closest friends. They all step forward and lift my mother's casket onto their shoulders. Max and myself move to follow as they carry her around the entire circle. I hold tightly onto Max's hand as we walk, and I can feel him shaking slightly, so I grip his hand a little tighter. He looks up at me and I can see the tears threatening to fall from his eyes. I smile and give his hand a small squeeze as he tries his best to smile back. As we make our way around, everyone bows their head as we walk past them—this is a sign of respect.

I notice Cody standing with Ava on our way around the circle. No one speaks as we walk, and the silence is deafening. Once we have made our way around the entire circle, Max and I make our way back to where Chase is standing in the circle, people moving aside so that we fit back in. My father and the others carry my mother's casket and place it on top of the pyre.

My father sends out a prayer to the Moon Goddess and then lowers the flaming torch to the dry wood at the bottom of the pyre.

The flames rise quickly and burn brightly. I can feel the heat from the fire licking at my face. I stare into the flames, absolutely mesmerized as they consume my mother's body. My father shifts into his wolf and others begin to follow. Some remove their clothes whilst others just change, tearing their clothing. I decide to remove my dress but leave my underwear on. I shift and wait, watching the flames. I feel Chase shift beside me and nudge my shoulder before licking behind my ear. Max remains beside me, placing his hand on my neck. I look around, noting that there are a fair few children who have never shifted that stand by their own families. Once everyone has shifted, my father lets out a sorrow-filled howl. The whole pack follows.

I'm sure that the howls can be heard for miles.

"Goodbye, Mum," I whisper to the stars.

CHAPTER TWENTY-EIGHT

MEETING ALLY

After my mother's funeral, I try to stay with my dad and Max, but he demands that I return with Chase to his pack. I don't think he wants to watch me wallow around like I have been.

I'm not sure how to be anymore. Everywhere I look reminds me of my mum. Every breath I take hurts my chest. I'm the reason my mum is dead. Those rogues had come for me, just like Cody had said. Me, not my mum. Somehow, they knew I was meant to be at my parents' house that afternoon. I would have been had Chase not asked me to go for a run.

Chase has a car come to collect us. I hug my dad tightly to me and bid him and Max a goodbye. The forty minute drive goes by slowly. The trees pass my window in a blur. I must fall asleep along the way, as I wake to Chase carrying me up the front steps to our house.

On entering, I can hear giggling coming from the kitchen. Chase rolls his eyes but has a cheeky smile on his face. My tiredness dissipates quickly, and Chase places me tenderly on my feet.

"Oh my God, she's here," a female voice calls. Suddenly, I'm enveloped by a slim blonde girl.

"Hey, Raven, I'm Ally," she says whilst squeezing me.

"Uh, hi," I say, smiling at her. I know right away that we will be friends. I just have this feeling about her. I watch as she walks back to Mark. She is about the same height as me with long flowing blonde hair and bright blue eyes.

"You didn't tell me she was that pretty." She smiles and slaps Mark's chest.

"Hey, I'm not allowed to look at her, or this big bad alpha will rip my balls from my body. And... well, I need them," Mark replies, holding onto the front of his shorts.

We all laugh loudly. It is the first time have been—the smallest bit--happy in over four days.

A small pang of guilt hits me. How can I feel happy when my mum is gone?

As if sensing my sudden guilt, Ally smiles at me and goes over to the fridge. She grabs out a bottle of wine, holding it up and nodding at me. I smile and nod back. This girl is after my own heart. Chase's phone begins to ring loudly next to us. Fishing it out of his pocket, he answers it, moving into the kitchen to grab a drink whilst he is talking. I pull my shoes from my tired feet, dropping them by the front door and make my way back towards the living room.

When Chase gets off the phone, he announces that his parents are holding a huge party in a couple of weeks, mostly to introduce me to the entire pack as I will soon become their Luna. It was meant to happen when I first arrived last week, but clearly, we had to postpone because of everything that has happened. After the party, Chase will be taking over the title of alpha, which is very exciting.

Noticing Chase move towards the couch, Ally moves back to me with the bottle in her hand. Grabbing my hand, she begins pulling me to the couch. Mark follows behind with two glasses. Holding his beer, he holds it up and tilts it towards Chase in a silent salute. Ally and I sip our sweet white wine and speak for hours whilst the boys chat about training and watch the football on the tele. It is just natural with her. Like I have known her my entire life.

It has been two weeks since my mother's funeral. As part of my becoming Luna, it is tradition that I plan my meeting party. The party planning has given me something to think about and focus on, which has been an absolute life saver. I know Chase hates seeing me so down, but he completely understands and has been ever so supportive of me. I seriously can't thank the Moon Goddess enough for mating me with Chase. He is the most amazing mate anyone could ever hope for.

Ally and I have been inseparable ever since I met her. She is almost like the female version of Cody. I can talk to her about anything and everything, and it's like we've been friends since birth. Cody hadn't even come to see me when my mother died. I had seen him at her funeral, but he didn't even try to speak with me or even look at me, for that matter.

Sitting on my bed, I keep thinking back to that day and I wonder if perhaps I should message him. He was—after all—one of my best friends and being around Ally just makes me miss him even more.

"Uh... hello, earth to Raven," Ally calls, laughing at me and waving her hand in front of my face. She's laying across my bed, looking through magazines.

"Sorry, I was just thinking," I reply, smiling at her.

"Check out this beautiful wedding dress," Ally says, throwing an open magazine at me.

I look over the page and yes, the dress is absolutely beautiful.

"You aren't even engaged," I tease, tossing the magazine gently back to her.

"One day I will be, and so will you," she says, pouting.

I know that her sad face is because of how long it's taking Mark to ask her to marry him. It's not like she hasn't been hinting ferociously over the past few weeks. She almost cleared out the local newsagents of all the wedding magazines and has been leaving them all over the house.

We hear the front door open and know it's our mates returning from their training. Looking at each other with huge smiles on our faces, we both leap up, hurrying downstairs. The boys have grabbed a bottle of water and are sitting on the couch by the time we make it downstairs.

Ally runs over and jumps straight into Mark's lap and starts kissing him heatedly. I smile down at Chase, and he pulls me into his lap before kissing my cheek softly. I turn my face to his and plant a chaste kiss on his lips.

Ally has started to grind herself against Mark and an occasional moan is escaping both of them. It is starting to get a little uncomfortable. But at the same time, I feel something warming low in my tummy. I want to do that with Chase. I can feel myself growing warm between my legs, becoming wet at the thought of rubbing myself against him. Chase's eyes snap to mine, and I realize that he can smell my arousal. Watching him carefully, he shakes his head as if trying to clear it of unwanted thoughts.

"Alright, get a room you two," Chase finally says—after two minutes of watching our best friend's kiss.

"Hey, don't hate on us, dude, it ain't my fault you haven't popped her cherry yet," Mark says, laughing at Chase.

Ally slaps his chest, growling at him. Her eyes snap to mine apologetically.

"Let's take this elsewhere," Mark says, wiggling his eyebrows at Ally. She giggles loudly as he stands up from the couch and carries her upstairs over his shoulder. Giggling, she waves down at us as they go.

I wave back, laughing. Once they are both out of view, I turn back to Chase, watching him carefully, worrying about what he was thinking. The silence is beginning to become uncomfortable. I squeeze my legs together to calm the burn I'm feeling.

Suddenly, I feel the need to break the silence, so I ask him how his training was.

"It was great, my little bird," he replies, smiling at me and running his rough hands up and down my arms.

"Little bird?" I reply, lifting one of my eyebrows at him.

"Yeah. *My* little bird," he replies.

"Where on earth did you get that nickname from?" I laugh, leaning in closer to his face.

He raises his hands to my face, and I think he is going to kiss me, but he turns my head to the side and whispers seductively in my ear.

"You do know that your name is also a type of bird, right?"

I can hear the smirk spread across his lips before I can see it.

Leaning back, I push his chest, laughing. "Of course I know that."

"So, my little bird it is," he replies, looking deeply into my eyes.

Suddenly, loud banging noises come from upstairs and loud moans start echoing down the stairs.

Covering my face, I begin to laugh uncontrollably in an embarrassed way. Chase pulls my hands away from my face and watches me carefully.

"If it makes you uncomfortable, we can go somewhere else?" he asks quietly.

"It's okay, let's just watch a movie," I say, standing up and walking over to the huge shelf full of DVD's, picking out, The Girl Next Door. I push it into the DVD player before moving back to the couch and laying down on Chase's lap. His hand rubs up and down my arm as we watch the movie. We are so comfortable, but the sound of the movie hasn't really covered up the noises coming from upstairs.

My mind keeps moving back to the thoughts of grinding myself against Chase. I try my hardest to think about other things. Chase has said he wants it to be special and I totally agree. After it almost happened with Cody, I realized that I wasn't truly ready yet. I laugh internally and a little voice in my head says, *"What are you waiting for, silly?"* I thought about it for a little longer and realized that I honestly didn't know why I was waiting. I guess mates usually mated within a day or two of meeting each other. Unfortunately, I had only just come to live with Chase and then mum passed... this wasn't usually how it happened when you found your mate. Akira huffs in my head as if pointing out how much she wants to mate with Chase and have him mark us.

Chase moves underneath my head, which is laying in his lap. I notice he seems to be a little uncomfortable, so I turn my head to look up at him. As I turn my head, I notice my head leaning against his hardness. Shocked, my eyes snap to Chase's.

"I'm sorry, my little bird, I can't help it. I can smell how wet you are. What are you thinking about?" he asks, looking deeply into my eyes.

Time to be brave.

"I was thinking about how it would feel to grind myself on you just like Ally was on Mark," I say shyly, looking away from him as I say it.

CHAPTER TWENTY-NINE

WHAT YOU DO TO ME

His eyes flash wider before he smiles down at me.

"That sounds amazing," he says, putting his hands over his face and laying his head back on the couch, making a groaning noise deep in his throat. I can tell he is struggling to keep Quinn at bay. After all, we should be mated already.

Laying there for a moment, he suddenly shifts, and my head falls from his lap onto the couch with a bounce. Suddenly, he is lying over the top of me. It would seem that Quinn has temporarily taken over. These eyes watching me are primal. I can sense the need emanating from Chase's body. His alpha genes are pushing him to mark me.

He makes sure to keep his weight off me as he leans on his forearms and his knees. As if he is starving, his lips crush down on mine, coaxing a moan out of me that makes its way into his mouth. He gently lowers his body over mine, pressing himself in-between my legs. I gasp at the sensation.

Chase gains back his control, his eyes flashing back.

"See what you do to me, my little bird," Chase says seductively into my ear.

He lifts himself back up off me. My hips lift of their own accord, moving towards him, trying to feel the sensation again. Watching Chase's face, I can tell by his eyes that he can see how needy I am, and he lowers himself again, rubbing his hardness over my throbbing core. I moan, bringing my hand up to my mouth to try and stifle it. My index finger lays across my lips and I bite down onto it, trying to stop any noises escaping my mouth as Chase teases me.

Chase soon stops rubbing against me and looks down at me as if he's wondering if what he's doing is okay. I reach up and pull him back to my lips hungrily. I don't know what I'm doing as I've never had sex before—since the last time I was even close, my dad walked in on me. Even if all this is new to me, my body seems to know what it's doing.

My body takes over and I push Chase backwards until he's sitting up. I climb down off the couch and kneel on the floor. Running my hands up his strong, muscular legs, I reach the top of his pants and I begin rubbing my hand over his hardness. He gasps, shocked by my boldness. I pull at the front of his pants silently, asking for them to be removed. As if reading my thoughts, Chase slowly pulls his pants down, watching me the whole time. I run my hands over the large bulge hidden beneath his underwear. He takes in a deep breath and closes his eyes quickly. When they open again, his eyes are burning with passion. I place my hands inside his boxer shorts, holding his girth in my hand.

My eyes move up his amazing body to see his face. He has his signature smirk on his face as if he knows what I'm thinking. I pull the thin layer of fabric aside. Leaning forward, I slowly caress around the tip with my tongue, causing Chase to push his hips forward and moan. I squeeze my legs together as the sound registers loud and clear in my groin.

Knowing that it feels good for Chase, I continue for a few moments before placing as much of him as I can into my mouth before beginning to move my head up and down his length, slowly at first. I feel Chase begin to move himself a little faster, pushing his hips up off the couch and pushing himself deeper into my mouth. I close my eyes, focusing on what I'm doing, loving the feeling of him inside my mouth.

"Open your eyes and look at me," Chase asks breathily.

I open my eyes and look up at him, watching him. The look on his face is making me so wet. I try to get some kind of relief for myself by leaning a little onto the heel of my foot that's currently underneath me. My core is burning hot and just hearing Chase moan is turning me on so much.

Chase reaches down and I realize he's trying to grab one of my hands which are resting on his thighs. He grabs my hand and places it around himself. Realizing what he wants, I use my hand and mouth in unison to pump up and down. He places his hands up behind his head as it rolls back onto the couch, and he closes his eyes.

"Raven, I'm going to come," he calls out to me. "If you don't want me to do it in your mouth, let go now."

I don't want to let go, so I continue, and soon, hot wet liquid squirts into my mouth and rolls easily down my throat.

"Nice, you got yourself a swallower," comes a voice from behind us.

Chase sits up and pulls me into his lap. We both look up, shocked, and see Mark leaning against the wall just at the bottom of the stairs, holding a bottle of water in his hand with just a towel around his waist.

"Piss off, Mark," Chase calls angrily.

Holding his hands up in the air, he replies, "Dude, it's not the first time I've seen you getting a blow job; besides, I've seen much worse," he finishes, smiling to himself before setting off back upstairs.

After Mark departs, Chase kisses my forehead and apologises.

"I'm sorry, my little bird, I didn't think he would be down for a while."

I smile shyly up at him, not really sure what to say.

I cuddle into him, and we watch the remainder of the movie. Mark and Ally go at it for a little while longer before coming down to make dinner. Mark makes himself comfortable on the couch, giving me a wink as he sits down. I smile at him and cover my face in embarrassment. Chase leans over, slaps him over the back of the head and we all laugh together. Ally is in the kitchen starting dinner, so I decide—to avoid the awkwardness—I will go and help her.

CHAPTER THIRTY

THE MONOPOLY GAME

Walking into the kitchen, Ally turns to me and squeals loudly, grabbing me and pulling me into a hug.

"Oh, my gosh, you little minx, tell me everything. Was it good?" She speaks so fast, I barely catch all of her questions. She holds me and basically squeezes me to death. I stare at her, not knowing what to say.

"Well, don't hold out on me, girl, how was it?" she asks after letting me go. I look at her and smile, and she squeals again.

"Shhh, okay," I say, grabbing her face between my hands. "It was just a blow job."

"What? So, you didn't have sex?" she says with a surprised look on her face.

"No," I reply, laughing at the newly changed look of disappointment on her face.

"Damn, I thought you might have lost your 'V' card," she says, pouting.

Shaking my head and smiling at her, I let go of her face, pulling her towards the bench and begin cutting up some ingredients to make a salad whilst she readies some steaks.

After a few moments of silence, she stops and looks up at me.

"So, he didn't even get you off?" she says, as if she's annoyed.

I shake my head at her, not needing to say anything. I continue to focus far too much on the salad ingredients I'm cutting. The capsicum that is meant to be in strips is now finely diced into tiny cubes.

"Chase, you are no gentleman," she yells, and I shove her with my elbow.

She laughs and puts the steaks into a preheated pan. Chase appears in the kitchen doorway, placing his arm above his head, his elbow resting on the wall.

"What?" he asks, a little confused.

"You didn't even get her off, that's a dog move, man," she says, laughing. She moves back next to me and nudges me with her elbow. I remain facing the bench whilst all the blood drains from my face in embarrassment.

"We would have gotten a lot further had your mate not interrupted us," he snaps back, speaking loudly so that Mark can hear from the lounge.

"I could have stayed quiet and watched," Mark yells back, causing Ally to burst into a fit of giggles.

I continue to stare down and focus on the cucumber I'm now cutting. I can feel the heat rising further into my cheeks. I hear Chase move towards me, and he grabs onto my hips from behind, and whispers into my ear, "Don't worry, my little bird, I will make you come for me later."

I turn to him and see he's glaring at Ally, who seems to be almost wetting herself she's laughing so hard.

"You know they are just trying to press your buttons, right?" I tell Chase whilst pressing my hands against his amazingly sculpted chest.

He continues to glare at Ally whilst he leans in and pecks my lips with a light kiss before leaving to go back into the lounge.

Our dinner was beautiful, and the boys made appreciative noises the whole time we were eating. We made small talk at the table about how our days were and, yet again, Ally dropped a few engagement hints into the conversation. Unfortunately, Mark is as thick as a post and isn't getting any of the hints. Chase looks over at me adoringly every time he misses one of her hints and winks at me. I roll my eyes skyward, wondering how daft someone has to be. It is almost like she needs a giant neon sign attached to her boobs in order for him to finally get the point.

After dinner, Mark and Chase wash up the dishes. Ally and I sit on the couch, waiting for the boys to finish up.

"So, are you excited for later?" Ally asks, taking a sip from the glass of wine she holds in her hand.

"I'm actually really nervous," I respond, taking a huge gulp out of my own wine glass.

"Why, doll?" Ally asks, scooting closer to me. "There's nothing to be nervous about, he's only going to eat you out," she finishes with a smirk on her face.

I slap her leg playfully and she begins to giggle loudly.

"What's so funny?" asks Mark as he comes back into the lounge, followed by Chase.

"Nothing," both Ally and I speak at once.

Mark and Chase both raise their eyebrows, not believing us.

Once the boys are done, they come and make themselves comfortable. Chase sits on the floor in front of me and I gently massage my hands through his hair.

"Let's watch a movie?" Mark suggests.

"No, let's play a boardgame," Ally announces, placing her wine glass down onto the coffee table. Getting up from the couch, Ally goes over to the hall cupboard, placing her hands on her hips as if the decision is really tricky.

"Monopoly, Jenga or Scrabble?" she calls loudly.

We all decide to have a game of Monopoly. We sit down on the floor in the lounge, placing ourselves around the long rectangular coffee table. Ally decides she wants to be the banker, so she hands out the money and I set mine up neatly, in little piles in front of me. I decide to be the top hat, Chase picks the shoe, and Ally picks the wheelbarrow—claiming it is to carry all her winnings home in. When it is Mark's turn to choose a piece, he quickly grabs the cat, claiming that he is the master of all pussies.

Ally and I laugh, but Chase just shoves his best friend and rolls his eyes.

We are about half an hour into the game, and Chase is kicking everyone's arse—although I'm slowly gaining some properties, it feels like Chase has pretty much bought everything on the board.

Ally is also doing quite well with a few hotels. Mark is almost bankrupt but still has two of the train stations and both of the utilities. I have two train stations and a few mismatched properties here and there, and it is my roll. As I move my way around the board, I'm the lucky one to land on Mayfair—which is currently unowned. Chase has Park Lane.

"Come on, little bird, sell it to me," Chase leans over and coos in my ear.

His warm breath on my neck makes the hair on my body stand on end.

I blink seductively at him before leaning forwards just a little, so that my cleavage is more on show. I watch as his eyes dip down and then come back up to mine.

I place my hand on his thigh in such a way that I know I'm not far from his crotch area.

Then, when I notice his breath hitch in his throat, I lean my face right into his with my lips just an inch or so away from his.

"You wish," I whisper before leaning back and sitting back on my bottom with an innocent look on my face.

Chase laughs and leans over, kissing my cheek.

"Fine, if that's the way you want to play," he says, shrugging.

I make eye contact with Ally, and she has a smirk on her face.

"Mark, babe, I really want more wine!" she asks, holding her empty glass in the air and batting her eyelids.

Mark doesn't really look like he wants to move but Ally's next words make him leap up from the floor.

She looks at me and winks. "It makes me really horny," she says in a really seductive voice.

I don't think I've ever seen Mark move as fast before. Running into the kitchen, he returns moments later with his wallet and his keys.

"I'll be right back, baby doll. There's no wine left in the fridge, only champagne," Mark says whilst motioning over his shoulder towards the kitchen.

Chase searches my face before asking, "Would you like more wine, little bird?"

I'm not sure why, but I look over at Ally quickly and note that she nods slightly. It is such a small nod that if I didn't know her so well, I would have missed it.

"Uh, yes, please."

Chase stands up from the floor and moves over to where Mark is standing. Patting him on the shoulder, he says, "Looks like a wine run, dude."

"Gotta keep the ladies happy," Mark replies, smiling at both of us.

The boys make their way out of the house, and soon, we can hear their car making its way towards the shops.

"Thank God they're gone. Come on," Ally speaks quickly, grabbing my arm and dragging me towards the stairs.

CHAPTER THIRTY-ONE

PREPARATIONS

eing dragged along like a ragdoll my arm feels like it's about to come off. "What on earth are we doing?" I call after her.

"Getting you ready," she says, almost pulling my arm out of its socket. Suddenly, she stops outside the bathroom, turning towards me just as I collide with her, not realising that she has stopped walking.

Giggling, she then turns and walks into the bathroom, pushing the door gently.

"Ready for what?" I ask, with a shocked look on my face, following after her.

"For Chase," she says, smiling at me with a cheeky look in her eyes. "Quick, get undressed and shower, you need to shave," she says, grabbing a towel and throwing it at me before taking a seat on the toilet.

What on earth is this crazy girl on about? I watch as a cheeky smirk crosses her face and I finally click. She wants me to make sure that I am presentable for Chase later.

My face heats a little before I realize she's completely right. I undress quickly and tie my hair up into a high bun; I won't have time to dry it. I turn the water on, sitting my hand underneath it, waiting for it to be a good temperature and stepping in once it is warm. I stand under the streaming water and take in a deep breath. I want this. I want to be intimate with Chase. After giving him a blow job earlier, I shouldn't be feeling so nervous about what is going to happen later. He knows what he is doing. He has done it before. A small pang of hurt crosses my heart but I banish it quickly. I reach for the razor and begin with my underarms and soon move on to my legs and groin area.

"Make sure you get right in there," Ally calls over the sound of the running water.

I had almost forgotten that she was still in the bathroom. "Oh my God, Ally, do you really need to be in here for this?" I say, laughing. We've definitely seen each other naked before, but really?

I smile to myself. Having only known her for a short time, I know that she is my best friend and always will be. We have a deeper level of connection that I have never ever had with another female. I can't even describe it.

"You definitely need my help." She laughs back, and I can just imagine her whipping her hair behind her shoulder and pointing her finger at me.

"Hurry up, you don't have all day," Ally calls, her voice seeming to be getting quieter as if she has moved out of the bathroom.

I roll my eyes.

After washing my body, I make sure that everything is pristine downstairs and that it's all cleanly shaven. I turn the water off and step out of the shower, reaching for a towel and wrapping it around me tightly. Ally suddenly returns, holding a small bag that looks to be from a lingerie shop.

"Here, put this on, the boys will be back any minute," she says before disappearing again.

I peek into the bag and find a beautiful black bra and underwear set with beautiful lace features and tiny crystal details.

I pop the underwear on and quickly put on a little bit of eye makeup before letting my hair down from the hair-tie. It looks a little messy, so I lightly brush it. Just as I think I am finished, Ally returns.

"Damn, girl, you look freaking hot as hell, even I would do you." She giggles. "Here, put this in your mouth," she says before popping a small breath mint into my mouth.

"Sit," she says, pointing to the toilet before picking up a curling wand. I quickly move over to the toilet and sit down.

Jeez, bossy much? I giggle lightly.

Ally begins placing light curls in my hair. It feels like only a few minutes before she taps my shoulder lightly saying, "Finished."

I turn to face her, and she places her hand on her chin.

"You need lip gloss," she says, turning and picking up a gloss before passing it to me.

After popping the lip gloss on, I look at my reflection in the mirror. The outfit is perfect. It is like it was made for my body. The small diamantes shine brightly under the bathroom light.

Running my hand through my hair and pushing it behind my ear, doubt hits me again.

"What's wrong, sweetie?" Ally asks, concerned.

"He's done this before," I stumble over my words.

"Sweets, we have been over this before. He didn't love those bimbos." She sighs. "He's made mistakes and you can't hold that against him."

I sigh. Maybe it isn't the fact that he has been with other girls that is getting to me. Maybe it is because I almost did the same thing with Cody and I'm feeling guilty about it.

Sensing me spiralling into a moment of mass overthinking, Ally drags me into Chase's and my bedroom.

Looking around, I gasp. It is absolutely beautiful. Ally has set up candles all around the room that makes the room shimmer and glow. It is just bright enough but not too bright. There are rose petals on the bed and champagne with a fruit platter and a can of cream on the bedside table.

"How the hell did you do all this in half an hour?" I ask, turning to her with a shocked look on my face.

She smiles at me with a Cheshire cat grin. "Well, the candles are from our bedroom, and I already had the fruit platter made for dessert. The champagne was in the fridge, and I had the lingerie to wear for Mark, but I never get a chance to put anything on because he's so impatient, so I figured you can have it," she says, waving her hands around the room like she's presenting it.

"Thank you," I finally breathe out.

"Now, when Chase goes down on you, don't feel like you have to be quiet," she says, winking at me and turning to walk back downstairs.

She hasn't even made it the whole way down the stairs, when I hear the boys opening the front door, laughing at something they were talking about. I hear Chase ask where I am and then I hear Ally letting him know that I'm upstairs waiting for him.

Hurriedly, I close the bedroom door, looking around the room, trying to work out whether to stand next to the bed or lay across it. I quickly decide that I'm just going to sit on the edge of the bed.

Sitting down, I cross my legs at my ankle and slightly bend my knees. I feel sexy. I truly hope that I look sexy.

I can hear Chase's footsteps getting closer to the door. When the door swings inwards, Chase looks around the room and appears to be a little shocked.

Then, his eyes meet mine.

CHAPTER THIRTY-TWO

I WANT YOU

Just this look alone makes my skin prickle with excitement. His eyes seem to flash between his and Quinn's. Akira makes a low moan sound in the back of my mind; she can sense that Quinn is present and she is ready to mate and be marked.

Small goosebumps spread across my skin like wildfire. A deep breath that I hadn't even realized I was holding escapes my lips slowly. Closing the door silently, Chase stalks towards me, like a lion on its prey. His eyes skim over my body before snapping back to my eyes. There is an electric charge moving between us and it is almost illuminating the whole bedroom.

As he reaches me, he leans in and presses his lips to mine all too briefly. Looking up at him, I try to stand to be at the same level as him, but he is too quick. He reaches down and pulls under my knees swiftly, so that I'm lying flat on my back on the bed. My legs are still hanging over the edge. Chase crawls up my body, supporting himself on his hands and kneeling with one knee on the bed and his other foot still on the floor.

Chase begins kissing my face lightly, avoiding my lips. He moves around to my ear and bites down on my earlobe sharply. I gasp softly at this action sending a shock straight to my groin. He then begins spreading kisses as soft as fluttering butterflies across my collarbone, moving down towards my covered breasts. He starts kissing my breasts over the top of the sheer fabric, and I can feel my nipples begin to harden and strain against the material.

Moving from my breasts, he makes his way down my torso, stopping just after my belly button.

Thinking he is going to continue down further, my heart is hammering in my chest like it is going to break free at any moment. I can feel my own wetness pooling down below, soaking the fragile material of my underwear. Instead of continuing down, he moves back up towards my breasts, hooking his fingers onto the top of the material and pulling it sharply down, taking my nipple into his skilled mouth. His tongue swirls around it. His breath warms it.

I swear, I almost come then and there.

Lowering himself so that his chest is against my sensitive skin, his body heat begins to warm me. Unexpectedly, he presses his pelvis into me. I can feel his hardness straining against the thin material that separates it from me. I lay panting below him. Suddenly, he releases my sensitive nipple and runs his tongue up my collarbone and to the sweet spot on my neck.

"I so want to mark you right now," he whispers against my sensitive skin. "I won't until you ask me to."

My body is so responsive to him, but no words come from in my mouth to respond. Did I want him to mark me in the throes of passion?

I have heard that it hurts, and I don't want to ruin the moment, so I cheekily lift my hips a little, rubbing my swollen clit against his hard length.

Chase smirks and leans forward, kissing me thoroughly before moving south. My body begins to involuntarily tremble under his expert touch. I begin to press my thighs together, trying to ease the pressure that is building between my legs. Chase moves down off the bed and kneels on the floor. I lean up onto my elbows so that I can see him, but I'm suddenly thrust backwards as Chase grabs my ankles, tipping me back against the bed. He spreads my legs slowly, holding onto my thighs so that my legs won't close. Chase kisses the very top of my right thigh before moving across, agonising slow, to my left thigh. His movements are slow and sensual. He swiftly kisses the centre of my burning core over the top of my underwear. This slight pressure is heavenly but gone all too quickly.

A small whine leaves my throat as I note the pressure has gone. I feel Chase lifting my bottom up so that he can remove my underwear. He is struggling a little and I'm getting impatient.

"Just rip them," I say breathily.

I can hear his sharp intake of breath before hearing the ripping sound of my underwear.

His fingertips begin touching my quivering flesh before I feel the tip of his finger slide a little way inside me before he removes it.

"You're so tight and wet for me, baby," Chase manages to say before plunging his tongue into the centre of my burning core. Tipping my head all the way back, I close my eyes and moan loudly. Unexpectedly, he slides the whole length of his finger inside me. He moves his finger slowly in and out until I'm trembling. Just as I become accustomed to one finger, he adds another whilst lowering his mouth back over my throbbing clit. I feel a tight pinch below and can smell a slight tinge of metallic in the air. I wince slightly, feeling Chase stop moving for a moment, and then he removes his fingers from me.

"Did I hurt you, baby?" Chase asks, sounding worried.

"No, I'm okay, it just stings a little," I say, breathing heavily.

I feel Chase use something to clean me quickly before using his tongue on my scorching hot core again. His tongue is relentless. He places two of his fingers back inside me. My hands are grasping at the sheet below me. Lifting my head, I see Chase's head between my parted thighs, and he looks up at me whilst using the tip of his tongue against my clit. His eyes are burning into mine, and that's when I notice my juices smeared across his gorgeous face.

I move my hands down into his hair and push his face back into my pool of moisture. He places his fingers back at my opening, plunging them deeply inside me. I tip my head back and arch my back into the air, meeting his fingers thrust for thrust.

"Ch…Ch… Ah… Se…" I scream as my body shakes involuntarily, almost bringing me to my peak. As my insides start to tighten, I know that I'm close to having an orgasm. Feeling that I'm close, Chase suddenly stops and removes his fingers from inside me.

I sit up slightly, staring at him with want in my eyes. I feel Akira flash through my eyes and Chase lets Quinn flash through momentarily. Our wolves were bonded from the moment Chase and I met. But mating and marking will bind Chase and I forever.

Gaining control back, Chase kisses the inside of my right thigh before saying, "I want you to beg me to make you come."

Looking down at him, I watch him struggle to control Quinn, his eyes flashing between his own beautiful blue ones compared to Quinn's midnight black ones with emerald-green sparks.

Shaking his head, Chase's ocean-blue eyes return looking deeply into mine, waiting for my response. I watch him carefully as he removes his shirt over his head, sweat shimmering on his face, and his—now bare—beautifully sculpted chest.

Sitting up fully, I draw Chase's mouth to mine, kissing him feverously. Tugging him to me, our tongues battle for dominance. I can taste my own saltiness on his lips which turns me on even more. Pulling away, I move my mouth to Chase's ear, and slowly, I run my tongue over his earlobe before biting down on it harshly. Feeling Chase's body rumble with a moan, I whisper seductively, "Make me come… hard," I finally manage to say. I'm not really sure where this sexual temptress in me is coming from, but I like her. She has such confidence.

Within moments, Chase has me panting like I have done a five-mile run. My insides begin to tighten, and I feel an overwhelming sensation come over my whole body.

"Oh my God," I call out, arching my back. Chase doesn't stop moving his fingers in and out of my tight wetness. I can hear the sound of his hand slapping against me. Suddenly, my orgasm shakes my whole body with shivers that I never want to stop. It is like the world has stopped. My ears ring as if there are no other sounds in the world than Chase's and my breathing.

Once my body stops twitching, Chase slowly removes his fingers. I can barely open my eyes, but I note in my mind that Chase now lays next to me. I open one of my eyes to see him sucking on the two fingers that have just been inside me. Both of my eyes burst open at this sight.

"You taste mighty fine, my little bird," Chase says with a clear smirk on his face.

Sitting up, I look deeply into Chase's eyes. I lean towards him, grabbing his fingers and placing them into my mouth. I suck on them, hard. Eventually, I let go of his fingers and lick my lips seductively.

"Mmmm, I really do," I say, smirking at Chase, whose jaw is now residing on the floor.

"You're so hot," Chase finally manages to say, wrapping his arms around me.

I yawn loudly and I fall back down onto my pillow. My eyes are barely staying open.

"Goodnight, my little bird," Chase says, kissing my forehead.

CHAPTER THIRTY-THREE

WHAT ARE BEST FRIENDS FOR

The next morning, I wake to a loud banging on our bedroom door. I roll over and slide out of bed begrudgingly.

"There better be a fire," I call to whomever is behind the door.

I pull on a robe and open the door. I'm immediately clobbered by one very excited Ally.

Chase sits up and Ally eyes him before saying, "Girl time, get out."

Chase throws his hands into the air and pulls the covers back; he's just wearing his underwear, but he pulls on a pair of track pants. Just as he gets to the door, he smiles at me before turning away and leaving.

"Sooo…" Ally asks expectedly.

I blush wildly and a huge smile spreads across my face.

"It was amazing," I finally get out.

"Clearly," Ally says, picking up the torn underwear from the floor and swinging it around before throwing it at me. "We could hear you moaning, so it must have been amazing."

I sit down on the bed and Ally throws herself down, smiling widely at me.

"We need to go shopping today to find a dress for the party," I finally announce, trying to get her onto a different topic.

After a well-deserved shower, I dress in a maxi-dress and pull on some sandals before heading downstairs. I find Chase sitting at the kitchen table, eating a bowl full of cereal. As I walk past him towards the kitchen, I plant a soft kiss on his cheek.

I grab an apple from the fruit bowl and settle into a chair next to Chase. I can't help but look up from the table and my eyes bore into Chase's beautiful blue eyes. He smiles at me before reaching his hand out to me. I place my hand gently in his and he pulls me from my chair and into his lap. Placing small kisses on my shoulder, he begins moving up my neck, grazing his teeth along my sweet spot.

"Alright you two." Ally laughs loudly whilst coming down the stairs, placing a large hoop earring into her ear as she goes. "You ready?" she asks, looking at me expectedly.

"Ready?" Chase asks, looking into my eyes.

"We're going shopping," Ally replies for me.

"What for?" Chase says, looking from me to Ally.

"Sex toys," Ally replies with a serious look on her face.

Chase's chin almost hits the floor, and he struggles to talk.

"Dresses for the party," I say, glaring at Ally, who is now holding her stomach laughing hard at Chase's reaction.

"What am I going to do with you," I mind link Ally before giving Chase a quick kiss on the lips and grabbing my car keys.

"You know you love me," Ally says out loud before grabbing her handbag from the table.

"Please be safe," Chase mind links to me whilst wrapping his arms

around me.

I smile up at him and lightly brush my hand over his cheek.

"*I will,*" I send back before leaving.

Running out to my car, I notice that Ally has already made herself comfortable in my passenger seat. Shaking my head, I slip in next to her and head off towards the local mall. It's quite large and much better than the one that's near my parent's house. It takes us about twenty-five minutes to reach the mall, and by the time we arrive, I am absolutely starving.

"Let's get lunch first," I whine at Ally, pulling on her arm in a childish way.

"You're always hungry," Ally responds, laughing. Unable to deny me food, she grabs my hand, and we head for the food court. I grab a seat across from Ally after buying some sushi. Ally scrunches her nose at me as she watches me eat.

"I honestly don't know how you eat that stuff, Ray," she says, putting her fingers down her throat dramatically.

"Shut up and eat your burger," I say back with sass.

After lunch, we decide to head to the toilet before we begin our shopping. I'm much faster at going than Ally, so I walk back out of the toilets and decide to wait for her just outside. As I am waiting, I have this weird feeling that I'm being watched. I look around, trying not to draw attention to myself but can't see anything out of the ordinary.

"Let's do this thing," Ally calls loudly as she loops her arm with mine, shaking me out of my trance. We float in and out of shops, trying on what feels like a million dresses. Ally finally exits the dressing room in a sexy black number with a heart-shaped neckline and a mermaid style bottom.

"I think this is the one," she calls to me, twirling herself in front of the mirror.

I leave the rack I was looking through and come around the corner into the dressing room to look at the dress on her.

"Oh, my God, Al, you look freaking stunning," I say with a big smile on my face.

"You think?" she asks, watching my face.

"If Mark doesn't ask you to marry him, I might just do it myself." I laugh and pull her in for a hug. "You look absolutely beautiful."

Ally goes back into the changing room and changes before paying for the dress. We head off in search of a dress for me. So far, I just haven't found anything that is screaming 'new Luna of our pack.' I want it to be beautiful but conservative, but also a little sexy. Who am I kidding? I'm never going to find something that's all of those things.

We head into yet another shop and Ally starts going through the rack. I walk over to the other side of the store and start flipping through the formal dresses. Again, I feel like there are a pair of eyes on me. I look up and see a set of brown eyes; someone I don't recognise. The guy immediately walks away, making me think that perhaps I just looked up at the wrong time.

"Ray, check this one out," Ally calls, holding up a dusty pink dress. "I think this one is going to look beautiful on you," she says, passing it to me.

I grab the dress from her and hurry into the change room. The dress is an off-the-shoulder with a tight corset-style top that clings to my waist and flows outwards towards the floor, with a slit up the side. There is also a small silver broach centred on a slim belt on the smallest part of the waist. It's absolutely stunning and as soon as I put it on, I just know it's the right one for me.

I come out of the change room to find Ally sitting on a couch, waiting for me.

"So, what do you think?" I say, twirling.

"Oh, hell girl, you look absolutely freaking jaw dropping," Ally replies, making winking faces at me.

I quickly change out of the dress and pay for it. Ally and I then begin walking back towards the car.

"Oh shit, I didn't get any shoes," I say, stopping in my tracks and nearly causing people to walk into me.

"I have to go pee again, so you go and look in there," Ally says, pointing to a nearby shoe store. "I'll be right back," she says before walking away.

Watching as Ally heads off, I wander into the shoe shop, hoping to find some lovely silver heels to go with my dress.

I round the corner to try and find my size when I notice the brown-eyed guy staring at me from just outside the shoe store.

CHAPTER THIRTY-FOUR

BEING FOLLOWED

This is starting to get weird. I rush out of the store and head for the toilets but find that when I look back, the man is following me.

"Someone's following me," I mind link to Ally.

"Where are you? I'm coming," Ally replies rapidly, and I can hear the concern in her voice.

Suddenly, my phone begins to ring. Looking down, I see that it's Chase.

I fumble to answer my phone whilst trying to keep a steady pace without falling down. "Hello."

"What's wrong, little bird? I can feel your fear from here, is everything okay?" Chase replies, sounding worried.

"Someone's following me," I whisper back.

"I'm on my way," Chase says quickly before hanging up on me.

Our bond is growing, I think, still moving. My fear must be strong for Chase to feel it from this far away. Chase being from an alpha bloodline can sense my feelings and emotions already. After we mate and Chase marks me, I will be able to sense his also.

In my hurry to get away, I had completely missed the turn off for the toilet, so I begin walking into a huge chain store. I look back, trying to check if I am still being followed, but I can't see him anymore. I look around, feeling frightened, and note that I can't see the brown-eyed man anywhere.

I walk slowly around the corner of one of the clothing racks and run straight into someone.

Looking up, I see that it's the brown-eyed man.

"I've got her," he says, pressing his hand against a small earpiece. He suddenly grabs onto my shoulders, his hard fingers digging into my skin. I struggle to get out of his grasp. He pulls me tighter to him and I notice that his scent smells off. Not like a wolf. It's almost invisible to my senses. I hit his chest and then bring my knee up towards his groin. The sharp pain causes him to let go briefly, and in my haste to get away, I trip and fall backwards onto the floor, letting out a squeal. As if sensing something, he moves back around the rack.

My hands cover my face, and I begin to cry. Suddenly, another pair of hands touch my shoulder. I look up to see a very worried Ally standing in front of me. The man with the brown eyes has disappeared.

"Are you okay?" Ally asks, holding her hand out to help me up.

I stand and check myself over. My eyes scan the nearby area. My breath is coming out in panicked pants.

"I'm okay, I think he's gone," I finally manage to get out.

Ally sniffs around me and suddenly stops when she sees a few humans watching us. They must think she's a little strange sniffing me, so we walk out of the shop and make our way back to the car.

I see Chase and Mark enter the mall, looking around wildly trying to find us. Our eyes meet and he rushes to me as fast as he can. Mark embraces Ally at the same time that Chase reaches me.

"Are you okay, little bird?" he asks, looking me over as if he's expecting to see injuries. "Mark and I were getting something from in town, and I could feel your fear. Did you see who it was?"

I replay the story of how I had seen him a couple of times before I realized that I was being followed. Chase hugs me tightly to his chest but then pulls me back at arm's length.

"You say that he grabbed your shoulders, but I cannot smell any scent on you other than Ally and myself," he says, looking a little confused.

I explain that the man's scent was off, he didn't smell right, like he was using something to cover his smell. Our senses are quite good, and we would have been able to track him had he not done something to alter his smell.

With no scent, we are unable to track down the brown-eyed man, which makes Chase very angry. I doubt I will be allowed to leave the house ever again after this. Cody had warned me that rogues would come for me one day. They have already caused the death of my mother, and now this.

We head back to my car. Ally decides to go with Mark. Chase holds his hand out for the keys to my car. I hand them over willingly; I am still shaking from my close encounter. He had communicated with someone. Someone was orchestrating this attack against me. The man's words echoing in my brain. *"I've got her,"* he had said.

We head home. Once we arrive, I realize that it's time to get ready for the party tonight.

After weeks of planning this party, I'm so excited for it to finally be happening. Tonight, I will be introduced to the entire pack as the future Luna, and Chase will take his rightful place as alpha. It is going to be a huge night.

Trying not to let what happened earlier ruin this momentous day, I quickly run upstairs to shower. Trying to forget about what happened at the mall is going to be hard. Chase follows me into the bedroom and closes the door.

I remove my shoes and pants and look up at him. His face is worried, and his eyes watch me in a way that I have never seen before.

I walk over to him, placing my hands on both sides of his face.

"What's wrong?" I ask in a quiet voice.

"I don't know what I would do if I ever lost you," he says, leaning forward and placing his forehead on mine.

"I'm not going anywhere, baby," I reply, leaning in a little further and pressing my lips to his.

"Come and take a shower with me," I say, pulling his hand. He follows me willingly, and soon, we are standing naked together under the steaming water.

Chase kisses my shoulder lightly before making his way up the side of my neck. I lean into him and moan quietly as I feel his hands move up my sides to caress my breasts gently. His fingers grip my nipples lightly, pulling them gently. This action makes my knees almost buckle. I turn and we begin to kiss deeply, our tongues colliding in this hot moment of passion.

Suddenly, we hear a loud banging on our bedroom door. Chase stops and moves to climb out of the shower, and before he leaves, he kisses my shoulder quickly, saying he will check who it is. I wash my hair and shave my legs. Stepping out of the shower, I realize that Chase isn't going to return. When I enter the bedroom with my towel wrapped around me, I find Ally laying across my bed in a towel herself.

"About time, I've been waiting for ages. Come to my room and I'll do your makeup and hair," she says, jumping up from the bed and heading out the door.

"Where's Chase?" I ask, following behind her. She shrugs her shoulders and pushes hers and Marks' bedroom door open.

I follow behind her and quickly squeal and cover my eyes.

"What the fuck? Mark, why are you naked?" I scream, turning around.

"Hey, you're in my room, Ray," he says in a mocking tone.

"Cover it up, babe," Ally says nonchalantly.

"Is it safe?" I ask, pressing my hand firmly over my eyes. "I never, ever want to see that ever again."

"It's safe," Ally replies, laughing.

Mark now has a pair of black suit pants on. I poke my tongue out at him as I walk over to where Ally is sitting at her vanity table, doing her hair. Mark just smirks at me and winks before exiting the room.

It takes Ally and me over two hours to do our hair and makeup. We blast tunes and sing along into hairbrushes and deodorant cans. I seriously love this girl so much. I missed having a best friend. Thinking about friends makes me think of Cody. I wonder whether he misses me or not? I have thought about him often, wishing that he had never had Ava as a mate… my life would have been so different.

When we're finally done, I go back into my room to pop my dress on. My eyes gaze over my figure in the mirror. I look at my dress and run my hands down my body, loving the feeling of the material against my skin. Doing a small spin, I smile at my reflection, until my face falls and I look down at my bare feet.

"Oh no, Ally, I didn't get shoes," I call to her down the hall.

She comes hurrying out of her room with two pairs of shoes for me to try on. Luckily, one pair is perfect, so I pop them on and check myself once again in the mirror.

"You look fab, lady. Let's go," Ally says, grabbing my hand. I still haven't seen Chase or Mark for the whole time we were getting ready, and I wonder where they are.

CHAPTER THIRTY-FIVE

MEETING THE PACK

I reach the bottom of the stairs with Ally and my eyes meet Chase's. My eyes flow up and down his body, noting just how handsome he looks. He is wearing a simple black suit that has been tailored perfectly to his body. He holds his hand out to me and I take it willingly. My heart begins to beat faster as soon as my skin touches his, igniting me from the inside.

"You look…" he starts. "Just… oh… wow," he finally gets out.

I smile widely and lean into him.

"You don't look so bad yourself, handsome."

"We've got a party to get to," Mark calls as he pulls a giggling Ally into his arms, kissing her.

We head out the door and get into Chase's car. The party is on the other side of the pack lands, and it is too far to walk in these heels.

Chase rests his hand on my thigh as he drives. His hand warms my thigh, causing me to melt into the chair a little. I feel a low vibrating feeling in my chest and I whimper, wanting him to touch me everywhere.

He looks over at me, sensing this, and mouths, "Later baby," whilst rubbing his thumb up and down my leg.

It doesn't take us that long to reach the site of the party. It is in full swing by the time we arrive. We can hear the beat of the music well before we arrive. I start feeling a little nervous the closer we get.

When we pull into a parking space, Mark and Ally jump out of the car excitedly and head straight into the party.

"What's wrong, little bird?" Chase asks, grabbing my hand in his.

"What if the pack don't like me?" I ask, looking down at the floor.

"They will love you," Chase says, leaning over and kissing my cheek lightly. "Come, let's go."

We get out of the car and Chase leads me into the party with his hand on my waist. Pack members bow their heads to us with such great respect. I smile politely and move through the large crowd. Looking around, I feel a wave of happiness come over me. Ally and I planned this party together... well, when we weren't planning Ally's imaginary wedding. It was my first task as an upcoming Luna... I had to plan a large pack event. I guess it is like a mini test to see how I would cope.

Looking around at the scene before me, I am so proud of how the whole night came together. There is a large marquee set up in a large field. The roof of the marquee is lined with beautiful shimmering fabrics. Tables are placed around with gorgeous floral centre pieces. The stage is placed at one end with a small space in front of it for those who wish to have a dance on the dance floor. The large black marquee is open at all sides except for the back part where the stage is set up.

Outside the marquee, old barrels are placed around with platters of food, beautiful strings of festoon lights hanging from perfectly placed poles that are all around. Waiters with silver trays of champagne wander around, making the whole night just look grand. The lights sparkle beautifully against the night sky that is slowly breaking through as the sun begins to slowly set.

Chase and I enter into the Marquee and are greeted almost immediately by his parents.

"You have done an outstanding job, Raven," Nicholas praises me as he leans in and hugs me.

I blush lightly saying, "Ally helped me."

Speak of the devil, Ally suddenly rushes over, squealing in my ear.

"Oh, my god, Ray, we did so awesome, the lights are just perfect."

Ally suddenly realizes that we're talking to Alpha Nicholas.

"So sorry for the intrusion. Alpha, Luna," she says, bowing her head in respect before being moved away by Mark.

Luna Alexandria smiles at me and hugs me swiftly before moving away to greet some new guests that have entered the marquee.

We spend the first part of the night moving around the party together, talking with many of the guests. Chase grabs two glasses of champagne from a passing server and passes one to me, smiling.

"My little bird, you have absolutely outdone yourself," he says, with a huge smile on his face.

"This is by far one of the best parties the pack has ever had."

I lean in and kiss his lips lightly. His eyes suddenly flash, and I know that I'm now looking at Quinn. "You will make a wonderful Luna," he says before his eyes change back and I'm looking at Chase again.

"Sorry about that, he's been trying to break through ever since we saw you in that dress," Chase announces, as if he's embarrassed that he lost control for just a moment.

Akira is panting in my mind, wanting so badly to mate with Quinn.

I smile lightly, knowing that I am ready now to be marked and mated. Chase is the love of my life.

I swing my arms around his neck and bring him to me. I press my lips to his and catch him by surprise. I press my tongue needily into his mouth and he opens it willingly. A low moan escapes into my mouth from his. Suddenly, we are broken apart by a loud voice booming over the speakers from the stage at the front of the marquee.

"Eh hmm, can I have everyone's attention, please," Alpha Nicolas announces.

"Chase, Alexandria and I, are excited to bring the whole pack together tonight for the long-awaited welcome and introduction of our future Luna to the pack. She has stolen my son's heart and Alexandria and I couldn't be happier to welcome her into our family. Please, put your hands together for Raven," Alpha Nicholas declares, waving his hands at me, asking me to move towards the stage.

Gracefully, I walk towards the stage with Chase trailing behind me, holding my hand. As I arrive on the stage, I look up to see Alpha Nicholas waiting patiently for the both of us with a huge smile on his face. He hugs me quickly before passing the microphone to Chase.

"Welcome everyone to this very special night," Chase speaks, looking out over the crowd. "I was beginning to think that I was never going to find my mate. Who knew that going to a neighbouring packs birthday celebration is where I would end up finding you," he says, turning and looking deeply into my eyes. "You are our future Luna and I could not be more proud of you for this amazing party you have put together for the pack tonight. Our pack welcomes you, my beautiful Raven."

Everyone cheers loudly for what feels like five whole minutes before the music starts up again and everyone begins to scatter. Some start to move towards the dance floor whilst others begin to slowly move off into groups to talk or eat. Chase places the microphone back onto the stand and we begin to walk back off stage.

"Before everyone disappears back into their festivities, I would like one more word with you all," Alpha Nicholas suddenly announces, catching everyone off guard.

People clearly weren't expecting to be called back but it didn't take everyone very long to return to the front of the stage.

CHAPTER THIRTY-SIX

BECOMING ALPHA

The crowd becomes silent. "Chase, my son," he starts. "You have proven to be a perfect replacement for me as alpha, and I don't see why we should wait until you're married for this to happen. You are twenty-one now, and I am passing my title to you this minute. All welcome our new Alpha and Luna," Alpha Nicholas shouts into the microphone.

Chase looks at me and I smile widely at him. He's in shock, I can tell. We knew that he would be taking over the title soon, but we didn't realise that it was going to be right now.

Unexpectedly, he lifts me and swings me around excitedly before planting a firm kiss on my lips.

The whole marquee burst into a loud roar of cheers and clapping.

Chase releases me and moves to his mum—who has tears in her eyes. He hugs her sweetly before shaking his dad's hand and hugging him.

I stand off to the side of the stage, just beaming with pride. *My alpha,*

I think to myself with a sigh.

"Now will you let him mark us?" Akira asks, bouncing up and down.

"Yes," I reply to her, and she howls loudly.

"What are you so excited about?" Chase asks me, wrapping his arms around my waist.

"You," I respond breathily before pressing my lips to his.

"Oh really?" he says with a smile on his face.

"Chase," Alpha Nicholas calls, waving Chase over towards him.

"Go, I'm just going to grab something to eat," I say, letting go of Chase's hand.

Chase moves over towards his dad who is talking to other members of the pack. I smile at him and watch as he moves away before I turn and leave the stage in search of food.

I wander around for a little while and get caught by many people welcoming me and congratulating me and telling me how wonderful Chase is. When I finally manage to get near enough to some food, it's pretty much non-existent.

I head off around the back of the marquee where the catering tent is to request dessert to be brought around. I'm honestly starving, so I'll take anything. On my way back to the inside of the marquee, someone steps in front of me. Shocked, I bump straight into them.

"You've taken my place, bitch."

Looking now, I realize it is Sarah that I bumped into.

"Excuse me?" I say, raising my eyes at her and placing my hand on my hip.

"I'm meant to be Luna," she spits. "Chase is mine."

"I'm pretty sure he's not," I say as I push past her.

Sarah grabs my hair from behind, bringing me to a halt and causing me to almost fall backwards where she has pulled me so hard.

"What the fuck, you crazy bitch," I say, taking a swing at her.

She steps back so that my fist doesn't make a connection, smirking at me.

"You will leave Chase alone or I will make you leave him alone," she screams at me. "He hasn't even marked you yet and I can tell by your smell you haven't mated. He's made love to me before. Many… many… times before," she finishes, sneering at me.

I ignore her comments and begin to walk away.

"He will come back to me," she yells after me.

I can't help myself. I walk back towards her and slap her straight across the face.

"I am your Luna, and you will respect me," I say, seething with anger. I can tell I'm barely holding Akira back. "You will stay away from my mate."

"Sarah, leave us," Alexandria's voice sounds behind me.

I turn quickly and bow my head down. Sarah almost chokes and walks away from the party quickly.

"I always hated that girl," Alexandria says with a small smile on her face. "Come, Raven, I'd like to have a small chat," she finishes, holding her hand out to me.

I reach forward and slide my hand into hers. She pats the top of my hand softly and we begin to walk.

"Don't pay any attention to that girl, she is power hungry. She doesn't want my Chase for love, she wants him for power," she finally announces after a few moments of walking in silence.

I don't really know what to say, so I stay quiet.

"Raven, I know that you have lost your mum, but I want you to know that you are already my daughter, even if you haven't married my son yet. If you ever want to talk or share anything with me, I will always be here for you."

Silent tears begin to form. One slowly releases from my eye and rolls silently down my cheek. I don't have any words, so I just throw myself into Alexandria's arms and hug her.

"Thank you," I let out with a breath I hadn't realised I was holding in.

Alexandria holds me against her and strokes my hair gently. "Oh, Raven, you have no idea how happy I am to have you as my daughter-in-law."

We stand hugging for what feels like forever before we're interrupted by a familiar voice.

"Is everything okay?" Chase asks.

"It's fine, dear, you take care of this girl, okay?" Alexandria says, releasing me into Chase's waiting arms before patting his shoulder lightly and moving away.

"Your mum is amazing," I sniffle into Chase's shoulder.

I can feel him smile into my hair. "She loves you, you know."

I nod and lift my face up to look into Chase's eyes.

"They are bringing out dessert now, so the party must be winding down. Do you want to go for a run?" Chase asks with a cheeky sparkle in his eyes.

"Are you serious? And miss dessert?" I say in a sassy way before heading back into the marquee.

I hear Chase laugh and follow me back into the marquee.

I locate the table with dessert and take a small cup of Crème Brule, which is just silky and beautiful.

Chase giggles at me and kisses my forehead whilst watching me eat. "What?" I ask. "I didn't get any other food at the party."

"Come on, my Luna, let's go for a run! I've been waiting all day to have you to myself, and I don't want to wait any more," Chase says, walking away from me.

I follow behind him and notice that he's walking away from the place where we parked the car.

Sighing, I remove my heels and run after him, jumping quickly, landing on his back.

Chase carries me on his back as he walks to the edge of the forest. He places me down when he gets to the tree line and begins removing his pants. I realize that I also will have to undress.

"Chase, could you please help me unzip my dress?" I ask, almost whispering.

I feel his hand on my shoulder before I see him. He unzips my dress slowly and it falls to the ground willingly.

As soon as my dress falls, I hear a sharp intake of breath behind me.

I turn to face Chase and note that he's struggling to keep Quinn back. His eyes flash between the two mesmerising colours and finally settle back on Chase's beautiful eyes.

Looking down, I remember the beautiful underwear set that I have put on. A gorgeous white strapless bra and underwear set with a small crystal detail hanging from the front with a large white bow on the back, right in the centre.

A small smile plays across my face, but it's soon swiped off when I met Chase's eyes. His breathing has changed, and he moves towards me, pushing me back up against a tree roughly. I stare into his eyes, and he pushes his mouth against mine harshly.

His hands entangle in my hair and pull my head back roughly. Moving his lips from my lips to my ear, my body convulses forward unintentionally, and I moan loudly as he bites down softly on my ear lobe. Moving from my ear, he makes his way down to my neck, right to my sweet spot. The spot where his mark is meant to be. His teeth graze my skin, leaving goosebumps all over me. Unexpectedly, Chase moves away from me, breathing heavily.

He shifts quickly.

"Follow me," he says through our mind link.

I swiftly follow Chase off into the night, absolutely loving the feeling of the breeze in my fur. After fifteen minutes of running flat out, Chase stops and I move in next to him, sitting down.

Looking around, I notice that we've come to a clearing in the woods. It is beautiful. The trees are all bright, with lights strung up in them, twinkling like the night sky. In front of us a small white marquee stands, and underneath it lays a blanket with a small basket overflowing with food and a bottle of champagne stored in a silver ice bucket. Suddenly, Chase shifts and I watch as he grabs a pair of shorts from the blanket. He holds up a flowy maxi-dress, silently letting me know that it's for me to wear. I shiver and change back, slipping the dress over me.

Chase sits down on the blanket and opens up the basket. Inside, I notice there are some strawberries and cupcakes. I sit down in front of Chase and lean against him.

"This is beautiful. When did you do this?" I ask, turning my head to the side and kissing his arm.

"I planned it out a few days ago and some of the members from the pack organised it during the party," he responds, kissing the crown of my head.

We sit in comfortable silence for a few moments. I can feel Chase munching on the strawberries whilst I pick at a cupcake.

I swipe my finger through the icing gently and place the sugary sweetness to my lips, eating it hungrily.

I can feel Chase's gaze on me. It's making the air around us sizzle and pop with excitement.

Staring into his beautiful eyes, my heart beats faster.

"I want you to mark me," I breathe.

CHAPTER THIRTY-SEVEN

MARK ME

Sitting up onto my knees, I carefully watch his face. Chase is clearly shocked but excited at the same time. He doesn't speak for what feels like forever. His mouth gapes open a little and I watch as he blinks a few times before finally responding.

"Nothing would make me happier, my little bird," he finally speaks.

I watch as Chase's eyes change colour. Quinn is clearly trying to take control. Shuffling forward a little, I lean forward and press my lips to Chase's. Akira is so very happy, and she flashes through, letting Quinn know that everything will be okay and that they will finally be joined together soon.

Once Chase marks me and we mate, our bond will be at its absolute strongest. We will be able to mind link no matter how far away we are, and I will be able to sense his emotions in the same way he can already sense mine. Male mates can sense their partner's feelings and emotions as soon as they find them, but she-wolves can't until the mating is complete.

I can tell that he is overthinking things. He gets this serious look on his face and a little wrinkle appears between his eyebrows. I wait, letting the information sink in.

"I really want it to be special," Chase finally requests. *So he won't mark me right here and now then?* I'm almost sad. I remember him saying that he wanted it to be special when we first met, and I would let him decide when and where. Clearly this means a lot to him.

Trying to diffuse the awkwardness, I move away and remove the dress I was wearing before shifting. Chase watches my naked body intensely until I'm in my wolf form. Walking over to him, I push my nose gently against his cheek. Reaching his hand up, he touches just behind my ear, scratching lightly. A low appreciative sound gurgles up from deep in my chest.

Smiling, Chase stands up and walks around me, touching my coat lightly as he goes.

"You're so beautiful," he declares proudly.

Removing his shorts, he shifts quickly and turns to face me.

"Quinn wants to jump on you right now, so I think it's best that we head home," he sends through to me.

Smiling internally, I take off back towards the way we came to collect my dress and get to the car.

"Just head home, little bird, it's been taken care of," Chase sends from behind me, realizing what I was going to do.

Turning sharply, I follow Chase until we reach our home. The lights are off, meaning that Ally and Mark aren't home. We both shift on the front doorstep and head straight upstairs. I'm grateful that they aren't home and that I didn't have to walk past Mark naked. I don't care about Ally, she's seen it all before, and I'm pretty sure that she's seen Chase many times also. I growl internally and Chase turns to face me just before we make it to our bedroom.

"Everything okay, little bird?" he asks, eyeing me suspiciously.

"Yeah," I respond, pulling him into the bedroom and pressing my lips to his.

"I'm going to take a shower." I sigh, releasing Chase's hair from between my fingers.

I sashay away from him, noticing his hard-on. I smile cheekily, my eyes travelling up his gorgeous body to meet his eyes. He smirks at me as I noticeably check him out as he stands proud in the middle of our room. He starts shaking his head, as if trying to clear all the dirty thoughts out of his mind of what he wants to do to me right now. As I turn to close the bathroom door, I notice Chase yawn widely. He must be so tired.

As soon as the warm water hits me, a huge wave of tiredness takes over my body. Today has been such a big day. The party turned out amazingly. When I step out of the shower, Chase is already in bed, fast asleep. I climb in next to him, and within seconds, I am asleep.

I wake unexpectedly to Chase rubbing my breasts softly. He brings one of my nipples between his fingers and pulls it lightly, causing my back to arch just to push my breasts further into his expert hands. His hand slides down over my stomach, lighting my skin on fire under his touch. Reaching down into my pyjama shorts, he begins to circle my swollen clit with his fingers. He brings his mouth to my ear and whispers breathily, "Come for me, baby."

I quiver as I feel myself building. My eyes roll back in my head, and I close them as my whole body begins to shake, my orgasm threatening to overflow like a boiling pot. I hear him moan loudly, and I turn to notice something moving under the sheet. He's wanking himself whilst getting me off. *That's hot as fuck*, I think as I watch his face. Suddenly, Sarah moves up from under the sheet, positioning her naked body over him, and she slides herself down onto Chase's waiting cock and begins bouncing up and down, screaming Chase's name as she rides him.

Suddenly, I sit up, screaming. My eyes fling open and Chase grabs at me, calling to me. "Raven, wake up, you're having a nightmare."

I hold my hand to my forehead, sweat dripping from my body. Chase turns on a light on the bedside table.

"What happened, baby? You were screaming," Chase says, holding both sides of my face and staring into my eyes worriedly.

"You were having sex with Sarah in our bed with me lying here," I finally say, still panting from the stupid dream I've just woken from.

"My little bird, I would never do anything like that to hurt you, unless you're into that," he says, smiling as I elbow him. "I'm joking. The only one I want to have sex with is you," he says as he runs his hand down my hair.

Chase smiles and pulls me to his chest. I feel him lean slightly to turn out the light. He falls back to sleep after a few seconds. I lay listening to the steady beat of his heart and finally drift off into an uneasy sleep.

CHAPTER THIRTY-EIGHT

LOVE IS FOREVER

The next morning, we are abruptly awoken with the sounds of Ally bursting into our room, screaming. Chase and I sit up quickly, and Chase covers his ears as I rub my eyes, trying to get them to stay open.

"I'm engaged, I'm engaged, I'm going to be a bride!" she screams excitedly, jumping on top of me and sitting across my legs.

My eyes finally behave, and I watch as she holds out her hand to me to show me her absolutely beautiful engagement ring.

Then, I start to scream.

Chase covers his ears calling, "I'm out," before getting out of bed and heading into the bathroom, closing the door behind him.

"When did this happen?" I ask as Ally moves herself into Chase's spot on the bed.

"Last night," she says proudly, holding her hand up in the air in front of her face to admire her ring.

"Mark asked me to go for a drive with him as the party started to wind down. We went a little way out of the pack's territory and came to this beautiful lookout high up on the mountain. The stars were shining so brightly and then he asked me to marry him." Her eyes start to fill with happy tears as she squeals again.

"I'm so happy for you, Al," I say, pulling her over into an awkward side hug.

"We're gonna go out for breakfast," she says, pulling me out of bed suddenly. "Get dressed, you have ten minutes," she shouts, leaving our bedroom.

I head downstairs after getting dressed to find Ally wrapped around Mark on the kitchen table, dry humping each other. I cough loudly, making them jump apart. I smile at them both when they look overly shocked. As if they didn't realise Chase and I were both still home. I shoot Mark a wink and he sends me one back.

I must admit, I was terribly intimidated by Mark when I first moved here, but now, after getting to know him, he's a great guy. Admittedly, he can be painfully flirty. Which I know he does just because he loves to piss Chase off.

I smile and think to myself just how beyond happy I am for him and Ally. I know that she's been waiting such a long time for him to propose. I should know, I'm the one who she's been complaining to about it not happening. I'm also the one who had read through enough wedding magazines to last me an absolute lifetime. Ally is very lucky that I just so happen to love her to death. She is the closest friend I have ever had who isn't Cody.

"So, Mark, a little birdie tells me that congratulations are in order this morning, and by little birdie, I mean your fiancé coming into my room screaming this morning," I say, trying not to giggle.

He nods and smiles down at Ally who is standing in his arms. "I had to do it eventually, she was about to up and leave me, or cut off my manhood in my sleep," he says, laughing.

Ally elbows him in the ribs and giggles shyly. *Come on, lady, you were just almost fucking your guy on our kitchen table.* I laugh to myself.

"Let's go, woman," Ally says, grabbing my arm and pulling me down the hall towards the front door.

"I didn't get to say goodbye to Chase," I call to Ally, trying to pry her hand off my arm.

"Oh, babes, he left already. Pack business. You know, now he's the alpha," she says, looking at my face with worry.

"But he didn't even say goodbye to me," I say, sighing.

"You will see him when we get back. Come on, I need food," Ally whines.

We head out to the shops, and I can't help but feel a little upset that Chase left without saying he was going. I guess I should get used to things now that he's the alpha. He will be called away for meetings and other issues. I will make sure he knows that he must say goodbye to me from now on.

Sitting at breakfast, I find myself listening to Ally talk about her upcoming wedding. Anyone would think that this girl had been engaged for months, let alone a few hours.

She has already considered so many wedding venues and asked me to come with her to look at wedding dresses in the next few weeks. I smile happily and agree to go with her. I wouldn't miss it for the world. She is going to make the most beautiful bride.

We do some shopping and decide to stay out for lunch before heading back.

When we arrived back, I call out, hoping that Chase is home but there's no response. Ally calls out to Mark, and again, no answer, so we decide to grab a drink and sit down to watch a movie. Part way through, I start to feel cold, so I run upstairs to grab the comforter off the bed. Walking into the bedroom, I realize just how empty it is. I can't help but feel a little sad that Chase isn't home. I walk over to the bed to grab the comforter, when a small purple piece of paper lying on the bed catches my eye.

I pick up the paper and realize that it's an envelope. On the front, it says, '*Raven*.'

Ripping open the envelope, I look down at the beautifully handwritten words. It reads,

Meet me on the front doorstep at six-thirty p.m., Love your Alpha.

I smile to myself, hugging the letter to my chest. *How romantic*, I think to myself before heading downstairs to tell Ally.

"What will I wear?" I ask Ally, smiling excitedly.

"Come, I'll have a look through your clothes," she says, grabbing my arm and dragging me upstairs.

We make it to my bedroom and Ally walks into the walk-in robe whilst I make myself comfortable on the bed. *This is going to take a while.*

"Uh, Ray," Ally calls, sounding a bit unsure.

"Yeah?" I reply, standing up from the bed, thinking to myself, *Oh God, what has she found in the wardrobe?*

Ally exits the robe, and in her hand, she is holding a dress bag. It's all black with some beautiful gold scroll writing on it. I slowly lower the zip to find the most exquisite gown. I gasp, my hands fly up over my mouth. I look at the dress in shock. There, on the top part of the coat hanger, is a small purple envelope.

The dress is a beautiful champagne colour, and it is completely made of sequins. It has spaghetti straps and a gorgeous plunging neckline that is bound to make my boobs look amazing.

I take the dress from Ally and lay it out softly on the bed, pulling the note from the coat hanger.

'This dress is going to look stunning on you. It shines beautifully, just like you do, my love, I can't wait to see you in it. There are shoes to match in the robe. Check the bathroom for your next surprise'.

"Eeeee..." Ally squeals, running into the bathroom after reading the note over my shoulder.

On the vanity sits a beautiful set of earrings.

"Oh. My. God," Ally says slowly. "Chase is a romantic, I never would have guessed."

I check the time and decide that I should probably have a shower and start to get ready, seeing as it is already four-thirty p.m. I climb into the shower and Ally and I chat about what we think might be on Chase's agenda.

Once I'm showered, I sit down in my towel whilst Ally does my hair and my makeup. Looking in the mirror, I smile softly.

"You look spectacular." Ally sighs, rubbing my bare shoulders.

"Let's get this dress on."

CHAPTER THIRTY-NINE

DATING THE ALPHA

Once I'm finished getting ready, I look down at the bedside clock, noticing that its six-twenty-eight p.m. I stand up and look at myself in the full-length mirror in the bathroom. I feel so beautiful. The dress fits me like a glove. The shoes are a lovely champagne colour, and they are simple. Ally helps me to put the earrings into my ears that Chase left me.

Taking a deep breath, I begin to walk downstairs. Mark is lounging on the couch. He looks up and does a complete double take.

"Holy shit, Raven, you look gorgeous," Mark comments, his chin almost on the floor.

"Doesn't she?" Beams Ally as she makes her way into Mark's arms.

"Thanks, guys," I say, walking towards the front door. I look back over my shoulder, a little nervous, only to find Ally pretty much eating Mark's face.

Sighing, I open the front door to come face to face with my magnificent looking alpha.

Chase stands waiting for me in a black suit. He looks so wonderful. My stomach feels like it is going to explode with all of the butterflies fluttering around in my tummy.

"Raven, you look beyond stunning. I can't even think of a good enough word to describe what you look like right now," Chase says so fast as he tries to speak in just one breath.

I spin around with my hands in the air and bent at the elbow, smiling. The dress sways easily and flows flawlessly down my body.

Chase's eyes shine brightly as Quinn flashes through.

"Quinn," I say, bowing my head lightly and bending slightly at my knee.

"You, my Luna, are exquisite," he breathes. I can tell he's clearly trying to not let Chase back through.

I can feel Akira pushing to get through, so I let her in briefly, as long as she is on her best behaviour.

I know what it must be like for her being kept from Quinn all the time. Just being away from Chase for today has had me on edge.

When we regain our true selves, Chase holds his hand out to me, pulling me to him and pressing his lips urgently onto mine.

"Thank you for letting Quinn talk with Akira."

"I know she was desperate to talk with him," I reply, smiling.

"Are you ready now?" Chase asks, reaching out and taking my hand before leading me silently to his car.

Holding the door for me, I slide in as gracefully as I can. Chase leans in after me and kisses my lips—all too briefly.

I watch as he walks around the car and gets into the driver's seat.

"Where are we going?" I pry, looking over at him whilst he focusses on driving.

"You'll see," is all he responds before turning on the radio.

I sit, nervously running my hands over my gorgeous dress. Chase reaches over, grasping my hand in his and bringing it over to his knee, rubbing his thumb across the back of my hand. He can tell that I am nervous, and this action calms me almost instantly.

We arrive at what appears to be a restaurant after thirty minutes of driving. I sit quietly and wait for Chase as he walks around the car and opens my door for me. Stepping out of the car, he places his hand gently around my waist, pulling me closer to him. We walk into the restaurant, my heels clicking lightly on the floor. We are greeted by a lovely young girl who asks us to follow her as if she knows exactly who Chase is.

As we walk, I notice the beautiful decor. The walls are filled with climbing vines, and they wind up the walls, as if searching for high ground. Each vine houses beautiful pink flowers.

The aroma filling the restaurant is to die for.

Round tables are scattered around the entire restaurant. The crisp white tablecloths look as if they are made from very expensive fabric. Each table holds a small crystal vase with beautiful floral centrepieces. The candles on each table make the crystal shine and reflect a rainbow of colours on each table. This isn't just any corner restaurant. This is easily something that is Michelin-star rated. Other patrons are scattered around, talking quietly.

We arrive at a beautifully set table outside on a balcony, overlooking the city. I notice that there is no one else seated in the outdoor area. The sun is still out but beginning to hang lower in the sky.

Chase pulls my chair out for me, and I sit swiftly. Feeling my tummy start to rumble, we look over the menu and both decide to order the seared salmon with cress salad. The meal is beautiful. I love being able to have this alone time with Chase. I sip on my lemonade, noting that Chase hasn't ordered any wine.

As if hearing my thoughts, Chase reaches across the table, grasping my hands. He smiles, saying, "This is only just the beginning of the night, my little bird, and I still have to drive us to our next destination."

My interest piques quickly, and I begin questioning him about what we are doing next. Just as I predict, he refuses to tell me. Once our beautiful meal is finished, Chase stands quietly and we make our way back to the car.

After what feels like forever, we arrive at a large gate. Chase pulls up to a pay station-looking-box and speaks with the attendant inside.

"Chase and Raven," he says to the attendant, who nods quickly and waves us through the gate.

Driving forward, I notice that we are at a large outdoor cinema. The sun is slowly setting in the distance and my heart hammers as Chase pulls the car into a parking space with a really great view of the screen. Looking around, I notice that there are no other cars at the cinema screen we have pulled in to.

"Either we got here really early, or we are at the wrong screen?" I ask, looking at Chase.

"There's no other cars," I add, looking around.

"There won't be any other cars, my little bird. It's just you and me tonight."

Suddenly, I jump in my seat, noticing a young man standing at the window. He's holding a tray filled with drinks and food. Popcorn, two cups of drink, and a bag of my favourite lollies—Skittles.

Laughing, Chase lets go of my hand and climbs out of the car, paying the man money before placing the tray of food on the roof of the car.

Chase leans into the car. "Stay here for a minute," he says before disappearing behind.

I hear him open up the boot of the car, rustling around, pulling things out. I stare down at my nails and check myself in the little mirror. I still look great, thank goodness.

Unexpectedly, my car door opens, and Chase holds his hand out to me. I take it softly in mine and climb out of the car, and he walks me around to the other side of it. It's then that I notice Chase has set up a large-sized bean bag on a picnic rug. There is a blanket folded off to the side.

Making myself comfortable, I slide down into the bean bag. Chase goes back to the car and grabs the tray of food. Sitting it down in front of me, I reach out and take a small sip from my drink.

Chase then grabs hold of one of the speakers and places it on the ground just behind us before taking a seat next to me on the bean bag.

The night sky is now in full bloom, and the stars are trying to peek out from behind small mists of clouds that linger in the sky.

Without warning, the screen lights up and some trailers begin to play. I watch the screen intently and notice Chase steal a few glances my way from time to time.

I wonder what movie we're seeing? I think to myself as Chase's hand snakes it's way around my shoulder.

I lean into him and put my head on his shoulder, smiling like a giddy schoolgirl.

This is my ideal date; I don't need all the fancy stuff to be happy. I just want to be with my guy and lay with him and watch movies.

The music from the movie begins and I gasp, looking up at Chase.

How did he know this was my favourite movie of all time? He smiles down at me and presses his lips to mine as we sink lower into the bean bag and watch, The Little Mermaid.

CHAPTER FORTY

THIS IS IT

Lying under the stars watching my favourite movie was beyond my expectations of a date. Chase is the perfect mate, and I don't think the Moon Goddess could have paired me with anyone more perfect.

As I lay in Chase's arms, watching the movie, I feel my heart swelling with love. Chase's soft breathing behind me is making me feel so relaxed, his chin resting on my head. I pick at the popcorn unconsciously and I can hear Chase chewing on some as well. *This is the most perfect night ever.*

As the movie comes to an end, a shiver creeps over my skin. The night sky is in full bloom and the wind has quickened, making it a little chilly. Noticing my skin is now crawling with goosebumps, Chase wraps his arms around me and rubs my arms up and down, gently trying to warm me.

"Thank you for a wonderful night," I say, reaching up and kissing Chase gently.

"The night is far from over, my little bird," Chase states, kissing me back quickly.

Standing, Chase pulls me to my feet. I bend down to put the heels back on that I had removed at the beginning of the movie.

"Don't," Chase says, grabbing them. "You won't be needing heels for what we do next," he adds, with a smirk on his face.

Intrigued, I try to pry.

"Oh, and what would that be?" I ask, running my fingers up his arm, causing him to visibly shiver.

With a tilt of my head, I question him with my eyes. I watch in amusement as Chase runs his fingers across his lips, zipping an invisible zip before dramatically throwing away an imaginary key.

Taking my hand again, Chase leads me over to the car before opening the door for me. Sliding in, I wait until Chase packs everything back into the car.

Sliding into the driver's seat, Chase flashes me a smile that just melts my insides.

We drive for a little while before pulling into—what appears to be——an area of forest. It doesn't look familiar to me, but Chase seems to know the area well.

"Is this the part where you admit you're not my mate and murder me?" I ask, chuckling.

Chase looks over at me, smirking, and silently shaking his head. I notice that we have come to a stop in a clearing. Looking ahead, I see a small portion of a lake, hidden behind a line of trees. The moonlight shining on the water is heavenly.

Chase hurries to get out of the car, rushing around to open my door. Chase takes my hand as I climb out of the car.

Lifting my dress a little so that it doesn't drag on the ground, we walk down to the water, hand-in-hand. *Thank goodness I left my shoes in the car,* I think to myself as we walk over the fine dirt path that is littered with leaves and sticks. Knowing me, I would have face planted easily if I had been walking in heels. As we come around the edge of some thickly spread trees, I notice a gorgeous boat tied to a long pier, floating peacefully on the water.

Gasping loudly, I look up at Chase who is smiling like he's just won the lotto.

"Your ride awaits, my lady," he says—in a fancy way—before a grin spreads back across his face, as if what he has just said has a hidden meaning.

As we reach the dock, I notice that the lake is huge. It goes further than my eyes can see. I silently take note to myself that I don't see any other boats around, which is interesting.

Chase gets onto the boat and turns, holding out his hand to help me hop on. *Such a gentleman.*

Standing on the deck, Chase stands in front of me, holding both of my hands. His skin touching mine just ignites me from the inside like a fire rushing down a hillside.

"It's my dad's, would you like a tour?" Chase offers, wrapping his hand around my waist.

"Yes, please," I say eagerly, as I gaze around at the beautiful sight before me.

The boat is lit up with festoon lights, just like my birthday had been. We wander around the boat as Chase shows me the upper deck. The boat is quite large. Chase tells me that there are two bedrooms and a kitchen on board, along with a spa.

It's absolutely luxurious.

When we finally go below the deck, Chase leads me into a lavish bedroom. The water from the lake is shining through the small portholes, filling the roof with a light blue glow. The water sparkles brightly, causing the reflections on the roof to look like twinkling stars.

The boat rocks calmly as the water laps at its side but it's not enough to make you unsteady on your feet or feel sick.

Looking over at the bed, I don't realise that I'm holding my breath until Chase moves in behind me, his hands skimming across my back gently. I let go of my breath, slowly turning to face him. Chase hastily crushes his lips onto mine the second that I turn around. Pushing his tongue between my lips, there is a sense of urgency in the air. I thrust my hands into his hair, pulling it slightly, causing a deep moan to escape Chase's mouth into mine.

Chase walks me backwards towards the bed, my calves meeting it roughly before we both fall backwards, landing on the pillowy mattress. Chase breaks away from our kiss, looking at me with what feels like all the love in the world.

Staring into his eyes, I just know it is the right time. I want to share my body and soul with him. My alpha.

Lifting my head a little, I lace my hands around the back of Chase's neck, pulling him back to my needing lips, craving his touch.

Our breathing is ragged, and I can feel a small knot beginning to form in my tummy. Chase moves his kisses from my lips and down my cheek, and towards my neck, grazing his teeth over my sweet spot. My body practically convulses under him.

"Mark me," I say breathily.

CHAPTER FORTY-ONE

THE MARKING

C hase sits up and I follow. His eyes meet mine, searching them wildly. I know he is checking to see if I really mean what I just said. I nod my head ever so slightly, letting him know that I am ready. He moves his lips back to the special spot on my neck. Feeling his teeth graze against my skin, I push my body closer to him.

It's like the world is standing still at this moment. All of the sounds have stopped. I can only hear our breathing. My heart is beating quickly. His teeth brush over my sensitive skin. They break through my skin excruciatingly slowly. At first, I feel pain, but it is quickly replaced by pure pleasure.

The instant his teeth break through my skin, I feel his presence in my mind become clearer. Like fireworks going off in the night sky, his presence breaks into my mind. I brace myself as he retracted his teeth and releases my skin. Chase steps back, wiping his mouth on his sleeve, and I watch as my blood smears across his crisp white shirt.

We're both breathing heavily.

"You have no idea how long I've wanted to do that," he says, panting. "I have always wanted this moment to be absolutely perfect. I have had it planned out like this ever since I was a young boy"—he pauses—"now everyone will know that you're mine," he adds, suddenly leaning in and kissing me desperately.

I can taste the slight zing of my blood on his lips. It sets off a chemical explosion throughout my body. I want him and I want him now.

I pull at Chase's shirt, trying desperately to undo his buttons. Becoming impatient, I pull the shirt sharply, sending the small buttons zooming all around the room. Chase's eyes are burning with passion, and I can tell he wants me just as bad as I want him.

"Raven, once we start, I don't think I'll be able to stop," Chase says between kisses.

"Then don't stop," I purr, pulling him into me again, shoving my tongue into his mouth aggressively.

Chase pushes his jacket from my shoulders, so that it lays flat on the bed. He pulls it sharply from underneath me, throwing it to the floor.

I stand and walk a small way from the bed. Chase whimpers but stays sitting and watches me intently. I turn away from him, looking back over my shoulder seductively.

I reach back, slowly dragging my zip all the way down, exposing my back to him. The dress slips from my body and lands artfully on the floor. My skin meets the cold air and I hear Chase stand from the bed and move towards me quietly.

My bra and underwear are still in place, and I feel Chase reach around from behind me. His hand rests on my stomach gently before I feel his breath on my ear.

"You. Are. So. Beautiful," he says, placing soft kisses against the skin of my neck and down over my shoulder.

I turn unhurriedly, his hand still wrapped around my waist. His skin against mine is sending electric signals straight to my core. Chase moves his hand up my back, quickly disposing of my bra before dropping to his knees on the floor. Placing his fingers into the top of my underwear, he leans forward unexpectedly and kisses my centre.

My breath catches in my throat and my eyes snap down to look into his. He watches me heatedly as he begins to slowly drag my underwear down my legs.

Once past my hips, my underwear plummets to the floor. I watch as Chase leans back in and runs his tongue up my centre, causing my knees to buckle underneath me. Placing my hands in his hair to steady myself, I pull ever so lightly, bringing his face back to me. I want more, I want him to ravish me.

Standing, Chase seizes me and pulls me to him, crushing his lips to mine. I feel myself being lifted and then laid gently onto the bed. He—surprisingly—flips me over onto my stomach and pulls me backward sharply, my exposed ass sitting in the air. I note that Chase's hands aren't on me anymore and I turn to notice him removing his pants.

Watching me closely, his eyes lock with mine. He walks towards me, and I ache for his body to be against mine.

He leans over me, and I feel him at my entrance. I think he's going to place it inside me, but instead, he runs it up and down over my centre, making me squirm.

Then before I know it, Chase has moved away, and his tongue is moving inside me. Chase presses one hand down onto my ass cheek, spreading me open more whilst the other curves around my leg and lands on my clit, rubbing it lightly in tiny circles.

I'm not going to last long like this. Being so open and exposed is completely different from the last time where I had been lying on my back. My body begins to shake with my impending orgasm. Stopping the assault against my clit, I feel Chase kiss my ass lightly before he stands.

Huffing, I turn over, wondering why he stopped. I had been so close to going over the edge, and he stopped. If I'm being honest, I'm a little pissed off.

Chase is standing in front of me, smirking down at me. He knows exactly what he is doing. *Asshole.*

My legs are now hanging over the edge of the bed. I watch as Chase begins crawling up my body, his knees next to my hips and his hands next to my head. He leans over me, and I watch him as he moves down a little and takes one of my nipples into his mouth. I observe him suck on it, hard, his eyes looking up at me.

Tangling my hands into his hair, I pull it lightly, causing a moan to escape from deep down in his chest. Holy hell, I nearly come right then and there. I've never felt this sensation before. I didn't know that I could get so turned on from someone sucking on my nipple.

Moving one of his hands downwards, I'm unsure what he's going to do, until I feel it meet my entrance. He rubs his finger around, making my wetness spread before he slowly pushes a single finger inside me. His thumb skims gently over my clit as he begins to move in and out of me, slowly.

The feeling of him sucking on my nipples and fingering me brings me closer and closer. I begin to shake; the feeling is exquisite. Sensing that I'm close, Chase releases my nipple and moves downwards replacing his thumb with his tongue.

Reaching down, I hold onto his head, pushing myself up into his face, craving the contact.

"Come for me, Raven," he says against my clit, making my legs shake uncontrollably as I spiral into a mind-blowing orgasm.

CHAPTER FORTY-TWO

MATE ME

Coming down from my orgasm, I pull Chase up to my lips, kissing him eagerly.

"I want you inside me," I say, panting against Chase's lips. "Please…"

I'm surprised at how brazen I'm being. Chase's mark on me is clearly driving my body to complete the mating process.

Once we are completely mated, I will be able to communicate with Chase from any distance, and also sense his emotions. I'm not really sure if being able to sense his emotions is going to be a good thing, but knowing that I will be able to communicate from far distances makes me feel so much safer, especially after the last time I was stolen and couldn't communicate with anyone.

I can't ever let myself forget that rogues will come for me. Not today, but one day.

I can feel Chase's hardness pressing into my hip. Lowering my hand down my body, I grasp his manhood firmly and begin to move my hand up and down his long shaft. Chase moans into my mouth, moving his hips in motion with my hand.

Biting down on my bottom lip, Chase pulls back taking my lip with him, releasing it just before it becomes too painful.

Chase lays back gently against the pillows. Watching him, I move next to him and kiss him gently before moving myself down the bed slowly. His eyes are burning with need. I love watching him like this, knowing it is me who makes him feel like this. Grasping the base of his member, I move it gently into my mouth, pushing it all the way to the back of my throat. I love the feeling of him in my mouth, and it makes me feel so powerful just knowing that I can bring him undone with my tongue.

Chase's hands snake around my hair and he tugs it lightly, causing me to moan deep in my throat. This action makes Chase thrust his hips forward, pushing himself further into my mouth.

Pulling away from me after a few minutes, I know it's because he isn't ready to come yet. He grasps my shoulders and guides me back to his lips, kissing me passionately.

Becoming impatient and needy, I arch my back, pressing myself into Chase's side just to feel some kind of pressure against my burning core.

Sliding myself backwards and making myself comfortable against the pillows, I watch Chase stand and walk to where his pants have been discarded on the floor. Stretching down to the floor, he picks up his pants before reaching into his pant pocket and taking out a condom. I observe as the packaging is ripped open and he pulls the small piece of rubber out before sliding it down over his length. His eyes flash between his own and Quinn. I know how long he's waited for this perfect moment. We could have just done it any old way but knowing that this is how he had planned for it to be makes it ever so special.

Catching his eyes as mine flow up his body, I watch as he begins stalking towards me like a lion on its prey.

Climbing onto the bed and manoeuvring himself over the top of me, Chase kisses me swiftly before asking, "Are you sure?"

"Yes," I breathe. "Please."

Chase grasps onto himself and positions his erection at my entrance. Looking deeply into my eyes, Chase presses the head of his hard shaft softly into my opening before moving swiftly and pushing the rest of himself all of the way inside me.

As Chase tears through my virginity, I let out a small cry of pain. It hurts like hell. Small tears form in the corner of my eyes, but they don't spill.

"It's okay, baby, it won't hurt for long," Chase coos in my ear, staying ever so still.

Needing friction, I place my hands on Chase's hips, pressing against them so that they touch against my skin, probing him to start moving slowly.

Chase begins to move slowly but soon his pace quickens. My hand grips his back and running my nails down over his skin leaves behind red marks. I moan in pleasure. This is amazing. I note mentally that once the first part of pain has gone, only pleasure remains.

Chase pumps into me at a steady pace, the sensation of him filling me up is absolutely incredible.

"Touch yourself," Chase breathes heavily into my ear.

I snake my hand down between us and begin making small circles over my clit. Chase continues to thrust into me, and I notice him looking down, watching my hand as I please myself with him inside me.

I lift my legs a little and Chase moves his shoulders to hold them up.

My head falls back at the new depth. Feeling Chase so far inside me feels incredible.

Finding myself climbing, I begin to move my fingers a little faster. The sound of Chase slapping against me is driving me wild. The smell of sex in the air is intoxicating.

My body begins to tremble slightly. Chase notices this and pounds into me even faster.

I orgasm loudly, screaming Chase's name incoherently before feeling his cock pumping his juices inside the condom. My orgasm rattles my whole body, bringing me undone.

Chase lays over me, still holding most of his weight, his breathing ragged and coming out in puffs.

This is the best feeling ever. I'm never going to be able to get enough of this. I'm never going to get enough of my alpha mate.

"I love you so much, my little bird," he says, breathing against my neck.

CHAPTER FORTY-THREE

WEDDING PLANNER

The next morning, I wake feeling warm and sated. Chase is lying beside me, sleeping soundly. I climb out of bed quietly, so as not to wake him. Wrapping myself up in Chase's white shirt, I wander up to the top deck. I note a small twinge of pain between my legs, but I smile at the memory of last night. It couldn't have been more perfect.

The cool breeze brushes against my skin lightly, bringing with it the smell of the nearby trees. Pine. It smells beautiful. Unexpectedly, I feel warm hands wrap around my waist. Chase brings his lips down onto my neck where his mark now lies. My skin is perfectly healed but still holds his mark. I will carry it with me forever. As his lips touch my skin, it lights up like a sparkler on New Year's Eve.

"Thank you for last night," Chase speaks softly in my ear. "It was the best night of my whole life."

Smiling, I lean my head back against his shoulder and sigh peacefully. The sun is still low in the sky, so it must be quite early. Its orange glow lights up the lake, making it sparkle like crystals. The boat rocks calmly on the water. Chase and I just stand together, enjoying this beautiful morning.

"We should head back soon," Chase says, releasing me and turning me around before kissing me lightly.

We dress and make our way back to the car. Chase holds the door for me whilst I climb in. Then he makes his way around to the driver's side. My stomach rumbles so loudly that even Chase can hear it, and he laughs, poking me softly.

When we arrive back at the house, we find Ally and Mark sitting at the table, eating pancakes. We sit down with them, and within seconds, Ally screams excitedly.

"OMG, you two fucked," she yells loudly.

Chase smirks at me just as Mark slaps him over the back loudly.

"Well done, mate, finally popped her good, hey?" Mark says, winking at me.

I place my hand over my face, sighing loudly.

"Tell me everything," Ally says, turning towards me and looking at me expectantly.

"I'm not telling you anything," I say, shoving my fork into a pancake and dragging it over to my plate before smothering it in maple syrup.

Ally tries to make a pouty face, pulling at my arm. I smile at her with a mouthful of food. I seriously can't deal with her sad faces, and she knows it.

Shaking my head, I watch her cross her arms and stomp her foot like a two-year-old.

"Well, fine then," Ally remarks. "Guess you can't be my maid of honour then."

My eyes fly up from my plate and stare straight at Ally. I hadn't even thought I would be in her wedding as she has three sisters.

"What?" I manage to choke out, without spitting out any pancakes.

I turn to face Ally. She has tears in her eyes. I just stare at her, shocked.

Finally, she nods wildly and flings herself at me.

"I want you to be my maid of honour," she says, sniffling in my ear.

"Oh my God, yes, of course I will," I squeal excitedly.

We finally separate and look over at the boys. Chase and Mark are just smiling at us.

"Hey, dude, best man, yeah?" Mark says, slapping Chase on the shoulder.

"Nah, man, I'm all good," Chase says swiftly before leaping up and grabbing Mark in a headlock. "As if I wasn't going to be up there with ya, man. Hell yes, I'll be your best man."

We all look around at each other, smiling like idiots. This is going to be epic.

Ally, of course, has been waiting so long to get married that she has been planning since she was like twelve years old, so this wedding isn't going to be in six months, it's going to be in six weeks. Yeah, you heard me right, six weeks.

It's a whirlwind of organising. Hen night, wedding dress, bridesmaid's dresses, centrepieces, the works. It's been a great distraction as Chase is always off doing his alpha duties.

Today, we're heading out to pick out Ally's wedding dress. I'm so excited. I booked ahead so that we would have one on one attention. Ally may have planned all of this out, but she can still be a major bridezilla when she wants to be.

Walking into the wedding dress shop, Ally squeals with excitement and runs across to touch the beautiful billowing dresses on the back wall. The shop is buzzing with people, and there are a few other brides trying on dresses that are coming in and out of dressing rooms.

After trying on over fifteen different dresses, we have narrowed it down to two. One is a mermaid style with beautiful lace detail and the other is a full ball gown with crystals sewn all over the bodice. Both are so different, so making the decision is going to be so very hard.

As Ally goes back in to swap from the mermaid back to the ball gown, I take a wander around the store, running my hands over the beautiful fabrics. My hands stop on a stunning gown. It is absolutely covered from head to toe in glitter. I pull the bottom of the dress out and hold it. It's absolutely stunning. For a second, I feel a small pang of jealousy. I wish I was marrying Chase.

"You should try it on," Ally's voice sounds from behind me.

"Oh no, this is your day," I say, letting the dress go and turning back to her.

"No way, this dress is screaming your name," Ally says, grabbing the dress from the rack and pulling me towards the dressing room. The sales lady looks a little put out, but Ally doesn't seem to be one to change her mind once it's set on something.

Ally starts pulling at my clothes, and I laugh. "I do know how to undress, you know?"

Minutes later, I'm standing in front of Ally in the most gorgeous dress I've ever seen. The lights from the roof are making me shine like a star in the midnight sky with every movement I make.

"Oh my God," Ally utters, looking at me in the mirror. "You need to put this on lay-buy. This is your dress."

I sway slightly, watching myself in the mirror, transfixed.

"Let's go look in the big mirror out front," Ally calls, grabbing my hand as she walks out of the dressing room.

I follow Ally out and stand next to her on the tall box in front of the large mirror.

"I think I like the mermaid one," Ally says, turning to her side to see how her bum looks in the dress.

"Yeah, me too," I say, facing her.

Suddenly, over Ally's shoulder, my eyes locked with another girl's. She is standing on a block with a wedding dress on.

Ava.

CHAPTER FORTY-FOUR

LET'S GET MARRIED

Seeing the shocked look on my face, Ally waves her hand in front of my face before turning to see who I'm staring at.

"Hey, who are you looking at?"

"Ava," is all I can get out. I feel like all of the breath has been sucked out of my body.

Ally's eyes flash quickly to her wolf. "I'll kill that bitch," she announces, getting down from the box she's standing on.

"No, please, let's just get changed and buy your dress," I plead, pulling on her arm.

"Fine, but if I see her again, she's gone," Ally spits, storming back into the change room.

I suddenly realise that Ava stands, wearing the exact same dress that I'm wearing. She has a smirk on her face and calls to the sales lady, "I'll take this one," before stepping down from her block and walking back into the change room.

I finally convinced Ally that she didn't need to cause a scene in the middle of the bridal shop, and we left having ordered Ally's dress. She questioned why I didn't want to buy the dress I had on, but I just told her I didn't like it that much. I could never love that dress now that I knew Ava was going to wear it. I knew that if I told Ally the real reason, she would possibly head back to the bridal show and decapitate Ava. Not that I would mind.

Maybe we should go back? I think to myself, snorting.

The next few weeks go by quickly. I have planned Ally and Marks wedding to a T. We had the occasional set back when Ally turned into a giant bridezilla, but overall, I haven't done too badly controlling her tantrums.

Today is the hen party. Ally—as we all know by now—is driven by penises. Not that I'm surprised with how much sex her and Mark have. I have organised a night filled with penis paraphernalia, and even strippers.

Mark is far from pleased, but Chase is a whole other story. I wouldn't be surprised if the boys totally crashed the party. Having a naked male around isn't going to exactly be easy on the boys, but hey, they get to see female strippers, so I think it's totally fair.

Ally is dressed to the nines in a stunning white dress with a giant bow on the back. I have adorned her with a veil with penis's all over it and a bright pink penis necklace. She has garters on her thighs and has started drinking way before I wanted her to. We have a group of about seven of us. It is nice and intimate.

We go out for dinner, which was so lovely, before heading off to the strip club. Ally is a mess by the time we make it, but she seems to be having the time of her life. I can't believe she's getting married in just two days.

Halfway through the night, we somehow end up at a local club. We are all fairly smashed—well, except me—as I know how bad Ally is right now and I need to ensure that she is safe. We stand at the bar, waiting for what feels like forever, trying to get a drink, when suddenly, a random guy comes over to us.

"Hey, beautiful ladies, want a good time?" he slurs.

"Fuck off, mate, I already have an amazing dick at home, no need for your pin dick," Ally responds with a high amount of sass.

The guy holds his hands up in a defensive way and backs away from us.

Poor dude never stood a chance.

The hens night goes by without a hitch, and luckily, the boys don't gate-crash.

"Never let me drink again," Ally utters, walking down the stairs. She looks wrecked. I am so glad that she's getting married tomorrow instead of today.

"Did you have a good night?" Chase asks, sitting down next to me on the couch and passing me a bowl of cereal.

"We had a blast," I reply, smiling and watching Ally cover her eyes, laying her head down on the arm of the couch.

"It was great," she finally announces. "Where's Mark?" she asks, looking up at Chase.

"We tied him to a tree, naked. He passed out, so he should be back around midday," Chase answers, grinning.

Chase was right, around lunchtime—a very naked—Mark enters the house. Ally dives on him, effectively covering his man parts from torturing my eyes. As always, they end up in their bedroom soon after, greeting each other. They seriously have way too much sex.

Finally, the morning of the wedding has arrived.

Ally began the day by running around, screaming through the house, "I'm getting married today," over and over. The boys departed yesterday to stay in the main pack house with Chase's parents. Ally and all her girls are all getting ready here at our house today.

We started our morning off with champagne and a fruit platter, which was really lovely.

The makeup artist and hairdresser have done an absolutely amazing job on each of us, and Ally looks like a princess. I watch as she grabs her dress from the wardrobe, bringing it over and laying it across the bed. She gently unzips the cloth bag. Looking down, she steps back, admiring it like she is falling in love with it all over again.

"Ray?" she asks. I look up from her dress, my eyes meeting hers.

"Thank you!"

"What for, Al?" I reply, tears starting to well in my eyes.

"For being my best friend and doing this with me," she says, letting out a small sob.

I walk to her slowly and bring her to me. We stand hugging for a while before someone interrupts us, saying that it's time to leave.

I help Ally into her dress and tie the back. She looks absolutely phenomenal.

She stands, staring at herself in the mirror. Her golden hair is in the perfect chignon, a small white flower pinned off to the side of it. Her dress hugs her figure like a second skin.

Taking her hand, I begin walking her downstairs.

Before we know it, we're in the car and heading to the ceremony.

I will be fourth down the aisle, and my nerves are running rampant. I'm chanting in my head, *Don't fall, don't fall, don't fall.*

Part way down the aisle, my eyes meet Chase's. I see him visibly take a deep breath at the sight of me in my beautiful maid of honour dress.

The ceremony is intimate, and I shed a few small tears. Ally looks stunning in her dress and Mark cries when he sees her walking towards him.

The reception is in full swing. Ally and Mark are dancing to their first dance as husband and wife. Chase holds his hand out to me, and I gladly take it. He spins me around the dance floor like a pro. Everyone seems to be having a wonderful time.

"May I?" Mark suddenly asks, reaching for my hand.

"Just remember which one's yours," Chase says, smirking, before handing me over to Mark.

Mark and I dance together whilst Ally is dancing with her dad. Chase makes his way over to the bar.

"I just want to thank you for being so amazing and helping Ally through this. I'm so happy that she met you and that you are her very best friend. I know she couldn't have done all this without you, even though she's been planning it for years," he finishes, watching his bride from afar with a twinkle in his eyes. "Also, now that we're married, it might be time for us to move out as we may need a little more privacy, you know, for all the extra sex… maybe in more public places," he says, smirking at me.

I slap his chest, giggling.

I suddenly feel a pair of hands on my waist and instantly know it is Chase. The heat from his hands sear through my dress and leave me wanting his touch all over my body.

"Can I have my mate back now?" Chase asks politely, even though I can tell he's becoming impatient having been away from me for even the shortest time.

Mark releases me and moves back towards Ally.

"What were you talking about?" Chase asks before wrapping his arms around me and kissing me sweetly.

"He wants to move out so that him and Ally can have more sex," I say, laughing. "All over the apartment," I add, shaking my head.

Chase stiffens a little when I mention Mark and Ally moving out. He begins to lead me from the dance floor.

"Come, I want to show you something."

CHAPTER FORTY-FIVE

OUR HOME

My eyes scan is face. "Are you serious? We can't leave our best friend's wedding," I say, pulling away from Chase's grasp.

"It's okay, they know, and we will be back before you know it," Chase replies, smiling and taking my hand in his.

The warmth from his hand fills my body with small tingles. Smiling to myself, I hope that this feeling never goes away.

I follow Chase out of the wedding, looking back over everything and feeling a small pang of guilt fall into the pit of my stomach.

Chase leads me over to his waiting car and we head back towards home. I have to admit that being part of this pack has definite pros. Chase's pack owns quite a substantial amount of land. The wedding was in the paddock in a marquee, so we weren't that far from home.

We travel a little way and I notice that we totally pass our house. I decide not to comment and just wait to see where Chase is taking me.

The car pulls over in a part of the pack lands that I have never been to before. Chase quickly gets out of the car and walks around to open my door for me. He takes my hand and I sense excitement and worry from him.

"Are you okay? You seem worried but excited," I ask, touching his arm lightly.

"Damn, I forgot you can sense my emotions now. I will have to be more careful in the future," Chase says, running his hand down his face.

We begin walking down a small path that's covered over slightly with beautiful flowers and shrubs. We come around a corner to find a beautiful house. The front lights are on so I'm assuming we are going to meet someone. Strange since I believed everyone to be at the wedding.

We walk up onto the front deck, and I note to myself how much I love the beautifully bright red front door. It has a striking brass style door knocker. I wait for Chase to reach out and knock, but instead, he just walks straight in through the front door.

Shocked, I follow in behind him. He is standing beside a beautiful hall table, holding a small box in his hands.

"Who lives here?" I ask quietly. "We can't just barge in," I add in a whisper, looking around for the homeowners.

Chase giggles lightly and begins walking towards me. When he reaches me, he hands me the small box he's holding.

I look down at the box then back up at Chase.

"Open it!" he says, smirking like he's hiding a huge secret.

I open the small box to discover a small set of keys inside. Confused, I look up at Chase.

"Welcome home!" he says, smiling at me, holding his hands up from his sides, his palms facing the roof.

It takes me a few seconds to realize what's going on, but I finally realize that Chase and I are standing in our brand-new house Squealing ear piercingly loud, I lift my flowing dress and dive into Chase's arms, wrapping my legs around him, causing him to stumble backwards a little. I push my lips onto his and kiss him wildly.

A little shocked, it takes Chase a few seconds to kiss me back, but when he does, heat rises throughout my whole body. My body reacts almost instantly. I can feel myself become damp.

I know I am affecting Chase the same way that he is affecting me. I feel him grow against my core. I keep my legs wrapped around Chase and I note that he turns and presses me against a nearby wall. Pressing his hardness against me roughly.

My body writhes against the firmness, trying to gain some friction. I can't get enough of this man.

Sensing my neediness, Chase reaches between us and unzips himself hastily before shoving my underwear to the side and swiftly slamming into me.

I scream out loudly, wanting him to take me hard. He doesn't disappoint. His breathing is heavy against my neck, and I hold onto him firmly. Taking every inch of him inside me.

"This is going to be quick, baby, come with me," Chase pants.

After a few minutes of pumping into me, Chase comes first. I feel him injecting his sperm into me as he calls my name loudly, the sensation and sound of him calling my name in pure ecstasy sets off my own earth-shattering orgasm.

We both stay in the position against the wall, breathing heavily for a few moments. Chase releases me after giving me a swift kiss.

"Well, I had hoped to christen our new home when we actually moved in, but hey, tonight is just as good as any," Chase announces, smiling at me. "I can't wait to fuck you on every surface of our new home," he adds smacking my behind gently.

Chase takes me on a quick tour of our new home. It's already furnished and it's absolutely beautiful.

"I started building it the day after I found you. I do hope you like it, and I'm sorry it's taken so long to complete," Chase says as we reach the front foyer again.

"I love it," I say, breathing a huge sigh and looking around, not really believing that this place is ours.

"We should head back, baby, they will be cutting the cake soon," Chase says, grabbing my hand as he pulls me out the front door.

When we arrive back at the wedding, I am glad that it is still in full swing. Ally is on the dance floor, shaking her booty wildly. As we walk back into the marquee, she waves me over. I kiss Chase swiftly and I move towards Ally.

"So, what did you think?" she asks with an expectant look on her face.

"You knew?" I ask, looking shocked.

"Of course I knew, I helped with the décor," she says, smiling.

I dive on her, hugging her firmly and whispering into her ear, "Thank you."

Ally and I dance for a little while longer before the MC announces that it's time to cut the cake and say farewell our bride and groom, so that they can head off to their honeymoon.

Ally and Mark have chosen to head off to Fiji for a whole month. I'm not going to lie, I'm a little jealous, but most of all, I'm really going to miss Ally.

After cutting the cake, Ally and Mark take their leave. I hold onto

Ally for as long as I can.

"I'm going to miss you," I whimper against her hair.

"I'll miss you to, my bestie," she replies, wiping a tear from her eye.

"Alright you two, I want to get to my honeymoon so I can mate the fuck out of my bride. Maybe you should have married her instead, Raven?" Mark jests. "Actually, dude, that would be hot as fuck," Mark says, slapping Chase on the chest.

Chase just shakes his head, grabbing my hand and bringing me possessively to his side.

"Back off, dude, you have your own," Chase adds, making a shoo like gesture with his hand.

They climb into a black car. Ally waves almost hanging all of the way out of the car window, and I wave back, wiping tears from my eyes as they leave down the driveway.

CHAPTER FORTY-SIX

LET'S DO IT

T he four weeks without Ally have been miserable. I missed her so much. She arrives back today, which I'm totally thrilled about.

My time has been filled with Luna duties, which I'm slowly beginning to learn from Chase's mum. She is just the most amazing lady, and I can only hope to live up to her standards of a fantastic Luna.

I have been down to the hospital wing a few days, helping with sick or hurt pack members. It feels so amazing to know that I'm a source of comfort and help to our pack members.

Chase won't let me anywhere near the dungeons as he said he is holding a few feral rogues and that they are dangerous. I totally agree with him, to be honest. I have had enough of my life being ruined by rogues so far, and I don't need to face any others. Nothing has come from that random brown-eyed guy in the mall that day, but I'm definitely not allowed to travel alone anymore. The pack doctors have been working on finding out different ways that we could mask our scents, but they are yet to come up with anything.

Chase and I moved into our new home, leaving the other house for Mark and Ally when they returned. We moved Mark and Ally's things into the master suite, and I made sure that the whole house was set up beautifully for when they returned.

I am seriously thinking that I need some kind of best friend ever award right about now.

Chase and I are just putting the finishing touches on the lounge when I hear a car pull up to the front of the house. I run to the front door, flinging it open quickly. I rush down the front steps and collide with my best friend the second she steps out of the car.

"Welcome home," I say, puffing out air quickly.

"Hey, you be careful with her," Mark chides me, his face impassive, and he doesn't smile like I expect.

I squint, wondering what his problem is, but I brush it off quickly, taking Ally's arm in mine and bringing her inside.

"I can't wait to hear everything. What did you do? Please tell me you didn't just have sex the whole time? Was it beautiful? Did you miss me?" I speak quickly, not waiting for Ally to reply.

Chase is standing on the porch and kissing Ally's cheek gently, he moves past us to help Mark get the bags out of the car.

We sit down on the couch. I hug Ally again excitedly, passing her a glass of wine that I poured minutes before they arrived.

"No thanks," Ally says, turning the wine down. I place the glass back onto the table and watch her quietly, thinking to myself that it isn't like her to turn down a wine.

Shrugging, I take a small sip from my own glass and look up as I note Chase and Mark walking in with the bags. Chase has a huge smile spread across his face.

"We moved your things into the master suite," I say, trying to break this weird tension that's going on in the room.

"That's great," Mark finally speaks, sitting down behind Ally. "We need our old room for a nursery," he adds, running his hand softly over Ally's stomach.

My eyes shoot straight up to Ally's and a huge smile spreads across her face.

I scream excitedly, realizing what is going on.

"Oh my God, I'm going to be an Auntie," I yell, jumping up from the couch.

No wonder Mark was so stern with me earlier about being careful with Ally.

Ally stands and brings me to her, hugging me tightly.

"I found out last week," she says holding me at arm's length. "I'm going to be a Mumma," she declares with a small hiccup in her voice.

"How many weeks are you?" I ask excitedly.

"Three weeks," she answers excitedly. "I can't wait to go shopping," she adds, pulling me back in for a hug.

After a chat and some dinner, we leave Ally and Mark to get unpacked and relax in their new home for the night and head off to our own home.

"I'm so excited," I say out loud as we enter through the front door.

I turn, noticing that Chase hasn't followed me inside. He's sitting out on the front porch steps, staring off into the distance. I sense something is up, but I know that he's trying to hide his emotions from me.

"What are you thinking?" I ask quietly, sitting down next to him and laying my head on his shoulder.

Looking down at me, Chase answers, "About how much I want to marry you. How badly I want pups of my own. About how I shouldn't be jealous of Mark and Ally and that I should be happy for them." He breathes out loudly. "I wish I had met you years ago, Raven."

I move myself up into Chase's lap, placing one leg on either side of his, holding his face between my hands.

"Let's do it then," I breathe.

"What?" Chase asks, looking shocked. "Do what?"

"Let's have pups."

"Are you serious?" Chase replies with a spark of hope in his eyes.

I nod and smile at him.

Abruptly, Chase stands up with me still wrapped around him, and he spins around in a circle, beaming at me. When he stops spinning, he crushes his lips to mine, pushing his tongue needily into my mouth. He tastes divine.

"I want you to have my pups," he speaks breathily.

"Well, my sexy alpha, let's go make pups, on all of the surfaces of our house," I whisper sensually before shoving my tongue back inside his mouth.

CHAPTER FORTY-SEVEN

UNEXPECTED ENCOUNTER

Ally and I head out the next day to do some shopping for the upcoming baby. Chase is a little sceptical letting us go, since last time I had that creepy guy following me, but I promised him that we would be fine.

Chase and Mark wanted to come with us, but they had to head over to a neighbouring pack to sort out some business with a rogue.

As soon as we arrive, we wander into the shops, when suddenly, I almost have to run. Ally has gained speed so quickly. Without hesitation, I notice that she is heading straight for a little clothing shop she's just spotted. She goes directly for all the little pink girl's clothes, holding them over her belly.

"What if it's a boy?" I ask, grinning.

"I guess I should find out the sex first, hey?" Ally replies sadly, putting the little dress back on the shelf.

We wander around for a few hours, picking out gender neutral items, like blankets, towels and even a few bodysuits in white. Until Ally decides that she's absolutely famished and needs food.

Just as we walk into the food court, I look around and decide that I want a burger. Whilst Ally tells me she is craving chicken, she heads off to get herself lunch, and I turn to go to the shop to get my burger. As I turn, I accidently bump straight into someone. Their scent is so familiar, and it assaults my senses. I turn to apologise, coming face to face with Cody.

"Raven?" Cody says, almost choking on the hot dog he's eating.

I stare into his eyes. How I miss those eyes. I can't believe it's been all this time and we haven't even spoken. My heart is heavy. This man used to be my everything, my whole world.

"Cody," I finally manage to say.

I can tell that he's trying hard to think of something to say but nothing seems to be coming out. Reaching out towards me, he grasps my hand in his.

"I've missed you," he finally says.

My breath catches in my throat.

Just as I'm about to reply, Ava appears, placing her hand over Cody's shoulder. Flashing not only an engagement ring but also a wedding band.

Ava glares at me like she's waiting for my face to disintegrate in front of her.

"Let's go, husband," Ava says before dragging Cody away.

Motionless, I stand there, shocked, probably looking like a complete idiot, when unexpectedly, Ally waves her hand in front of my face.

"Hey, was that Ava?" she asks, biting hungrily into her chicken.

"Yeah, and Cody," I reply, still dumbstruck. "He said he misses me, Ally."

"He what?" Ally replies, almost spitting her chicken out. "Do you miss him?"

"I really do, he was my best friend, Ally… Before you," I add quickly, when she raises her eyebrows at me.

After lunch, Ally complains that her feet are hurting, so we decide to head home. I was just going to drop Ally back at hers but because I know Chase is still away, I decide to go in for a bit. After getting comfy on the couch, we start to watch a movie together.

We decide on Bridesmaids as it's such a funny movie. I'm so glad that Ally wasn't a crazy ass bride.

Halfway through the movie, my phone buzzes softly in my jacket pocket. I grab it out quickly, hoping that it's Chase. I miss him so much already.

Looking down at my phone, I see Cody's name sitting on the screen of my phone.

"What's up?" asks Ally, putting a chip into her mouth. "You look like you've seen a ghost."

"I just got a message from Cody," I say faintly.

"Well, what does it say?" Ally asks impatiently.

I open the message and read it, not really knowing what to expect.

"He wants me to meet him by the lake, to talk."

"Are you going to go?" Ally asks, moving to face me on the couch.

"I don't know, what do you think?" I ask apprehensively.

"I think you need to talk with him and fix things up, Raven. I know things went a bit too far with you both, but he has been your best friend for your whole life," Ally finally says.

I think back to the last time that I spoke to Cody. We didn't exactly leave things in a good way.

"I don't want Chase to know that I've gone to talk with Cody, he will follow me and rip him apart out of jealousy," I say, standing quickly. I grab my bag and shove my phone inside it.

Ally wishes me luck before I head out to my car. I quickly drive home. I place a change of clothes in a small bag before shifting. Carrying the bag in my mouth, I run towards my father's pack grounds to meet Cody at the lake.

As I run, I think about all of the years that Cody and I have been friends. About all the good times. He was always there for me, he listened to every single one of my problems, gave me hugs when I was feeling sad. I can't believe that I let his mate come between us.

"No, it wasn't just Ava who came between us, it was your feelings," Akira reminds me disdainfully. *"Remember, you nearly mated with him."*

She's right, I think to myself. It's my fault. *I told him how I felt, I let myself fall in love with him, but I blamed Ava for coming between us.* I'm a huge hypocrite. Imagine if Sarah did with Chase what I did with Cody, knowing that he had a mate... I would have been furious. These words replay over in my head like a broken record.

I stop walking and consider whether I should head back home and forget about going to see Cody.

"Do you still love Cody?" Akira asks me softly.

I sit down and think for a moment.

"Do I still love him?" I ask myself out loud. "Of course not, how can I love anyone else but Chase?"

My feelings for Cody went away the minute Chase's eyes met mine at my birthday party, but deep down, I still do love him as a friend.

I begin walking again. I will talk with Cody and clear the air. He's still my best friend after all and we need to fix our relationship. I do really miss him.

I arrive at the lake and sit down by the tree that we used to meet at. I can smell many different scents around the area from my father's pack. Clearly, the lake has become a lot more popular since I left.

I place my bag down and shift back. Putting my clothes on, I sit down again, resting myself against the tree to wait. I had expected Cody to already be here, but I guess he got caught up.

I sit for half an hour, skipping rocks over the lakes surface whilst I wait. Perhaps Cody has changed his mind about meeting me? Sighing, I stand and begin to walk around a bit.

Unexpectedly, something painful stings my neck. I reach up and pull a large dart out of my neck.

Before I can scream for help, I feel my legs buckle underneath me. My mind slowly slips into sleep. My eyes close and darkness overtakes my senses.

CHAPTER FORTY-EIGHT

WHERE IS MY MATE

(Chase's Perspective)

We are heading home from yet another pack meeting. I drive speedily down the road with Mark in the passenger seat. Our business with Alpha Jordan, regarding the rogue, has been sorted. Alpha Jordan called me two nights ago, saying that a rogue had mentioned Raven. Quinn had gone absolutely wild after hearing this, and I struggled to control him. I decided that it was best that I didn't show Raven how stressed I was and didn't inform her of what Alpha Jordan had told me. I will hunt down and kill anyone who wishes to harm my Luna.

I look down at my phone and notice that its battery has died. Frustrated, I ask Mark to call the girls and check in with them, only for him to tell me that his phone has also died as he's been playing candy crush too much. I growl angrily, deep in my throat, aggravated. I try to call out to Raven through our mind link. Now that we have completed the mating ritual, I can contact her through our link no matter the distance. Either she's asleep or she's blocking me out as I can't seem to get through.

The car ride seems to be taking forever and now that I can't contact Raven, I begin to stress a little. My thoughts stray from the situation at hand and straight to my mate. I can't wait to get home to Raven.

After last night's remarkable bout of sex, I can't wait to bury myself inside her again. I mean, I have had sex quite a lot before Raven, but with her, it's just a whole new level. It's like her body was made for me and mine for her.

I can't wait to be a dad.

After the hour and a half drive, I finally turn down the drive and head into our pack lands. It is night, and the sun has not long set over our lands. I can sense Mark's anxiety about getting back to Ally. He tried to link with her earlier, but he never actually told me if he got through. When we pull up out the front of their house, I notice that Ally is running down the front steps and she looks panicked.

I haven't even got the car to a complete stop and Mark is out and running towards Ally. The look on her face is telling me that something is definitely wrong.

Mark brings Ally to his chest, and she begins crying. I hurry to their side now, really worried.

"I'm so sorry, Chase, I'm s...orry," Ally says as she sobs against Mark's chest, tears streaming down her face.

"What's happened?" I demand.

"It's my fault, I told her to go," she says, finally meeting my eyes.

"Where is she?" I snap, becoming impatient.

"We bumped into Cody whilst we were out shopping and when we got home, she got a message from him. He wanted to talk with her by the lake back at her old pack. She's been gone for hours and hasn't come back," she blurts out quickly before she starts crying again.

I shift so fast I hadn't even noticed that I'm running. Running to find my girl. My Luna.

How dare he want to speak with her. I feel the pinch of pain in my chest, knowing that she decided to go back and talk with him. A hint of jealousy stabs at my body like small needles in my heart. What if she chooses him? My mind swims with questions and I push myself harder to get to her.

The minute I enter Alpha Damon's pack lands, I can smell her scent nearby. I run full pelt towards the lake, my eyes anxiously scanning the area, but to my disappointment, she isn't there. I can smell her, but I cannot see her anywhere. I decide to go straight to the pack house to see if she is just visiting her father and brother.

Reaching the pack house, I shift and storm through the front door, my panic to find Raven overshadowing my manners. I come across Max first, who finds me a robe quickly before pointing me towards his father's office. I push through the door to find him sitting at his desk on the phone.

The minute he sees me, he apologises and puts the phone back onto the receiver. Standing, he rushes towards me.

"What's happening? Where's Raven?" he demands.

The look on my face and my unannounced arrival must have tipped him off that something is wrong.

"We need to find Cody," I say sharply.

Before I know it, we are at a house not far from the main pack house. Alpha Damon pounds on the door.

Within seconds, Cody answers, smiling at his alpha, but his face drops when he sees mine.

I rush towards him and wrap my hand around his throat.

"Where is she?" I scream, my voice filled with anger. "Where is my mate?"

"Hey, I don't know what you're talking about," Cody says, struggling to breathe.

My grip tightens and he makes a small choking sound.

Damon places his hand on my shoulder, and I release him reluctantly.

Looking deeply into Cody's eyes, Damon uses his alpha tone to demand where Raven is.

No wolf can deny their alpha's tone, they must do what their alpha says.

"I don't know where Raven is, the last time I saw her was at the shops this morning," Cody says, holding his hand tenderly against his—now—red throat.

"You messaged her to meet you by the lake," I spit at him, lunging for him again.

"I never messaged her," Cody announces, holding his phone out to Damon.

Damon looks through the messages and shakes his head. "There are no messages on his phone to Raven."

Growling angrily, I exit the house. Alpha Damon follows me. The door bangs loudly as Cody angrily closes over his door, leaving the alpha and myself standing alone.

I start to pace back and forward, anger rising inside me.

Alpha Damon places his hands over his face, realizing what has happened.

He rushes away, and soon, I hear howls all around the pack lands.

"Where is she?" I scream to the sky before dropping to my knees. This pain is nothing like I've ever felt before. Tears begin to streak down my face.

Raven...

Quinn howls deep in my mind, pining for our mate.

Someone has taken her from us.

I have failed to protect her. I have no one to blame but myself. I knew that one day the rogues would come for her, and I did nothing to stop them.

My hands clench into fists so tightly that my claws begin to spring from my fingertips, piercing through my skin.

I adore you, Raven.

I'm so sorry.

She is my whole world, and she's gone. She is the light to my dark.

How can I possibly forgive myself? How can I live without her?

"I refuse to live without her," I cry out into the night, shifting quickly. I run. I have to find my Luna.

CHAPTER FORTY-NINE

TAKEN

My head hurts.

Where am I?

My eyes won't open. I will them to in my mind, but nothing happens.

I try to move my arms, but they don't seem to follow my brain's command. I can manage to move my fingers. I can feel a cold surface underneath me.

Pain rises in my chest, and I can hardly breathe.

Come on, Raven, wiggle your toes. Nothing happens.

My head is hazy, but I try to call out through mind link.

Chase…

Pain rips through my body as I feel the bones in my hands break. Screams roar from deep down in my chest. My eyes flutter open slightly, but I can't see who is standing over me. Their shadow is blurry. I watch as their hand raises again, and now I know that they are hitting me repeatedly with a long hard item that resembles a hammer.

"Help me," I scream out through our mind link.

Nothing comes back. It feels like my mind is disconnected. Fuzzy, like being drunk, but in a bad way. What have they given me? Why are they doing this?

I knew one day that the rogues would come for me, but I wasn't expecting it to be so soon after finding my mate. A voice is talking to me as they torture my hands, but my mind is fuzzy, I can't even make out if the voice is male or female. My werewolf healing kicks in, resetting my broken bones. It is working far more slowly than normal but I can feel each of my fingers clicking back into place before being smashed apart again as the tool comes down harshly onto my hand. Time is passing slowly. After what feels like hours, my attacker decides they are clearly bored of breaking my fingers.

The tool they have been using to inflict my pain is placed down on something metal beside me with a loud clatter. The sound makes my head hurt even more. I can't even hear Akira in my mind. It's like she is being blocked from me and I'm not able to reach her.

The pain is becoming too much. I try to clear my mind to make a connection. I try again to call out to him, but nothing happens.

Suddenly, I feel a large amount of pressure on my left leg. The bone breaks under the force. I hear a vicious laugh. My torturer clearly finds pleasure in my pain.

A scream rips through my lips, and my throat is as dry as the desert. I pray in my mind for this to end. For them to just kill me. It would be welcome after all this torture. I feel a small tear streak down my face and into my hair. I try to speak to my attacker. Beg them to stop, but nothing but screams come out of my mouth. Before I know it, pain takes over my body, shutting it down, the darkness taking over again.

(Cody's Perspective)

A loud banging comes from my front door. I stand from my chair, the sharp motion makes it scrape noisily against the floor. It must be urgent as the person behind the door bangs again even more loudly. I realize that I can smell Alpha Damon and quicken my pace to answer the door.

The door squeaks in protest as I open it. I smile widely at Alpha Damon, but my face falls when I see Chase standing behind him.

Unexpectedly, he rushes towards me. I watch as his hands wrap quickly around my throat.

"Where is she?" he screams angrily. "Where is my mate?"

I watch as his face fills with anger and begins to break into sorrow.

"Hey, I don't know what you're talking about," I squeak, struggling to breathe as his grip on my throat tightens.

Alpha Damon suddenly places his hand on Chase's shoulder. He releases me, but I can tell that he doesn't want to.

I know what's coming next. Alpha Damon looks deeply into my eyes. He asks me quickly with his alpha tone, demanding to know where Raven is.

I raise my hand to my throat, unsure if I will be able to answer after Chase's hands almost cut off my air supply just a moment ago.

"I don't know where Raven is, the last time I saw her was at the shops this morning."

"You messaged her to meet you by the lake," Chase screams, immediately lunging for me again.

"I never messaged her," I say sharply, fishing my phone from my pocket and handing it to Alpha Damon.

I watch him as he looks through my messages and shakes his head. "There are no messages on his phone to Raven."

Chase growls angrily before exiting my house. Alpha Damon follows behind him.

I close the door angrily. How dare they come into my home and accost me. I haven't messaged Raven since she left. The last message I sent her was that I wished she hadn't left. She never replied.

Deep down in my heart, I truly meant that. I wish that I had never met Ava down at the lake that day. I want Raven. I have loved her my whole life. I would do anything for her.

I run my hands through my short brown hair in frustration. I want to scream. Why did the Moon Goddess do this to me? Why did we have chosen mates? Why couldn't we choose our own love?

Raven is my whole world and I need to find her. I had been the one to save her when Rhys took her, and I would be the one to save her this time.

Shifting, I begin running.

To the place where we shared.

Our special place.

The lake.

CHAPTER FIFTY

THREE WEEKS

(Chase's perspective)

My whole body is tense. "It's been three fucking weeks," I roar at Mark, throwing my desk lamp across the room. It smashes loudly, causing the lightbulb to burst, shattering into small particles, spreading glass all over my office floor.

"Where could she be?" I ask, moving my hands into my hair and pulling it sharply. I heard her call out to me a few nights ago through our mind link, but when I called back, I got nothing.

My Raven is missing. We have no leads. I followed her scent back to the lake, but from there, it's like she just vanished. Her scent had disappeared. Just like that strange wolf who had tried to take Raven from the Mall.

I have some rogues down in the dungeons. I decide to head down and question them again for the second time today. Even if they don't give me answers, hurting them helps my rage. I am not a nasty alpha, but the loss of Raven is pushing my animal instincts to the maximum.

Pushing through the front door, it bangs loudly against the frame, almost threatening to come completely off the hinges. My footsteps fall noisily onto the ground. I nod to the guard on the door to the dungeons and they bow to me, showing respect before stepping aside.

The cells hold three rogues. Their stench fills my nose as soon as I come near. Part of me actually believes that they don't know anything as I can smell each one of them. I feel that the rogues I am looking for are those who have masked their smell somehow.

I have teams out constantly searching our lands and those near us with the other alphas' permission. My pack is tired and I'm beginning to lose hope.

Quinn has hidden away in the deepest part of my mind and is refusing to come out. He is heartbroken. His mate is missing, and he can't even function normally without her.

Come to think of it, I can't function without her. I have had to send a clean-up team out to our house to remove everything that I have broken over these last few agonising weeks.

Mark and Ally have let me stay with them, but I know this has been hard on them. I have barely slept a wink. I constantly search for her. Trying to pick up any information I can as to her whereabouts.

I have killed many rogues for information, but so far have come up empty-handed. Someone must know what happened to her.

I have been to speak with Alpha Sam who took over for Alpha Rhys, but nothing. He hasn't seen Raven since the day she was rescued. He mentioned that a few members had turned rogue after Alpha Damon killed Rhys. But he had banished them and didn't know where they had gone.

My insides are screaming for sleep, but I continue to keep myself awake. With Quinn deciding to become a recluse, I'm unable to shift. He's too broken to come forward when I ask him to.

Mark stares at me after my spat. He doesn't seem like he knows what to say to me, so he just listens.

Suddenly, a call comes through from Alpha Damon.

"Yes?" I call down the phone. "Have you found her?"

I stand and begin pacing, waiting for his response.

"No, son, but I do have information. I will enter your pack lands momentarily and meet you in your office," he says in a solemn voice before hanging up.

"No, she can't be, I can't lose her," I scream, picking up a tray of documents on my desk, sending them flying.

Mark stands and moves around my desk. Grabbing my shoulders, he looks at me.

Like, really looks at me.

"Mate, we will find her," he says earnestly.

I huff and sit down roughly in my chair, making it squeak in protest.

After a few minutes of watching Mark pick up the lamp and the papers I had thrown in my outburst earlier, there comes a knock on my door.

Mark opens the door and allows Alpha Damon to enter. I stand, taking his hand, shaking it before I notice Cody standing behind him.

"What is he doing here?" I roar.

"He knows who took Raven," Damon announces before forcefully sitting Cody down on a chair.

I move forward, ready to strangle him, when Damon's hand comes to rest on my shoulder, stopping me.

"He has only just worked it out, today, son. He came straight to me and let me know. Listen to him," he says quietly.

Had anyone else touched me that way, I would have torn their face off, but Damon is Raven's father and I give him the respect he deserves by sitting back down in my chair.

"Speak," I order Cody, who looks over at me in fear.

"It was Ava," he squeaks uncomfortably.

"She messaged Raven and then deleted it from my phone. I found it in the junk folder," he adds. "She's been disappearing a lot lately after I fall asleep, and to be honest, I never thought much of it, but I also never asked where she was going," he says, looking down at the desk as if studying its woodgrain.

"So, last night, I pretended to be asleep, and when she left, I followed her. She went off our lands to the West and travelled for about forty minutes before going into an underground mine in unclaimed territory. I waited outside. I could hear screaming." He breaths out sadly.

"I hid." He pauses and looks at my face. I nod, letting him know to continue.

"Ava exited just after morning. I had been waiting for over six hours, and she looked to be heading home. Two other male wolves followed her out but there didn't seem to be anyone else around, so I decided to check out what was down in the mine and who had been screaming.

"I searched many different rooms down there. The mine looks like it's been turned into some kind of lab. It's abandoned and the rooms don't have much in them besides a few tables and some medical equipment that doesn't seem to work."

"Get on with it," I yell, balling my fists. "Where's Raven?"

"I… I found Raven," he adds nervously.

I sigh appreciatively, placing my hands over my face and running them up through my hair.

"But I couldn't move her, she was unconscious. I heard people returning, so I hid and waited. They moved Raven to another room, and I snuck out and came straight to Alpha Damon."

"Take me to her," I demand, standing and moving to the door swiftly.

Quinn comes to the forefront of my mind.

"Let's go and get our Luna," he speaks eagerly.

I shifted mid-run out of the house and am soon followed by Cody, Mark and Alpha Damon. I send mind links through to other strong pack members to follow behind. We have a team of thirty strong wolves from my pack alone, and soon, another twenty added on from Alpha Damon's pack.

Cody leads us to where Raven is being kept. We watch—hidden— to see if anyone is entering or leaving the mine. Shortly after arriving, a tall man exits the mine on his own, lighting up a cigarette and taking a deep pull from it. He rests against some large rocks and seems deep in thought. He doesn't even notice Alpha Damon until it is too late. I watch on as the man's throat is ripped clean from his body before he crumples to the ground.

The man lets out a strangled sound, alerting some other men inside the mine. They exit quickly, running at us. I note they have no scent and feel relief wash over me as I know Cody is telling the truth. These people are who took Raven. She is here somewhere.

A dark brown wolf runs at me, catching me off guard as my mind drifts to thinking about Raven. His claw rips into my leg painfully. I whip around quickly grab another reddish coloured wolf before throwing him harshly to the ground. No one is going to stand in the way of me getting to my mate. The warriors we have brought with us dispose of the seven rogue wolves quickly.

The heavy breathing of everyone fills my ears. I look towards the door to the mine as if waiting for the second wave of rogues, but no one comes.

Cody begins walking towards the door ahead, and I follow closely behind. Soon, we come to a room. I shift and so does Cody. Grasping the handle sharply, I turn it. But the door is locked. With all of my strength, I barge my way through.

The sight in front of me almost makes me buckle at my knees.

There, on a sterile-looking medical table, lays my girl. My little bird. My Luna.

She looks so helpless, lifeless.

I should be able to hear her heartbeat from here. Why can't I hear a heartbeat?

I rushed forward, shoving my ear to her chest. Her heart is still beating but only just. I look around and notice that she is attached to a drip. I rip it from her skin, the liquid seeping from the tubes onto the floor, the machine it was connected to beeping incessantly. I sniff wildly, smelling that it is Wolf's bane mixed with some kind of sleeping drug.

This is why she wasn't able to mind link me, they have been keeping her painfully asleep. I lift her small, frail body into my arms and carry her from the room.

I have a car waiting for us up by the main road.

Alpha Damon and I rush her back to the closest pack hospital, which happens to be Damon's.

The doctor and nurses push us from the room, and we try to wait patiently.

After two hours of pacing, Alpha Damon stands hurriedly, and I notice that the doctor has returned. I look up at him expectantly.

"She's okay," he announces loudly. "I have given her an antidote, but she needs rest."

"Also, if I may have a word Alpha Chase," the doctor notes, pointing to a small corner of the waiting room.

I follow him and wait expectantly for what he has to say.

"Raven has been tortured horribly. Her body is very weak, bruised and she has lost a lot of blood from small cuts made to her wrist area. She has three broken ribs that remain unhealed due to the wolf's bane. They will heal in the next few days due to the antidote, but there is one small thing that I noticed whilst examining her…" The doctor pauses and I stare at him.

"Yes?" I prompt harshly. *Seriously, I'm about to rip this guy's head off if he doesn't speak.*

"Well, sir, Miss Raven appears to be pregnant," he announces proudly.

CHAPTER FIFTY-ONE

MURDEROUS RAGE

I stand there in shock, letting the doctor's words sink in. *I'm going to be a dad,* I think excitedly, placing my hand on my forehead.

Alpha Damon, having clearly overheard, comes over and claps me loudly on the back.

"You better marry my girl before this baby comes along," he says, grinning. His eyes appear glassy. I watch as his hand slides over his child thoughtfully before he walks away, whispering to himself, "I'm going to be a grandpa."

The hours seem to be ticking by slowly as I wait for Raven to wake. It feels like my life is moving in slow motion, watching her lay there helplessly and knowing I can't do anything to help her. The doctor said she would wake from the coma once she was ready to.

I hear a sound by the door and look up.

"We found her," Alpha Damon announces, and I realize he's talking about Ava.

"I have interrogated her." He sighs. "I found out that she decided to continue to follow Alpha Rhys orders even though he's dead. She continued with them because she hates Raven for trying to steal Cody."

A rumble erupts from me involuntarily, Quinn clearly upset with hearing Cody's name.

"I've got her locked up down in the cells for now, I'm not really sure what to do with her as Raven is no longer officially part of our pack. The decision is yours, son." He breathes, visibly worried as his eyes watch his daughter's sleeping body.

"I will think it over for now, but no food or water," I state, watching him take leave. He has barely slept in days. He sits with Raven whilst I sleep, which has only been about four or five hours over the past three days.

I begin to pace back and forward. The beige colours of the room are plain and boring. I make note to myself to have some flowers brought to the room to brighten it a little for when Raven wakes. My pacing is short lived. I slump down in my chair, my elbow and hand supporting my chin. Stubble scratches at my hand. I need to shave.

I sigh loudly, leaning forward in the chair and placing my head in my hands. Sitting here, waiting for my girl to wake up, is the most excruciatingly painful time in my life. Waiting is hard, especially when what I really want to do is go over to the cells and rip Ava's head from her body.

My eyes glance back over to my sleeping girl.

Please wake up, Raven.

My eyes flutter open and closed. The light is so bright. I try again, blinking a few times to help my eyes adjust. My eyes roam around the room… it smells medical. *I know this roof… I'm in my dad's hospital wing… How did I get here?*

A small cough escapes my throat as I try to talk. My throat feels dry and cracked like I breathed in a whole heap of dirt. I need water.

"Raven?" Chase says, leaning over me. "Oh, Raven," he says, tilting down and kissing me desperately. I scrunch my eyes at the pain in my chest as he presses against me.

Realizing he is hurting me, Chase leans back, staring down at me. I watch his eyes, and they are watching me like I'm going to disappear.

"W… water," I croak.

Chase quickly brings me some water and tilts the cup gently to my lips.

The water flows down my throat and begins to soothe the soreness instantly.

"Why are we in my father's hospital?" I ask, bringing my hand up to my throat when it still stings a little. I sound like I have a cold, which is annoying.

Chase stares at me for a moment, like he's struggling to think really hard about how to answer me.

"You don't remember?" he almost whispers.

I think back. "I remember going to see…" I pause, not wanting to finish my sentence.

"Cody," Chase finishes for me. "You went to see Cody and you were taken; you have been missing for three weeks, Raven."

I look up at him, shocked. I try to sit up a little and notice tenderness across my whole body. A flash of a room and a hammer being slammed into my fingers breaks into my mind. I shake my head. *I was tortured.*

"No, baby, stay still, your body is weak because they had you on a wolf's bane drip," Chase slowly coos to me, pressing his hand gently to my forehead.

I stay still, loving the feel of his hand on my skin. I lean into his hand slightly, relishing it.

"Who took me?" I ask, looking up at Chase. "Was it the rogues?"

"Raven, it was Ava all along, she's been behind the whole thing."

"Ava sent the rogues after me?" I question, looking at Chase with disbelief on my face.

Another flashback of someone injecting me with Wolfs bane breaks into my mind, but it comes and goes quickly.

"Raven, are you okay?" Chase asks, moving closer to me and holding my hand in his.

"I keep having flashbacks of things that happened to me," I say, breathing heavily.

"It's okay, baby, you're safe with me now. I will always be your safe place." He smiles and then adds with a stern look, "Ava is locked up in the dungeons." I watch as Chase starts rubbing his hand over mine. A huge yawn escapes his mouth as he tries to smother it with his other hand.

"You look so tired, my Alpha, you should rest," I say, reaching up to touch his face gently.

Chase climbs into the hospital bed next to me and I rest my head against him gently.

"Raven, there's something I need to tell you," Chase says softly, sitting up enough to look deeply into my eyes. "When you came back here, the doctor did a check on you, and well…" He pauses.

"You're pregnant." He beams.

I look up at him and a huge smile spreads across my face. "I'm going to be a mum?" I ask, beaming at him.

He nods excitedly. "And I'm going to be a dad," he adds before resting his hand on my belly and resting his chin on my head. Within minutes, he is asleep, breathing heavily. I can feel his warm breath fanning over my hair.

"You are my safe place," I whisper softly. "My Alpha."

In the morning, I wake to an empty bed, and Chase is nowhere to be seen. I climb out of bed and note that I don't have any pain.

My accelerated healing must have kicked back in now that all of the wolf's bane is out of my system.

I stretch my hands high up over my head and then bring them back down to my belly, running my hands over it softly.

I can't believe that I'm going to be a mum.

I walk out into the hospital corridor and note that no one is around, which seems strange. I wander back into my room and grab a robe. Wrapping it around myself, I decide to head out into the pack grounds to find someone, anyone. Again, it's eerily quiet. I can even hear the sound of my own footfall on the path.

"Chase?" I call out through our link.

"Raven, stay where you are," he replies back quickly, and I can sense that he's angry.

"Where are you? I'm outside the hospital?" I send back.

Suddenly, anger grips me as I feel it rolling off Chase through our link.

I begin walking towards the dungeons, feeling drawn there. It's almost like my body is being drawn to Chase. The overwhelming need to calm his anger takes over my body.

Remembering Chase mentioned that Ava was in the dungeons, a

new wave of determination takes over. I'm going to confront this bitch once and for all.

As I walk towards the dungeons, I can see Chase and my father with a few other pack members circled around two figures. I realize that it's Ava and Cody.

"Just let her go," Cody calls empathetically. "She doesn't know what she's doing. Alpha Rhys damaged her mind."

I run to Chase's side and note the look of fear on his face when he sees me.

"Raven, go back to the hospital and lock your door. Ava has managed to poison some pack members and they have died. She's dangerous," he sends to me, trying to push me away.

Ava's eyes meet mine; they are full of loathing.

"A few more hours and I would have killed you," she spits at me.

"Why do you want to kill me so badly?" I ask her heatedly.

"You want my mate, you're going to steal him away from me, he's all I ever wanted, and you want him for yourself, you selfish bitch," she screams.

Cody holds onto her like if he lets go, she might break.

"I sent the rogues to kill you, but your stupid mother interfered. You should have died months ago," she screams so loudly that she almost falls forwards.

I stare at her in shock, realizing what she has just said.

My dad's face contorts as he also realizes what she has just admitted.

"Aveave" my dad says breathlessly. "She wasn't asking for you Raven, she was trying to warn me that it was Ava." He shifts and moves to face Ava.

Before I even notice it happen, I shift angrily, charging at Ava. I collide with her, and she spins wildly, shifting into her wolf, sending me flying backwards. My paws skid in the dirt. As I come to a stop, I turn to face her.

My father waits. It's almost as if he is in complete shock having learnt that one of his very own members could have killed their Luna. His Luna. He watches like a statue as Cody and Chase shift also. My rage is driving me. She killed my mum.

My attention quickly slips to Chase as I sense a wave of anger and worry flow from him. Noticing my attention on her waver, Ava runs, crashing into me, sending me flying to the ground. I feel something break and a sharp pain rips through my side. She picks me up by the scruff of my neck, hurling me into a nearby tree. I howl out in pain.

I spin and run back at Ava, scratching at her left flank, leaving a gaping wound. A sharp snarl erupts from her as she grabs hold of my paw as I move past her, biting down hard. I can feel bones break as her jaws squash my bones. Yelping as I rip my paw from her mouth, I stand with my paw raised. It hangs in an unnatural way, clearly broken.

I watch as her muzzle moves into a smirk. A new wave of resolve takes over and the pain seems to dissipate. I run back again, skidding underneath Ava's chest. She is too slow and misses grabbing me. I grasp hold of her roughly. I rip straight into Ava's throat, killing her immediately.

Her body slumps to the floor and automatically shifts back to its human form.

My muzzle is dripping with her blood. Driven by fury, I walk over to her small form to make sure that she is dead.

I shift back and stand over her body like a trophy hunter. My breathing is harsh and coming out in pants.

Chase hasn't moved from his place; he shifts back and begins to move towards me.

Without warning, a loud howl breaks the silence. My eyes land on the source of the sound.

Cody.

He is still in his wolf form. I can almost sense his despair just from the sound omitting from him. Losing your mate is apparently the worst pain a wolf can go through, and I have just killed Cody's. Part of my heart wants to sooth his pain. I watch as his eyes meet mine, a whimper breaking from his throat.

He turns and runs. I step forward to follow him, but my body falters and I fall forwards. Catching me, I watch Chase's face full of worry as he lifts me gently and runs as fast as he can back to the hospital.

CHAPTER FIFTY-TWO

DEVASTATION

(Caution this may be a trigger for some)

My hand lands over my stomach as I lay in bed at home. It's been four weeks since I killed Ava. Her attack against me has wounded me so badly that my body could no longer support my pup.

I haven't wanted to see anyone.

I have hidden myself away in my bedroom.

Chase has remained by my side at all times, only leaving briefly for pack work and he then returning straight after. I know how hard it is for him to leave me, but I feel like he needs to get away from my grief. I had only been five weeks pregnant but the pain and hollow feeling that I have inside me won't go away.

I lost my pup.

Akira is absolutely devastated. She hasn't spoken in weeks. I know she feels like it is her fault as she shifted out of anger at Ava and killed her. But we both know that the only person to blame is Ava. Had she not thrown me into the tree, our pup would still be here.

I haven't seen Ally. I asked her to come but I know she doesn't want to be around me since she is now six months pregnant, her bump clearly showing. She has told Chase she can't bear to come near me, saying that it is her fault that I was taken by Ava and her rogues and also knowing that she still has her baby and I don't have mine. Chase has told me that she is absolutely wracked with guilt.

In a way, it hurts to know that she won't be there to comfort me, but at the same time, I try my best to understand her reasoning. I don't know how I will react seeing her beautiful baby bump, but I know deep in my heart that I am still so happy for her to be growing a beautiful baby girl and that I don't for one second blame her for what happened with Ava.

The days seem to be melting together, and soon, I have lost all sense of time.

There are times where I just want to be by myself, hiding away, letting my sorrow eat me alive.

From our bedroom, I can hear Chase in the living room, watching a movie. He had asked me to join him earlier, but I had silently declined. My head told me that I needed to go downstairs but my heart just can't cope.

It must be an action movie, as I can hear a few explosion style scenes. Suddenly, the movie goes quiet. I wonder quietly why he has turned the movie off, when I hear a knock on the front door.

I overhear Chase get up to answer it.

I haven't seen anyone for over six weeks now. So when I hear my bedroom door creek open, I'm shocked to see Alexandria. She pokes her head around the edge of the door as if she needs to make sure that she's allowed to come in first.

I look into her eyes and tears start to stream down mine. Alexandria rushes towards me, sitting on the edge of the bed. She holds her hands out to me and I go into them willingly.

"Oh, my sweet girl, I'm so sorry," she coos to me whilst running her hand over my hair gently.

"I'm sorry that I haven't come sooner, Chase wouldn't let anyone near. Quinn has been very possessive and refused to let anyone near you."

I don't answer, I just sob louder and let her hold me.

We have been sitting for ages before I stop crying and sit up a little. Alexandria just holds me and lets me cry. I am so grateful for her.

"We need to get you up and out, beautiful girl. You have been locked up in here for six weeks," she says seriously.

I look into her eyes and know that it's time. Time for me to get out of bed, time for me to shower... I seriously stink. Time for me to go and support my best friend.

"I don't know if I ever told you, Raven, but I too have lost a child."

My eyes widen at her confession. I don't speak, I just listen.

"Chase was a twin. His brother never made it. I understand just how hard this is for you, my girl, but I promise it will get better. You will never forget your pup; they will be in your heart and your memory always. Don't let your life move on without you. Our pack adores you; they need their Luna, Raven, we need you," she says, patting my leg before getting up and kissing my forehead before leaving the room.

I sit for a few moments before lifting myself out of bed with a new found energy. *I can do this.*

I shower, dress and head downstairs. Chase is in the kitchen, fixing a small plate of food.

Noticing me in the doorway, he slowly saunters over to me.

"Hello, my little bird, how I have missed seeing you around the house," he says with a swift kiss to my lips. "I have made something to eat for us," he adds, waving his hand towards the couch.

We sit together peacefully, and I smile to myself before taking a bite of the sandwich that he's made me. I can't believe how I am so lucky to have such an amazing mate.

When Chase got me to the hospital—after Ava slammed my body into the tree—he was so worried. I didn't even have a chance to fully process the fact that I was pregnant before my baby was taken from me. As much as everyone tells me not to blame myself, I still can't help but feel like if I hadn't lost control of my temper and shifted, then she never would have attacked me. I still can't believe that I actually killed someone, to be honest.

A wave of sadness begins to swamp my insides again, but I push it away quickly.

I know Chase is absolutely devastated about losing our pup. I can feel his sadness and it doubles my own. We both lost our baby, and I must admit I could quite easily have hidden away and buried myself under pillows and blankets in bed for a few more weeks had Alexandria not come and talked with me.

The pack needs me, the pack needs their Luna. I have taken my time to mourn my loss and Alexandria is right, the pain will never go away but I can learn to deal with it and move forward, always keeping them in my mind and my heart.

"Ally and Mark are coming over for dinner," Chase suddenly announces, breaking me out of my thoughts. "I hope that's okay?" he adds, looking deeply into my eyes as if he's waiting for me to decline the idea.

"Sounds wonderful," I reply, smiling. "I have missed Ally so much."

Chase and I prepare dinner together. We decided to make lasagne with garlic bread.

Alexandria was right, getting out of bed and keeping myself busy has really helped me. I feel much calmer and in control of my feelings. Even though Chase has stayed with me during the past few weeks, we haven't really been connected in the same way. We have been there together, in the same place, but we haven't really been *all* there.

I haven't laughed in weeks, so seeing Chase dance around the kitchen to the radio makes me giggle so hard I almost wet myself. It is just a huge reminder of how much I truly love him and how we are always going to be together, during the good times and the bad.

Whilst Chase dances around with the herbs in his hand for the garlic bread, I stir the meat sauce around in the pan, watching it blip and bubble away like a mini volcano. Once the sauce is done, we layer up the lasagne and I place it in the oven.

Chase appears behind me, wrapping his hands around my waist, bringing his face down into the crook of my neck. He kisses me tenderly before using his hands to turn me around. I place the oven-mitts gently back onto the bench and wrap my arms around his neck.

Bringing me in, Chase places his lips onto mine ever so sweetly. His lips light a fire deep down in my stomach, and soon, our kiss becomes heated. My hands grasp his hair desperately and pull it roughly. I hear a low deep growl erupt from Chases chest, to which I respond with a moan.

Chase lifts me from the ground, placing me onto the bench, his lips never once leaving mine. His hand leaves my waist and travels up my shirt. Chase grasps the edge of my bra, drawing it down slightly, allowing my nipple to escape. He uses his fingers deftly, teasing and pulling it, making me squirm under his touch.

It's been too long since I've had him.

I push my body flush against his, pulling him to me. I need some kind of friction against my burning core as I'm now writhing under his expert touch. He knows just how to turn me on and he's barely doing anything.

Wanting to hurry things along a little, I slide down from the bench and kneel in front of Chase, and bringing my hands up to his zipper, he watches me intensely.

Just as I'm about to release him from his boxers, the doorbell rings.

CHAPTER FIFTY-THREE

NEW LIFE

Chase groans loudly before re-zipping his pants. He places a quick kiss on my lips before begrudgingly leaving me to open the front door.

I busy myself getting out the cutlery before I hear small footsteps enter the kitchen behind me. Turning, I see my beautiful best friend. Her belly looks so big now and I can't believe how much her bump has changed.

I need to remind myself that I haven't actually seen her for almost two months. The last day that I saw her, was the day I went to go and meet Cody.

She stands in the doorway, unmoving. Her eyes meet mine but instantly they move to the floor.

I run to her and gently wrap my arms around her whole body, even though her tummy keeps me from getting too close.

"I missed you," I breathe softly.

I move her back to arm's length and notice she has tears in her eyes.

"I'm just so sorry, Ray, it's all my fault," she stutters before pulling me back in for another hug.

"Shhh," I coo in her ear and hold her gently. "It's not your fault."

Unexpectedly, I feel a very small push against my tummy.

"Ohhff," Ally says, taking a step back and rubbing her tummy joyfully.

I look at her and smile, realizing that the baby has been kicking Ally so hard that I can feel it.

Her eyes snap up from her tummy to meet mine. I can tell that she is feeling a little stressed about the situation we are in.

"May I?" I ask. Stepping forward, I hold my hand up, just hovering over her tummy. Ally nods ever so slightly. I lower my hand gently and begin to rub my hand over her belly softly.

After a few moments, I felt a small kick and then the whole baby rolls over. My eyes widen and I look up at Ally, surprised.

Ally giggles lightly at my expression, and soon, we are both laughing together.

The dinner goes by smoothly. The lasagne was so beautiful, and Ally and Mark have brought over dessert. Scrumptious apple pie with ice-cream.

After dinner, the boys play a game of pool whilst Ally and I sit on the games room couch and have a real heart to heart chat. We decide that we need a girls day. I thought it might be nice to go to a local day spa. Ally loves the idea and we promise to see each other every day.

We walk them to the front door around eleven p.m., and then go off to bed. I am absolutely drained from the day. As soon as my head hits the pillow, I'm asleep right away.

Ally and I keep our promise and spoke every day. She decided that she wanted a baby shower after all, and I said I would organise it for her—much to her sister's disgust.

My life slowly goes back to normal, my Luna duties becoming more prominent in my life, and I work along-side Alexandria as she teaches me how to be the best Luna possible. I still think about my mum every day and how much I miss her. I wish that she could see me now. A Luna.

Three months have absolutely flown by, and before I know it, Mark is calling me, letting me know that Ally's waters have broken. Ally has asked me to be with her in the birthing suit, along-side Mark. At first, I wasn't too sure about being in there with her, as I felt like it was a private and special moment between her and Mark, but she insisted.

I hang up the phone, almost tripping over, trying to pull on my shoes. Once they are on, I race out and jump into my car, zooming straight to the pack hospital.

Once inside, a nurse leads me to her room. Not that I really need directions. I merely have to follow the intense screaming that I know is my best friend.

Once I arrive inside the room, I can see Ally mid-contraction. Mark is holding her hand but clearly in pain himself. I can see that he is trying really hard not to complain, but his facial expressions aren't really helping.

When Ally finally sees me, she holds out her hands to me and I walk over to her willingly.

"Hey, Al." I smile, kissing her on the forehead. "You are so amazing," I coo to her.

She smiles up at me before another contraction takes hold of her. I'm not really sure how to help her, but I have read somewhere about a pressure point in the back.

I try my best to explain how it works to her.

"I'll try anything, Ray, it hurts so bad," she says through gritted teeth.

I help Ally get into a more comfortable position on her knees, so that she is leaning over the back of the bed, aided by a pillow pressed firmly to her back.

"Oh, that helps so much," Ally breathes out in puffs.

Mark lets out a tense breath that he had been holding, clearly happy that Ally isn't in as much pain as before.

Ally was in labour for over six hours before a beautiful little baby girl entered the world. She is so tiny. As soon as she lets out a small cry, tears stream down my face. Mark follows her protectively over to the nurse's station to watch her closely.

I hold onto Ally's hand, looking down at her. She is exhausted. Her hair is absolutely crazy, but I'm not about to tell her that.

"You did it, Mumma," I say, smiling and trying not to sob as I say the words.

Ally looks up at me and smiles tiredly. "Thank you for being here with me, Ray."

I hold her hand and we just stare at each other, smiling before we are broken apart by a tiny little girl being carried by her father, coming between us.

Mark passes the baby to Ally, who takes her greedily. Her eyes wave over the baby in such awe.

Mark moves around to the other side of the bed, settling in next to Ally.

"What's her name going to be?" I ask quietly, leaning over to stare at the beautiful little bundle in front of me.

Mark and Ally look at each other and Ally nods slightly.

"Her name is Haylie Ray," Mark announces proudly.

My eyes snap from the baby up to Ally and Mark. They both smile at me widely before I look back down at the baby.

"Welcome to the world, Haylie, your Auntie Raven loves you."

CHAPTER FIFTY-FOUR

SURPRISE

Life was good again. I hadn't forgotten the past, but I'm so excited for my future. Haylie is just the light of everyone's lives. She is almost nine months old now. I helped Ally in the first few days of being home as Mark had to attend to some important pack business with Chase. I was so glad to be there for her. It gave me a taste of what it was like to have a new-born, and well, let's just say I was super tired after the first few days, and I wasn't even the one who was breast feeding.

Ally is an amazing mum. I always knew that she would be. From the first moment that I met her, I knew she was going to be a fantastic mum. She has a way with people. She's so kind, caring and considerate of others. The perfect beta female. My best friend.

Chase has been away from the pack for a few days now, overseeing something in the city, but he called earlier to let me know that he is returning later in the afternoon and that he wants to take me out for dinner.

I have missed him so much.

I pull into our driveway and head inside after returning from Ally and Mark's house.

I had gotten Haylie to sleep so Ally decided that she also needed a nap, and I couldn't have agreed more. I could use one also, but I know that I need to do a quick tidy up at home before Chase returns.

After cleaning the house, I decide to have a shower. The warmth of the shower makes me feel tired, but the second I step out, the cool air brushing against my skin makes me feel instantly awake.

Fresh and clean, I wrap myself up in a cuddly robe before lying on the sofa and reading a book. Sitting still for a while, my body relaxes into the cushions.

I must have fallen asleep because soon, I'm woken to our doorbell ringing.

I answer the door, rubbing my eyes to find Mark standing with a box in his hands.

Seeing Mark makes me jump for joy, as he was with Chase, which means they are both home. Looking behind Mark, I notice that Chase is nowhere to be seen.

Pouting slightly, I hold out my hands as Mark hands me the box and turns to leave without saying anything to me.

"Hey?" I call. "What's this?"

"Open it and you will see," Mark replies with a smirk before running off.

I close the front door with my foot, causing it to bang loudly before heading into the lounge.

I lay the box gently on the sofa next to me before opening it up. Inside is a gorgeous set of bathers and two airline tickets.

Holding them up, I see that they are for a trip to Bora Bora, and they leave tonight.

I scream excitedly before running around the house.

I was going to call Ally but decided I shouldn't as I don't want to wake her.

I drop my phone onto the couch as I hear the front door open. Running, I collide with Chase at full speed, kissing him furiously before stepping back.

"Hey, my little bird," he says in-between kissing my lips. "Ready for a holiday?" he asks, smiling.

I nod swiftly before throwing myself into his arms, wrapping my legs around his waist.

We head off to the airport later that afternoon. Our flights don't leave until ten. I'm a little sad that I didn't get to say goodbye to Ally and Haylie, but Chase said we didn't have time and that we were only going for five days so it wasn't that long.

Walking through the airport, we check in our luggage and watch as it is taken away on those cool little escalators.

We make our way to the waiting lounge and just as we're finding seats, I look up and two eyes meet mine.

Shocked, I just stare.

"Ally?" I yell loudly before squealing.

"Surprise." Chase giggles next to me.

My mind whirls for a few moments before I click that Ally and Mark are coming on the holiday with us.

Then, I notice one small detail. Where is Haylie?

Sensing my worry, Chase mind links, me letting me know that Alpha Nicholas is going to look after the pack whilst we're away and Haylie will be staying with Ally's sisters.

I grab my best friend, jumping up and down excitedly. This is going to be the greatest holiday ever. The four of us together. I know Ally will miss Haylie, but she is so excited to come away with us. The wait in the airport isn't very long, thankfully, but the seats are uncomfortable.

The flights are long, but I manage a little sleep on the way. When we arrive, Chase wakes me, gently we wander through to the baggage claim. As soon as we all have our bags, we walk out of the front doors to find a beautiful black sleek limousine waiting for us. It drives us to a beautiful resort with stunning over-the-water bungalows. As we begin walking to our room, I take in the amazing scenery. The water is a clear crystal blue, and I can see small fish swimming around beneath us.

Ally squeals excitedly when she sees a turtle swimming below the deck.

This place is absolutely beautiful.

Mark grabs Ally from behind and she squeals again. "Here's us, babe," he says, pointing at number forty-four bungalow. He lifts her over his shoulder and smacks her loudly on the bum.

"Have fun you two," I say, waving to Ally with a smirk on my face.

"Oh, we will," Mark responds, wiggling his eyebrows seductively.

Chase grabs my hand and pulls me away from the other two, who have already shut their door.

We walk a little further down the boardwalk and I notice that the bungalows seem to be getting larger and further apart.

"What number is ours?" I ask, looking at each of the doors.

"Uh, we're number fifty," he says, looking down at the keys in his hand.

We soon arrive at our beautiful bungalow. Chase places the key into the door.

On entry, I take a few steps inside and spin around. I'm absolutely blown away by the grandness of this place. The windows are all huge and I can see the ocean for miles. There are bi-fold doors that open out onto our own spa and our bed is basically hanging out over the water as the floor is all glass.

On the bed lays a note, welcoming us with a beautiful bottle of champagne and a plate of chocolate covered strawberries.

I throw myself down onto the bed and sigh loudly. This is picturesque and just what I need.

The first two days of our holiday, Chase and I decided to explore the island, and we even did a little snorkelling and swimming. We didn't see Ally and Mark much. Anyone can guess what they were doing the whole time.

On the third night, all four of us went into town for a luscious steak and seafood dinner. The food was to die for, and I was definitely going home a few kilos heavier.

After dinner, we went for a walk along the beach together. With Chase's hand in mine, the water lapping over my feet, the sound of the ocean splashing against some nearby rocks, I was completely at ease.

On the fourth day, Ally and I decided on a girl's day. We had massages, facials, manicures and pedicures. We then sat on the beach and drank cocktails together, talking about all kinds of girly things. It was so great to just sit and chat with her like we used to.

We went our separate ways just before dinner time. I dropped her back to her bungalow and began walking back to mine with the wind blowing in my auburn hair. My mind felt so at ease here. The only sounds were that of the water brushing against the wooden supports holding up the bungalows and boardwalks, and the sound of my shoes landing gently after each step. It didn't take me long to reach our room.

I place the key haphazardly into the slot and turn the handle gently. The door swings open gently. Looking up, I gasp at the sight in front of me. The room is filled with small flickering candles and rose petals lying on the floor.

In front of me, I find a note.

CHAPTER FIFTY-FIVE

MYSTERY CARDS

L eaning down, I pick up the delicate piece of paper. My stomach turns with anticipation. Opening it, my eyes scan over the words reading, *Follow the rose petals and you shall find me.*

My heart is pounding in my chest out of excitement.

I follow the rose petals around and into the bedroom. On the bed lays a heart made out of the delicate crimson petals, and in the centre, another note.

Rushing forwards, I scoop up the letter and begin quickly opening it up. I find another note like the first. It reads, *You will find me in the water.*

Rushing out past the bi-fold door that stands open, I walk out over the decking.

There, laying in a colourful pink donut, is Chase. Next to him is a bright purple donut. I smile down at him and he winks at me.

"Go get changed and jump in," he calls, holding up a bottle of champagne.

Walking back inside, I feel a small sting in my heart. I was expecting to find him down on one knee, ready to propose to me, but instead, he wants to go swimming.

Walking back into the bedroom, I feel heavy. I guess I got myself all excited for no reason. Realizing that he isn't going to propose makes me realize that I really do want to marry him.

Doubt suddenly bursts into my mind. What if Chase doesn't want to marry me?

"No, that's silly, of course he does, I'm his mate," I say out loud to myself before taking a deep breath and letting the silly idea go before searching through my bag.

I find two of the bikinis that I packed and hold the blue top up in front of me. Throwing it down onto the bed, I select the beautiful purple top, holding it up to my chest and looking at myself in the mirror in the bathroom. I decide to wear the purple set. I quickly change into my bikini before walking back out and jumping into the water. The second I break through the cool water; a shiver runs over my body. I try to sense Chase's emotions but I'm not sensing anything but calm from him. I hope he didn't feel my disappointment earlier. I break the surface of the water and take in a lungful of air. I swim over to the purple donut and squeeze my way into it.

Chase also has a floating tray attached to his donut that I hadn't seen before. It's filled with tropical fruits and holds two champagne flutes. Chase pops the cork and fills a glass for me before filling one for himself. Sipping it, I take a piece of pineapple and add it to the champagne before eating a second piece.

We float around peacefully, eating fruit and sipping our champagne for a little while before Chase jumps out of his donut and swims over to mine. Jumping up, he lays with his elbows over my legs.

Looking down into his glorious blue eyes, I can't help but think how lucky I am to have him as my mate. Akira purrs in my mind, agreeing with me.

"What are you thinking about?" Chase asks softly, rubbing his thumb over my skin, setting off goosebumps all over my body.

"You," I reply, staring at him with a burning passion in my eyes.

Akira flashes through quickly. She's like a beacon calling to Quinn––who also flashes through.

Our souls forever intertwined. Destined to be together.

The next thing I know, I'm flying through the air.

I splash into the water unceremoniously.

Coming up for air, I take in a breath loudly. My hair is covering my face, and I pry it away with one hand and use the other to feel out in front of me for my donut, which I can't seem to find.

Then, I hear laughing.

My eyes settle on Mark's face.

Anger burns inside me, and I push both hands forward, splashing him.

"What the fuck, man?" Chase queries, coming up to the surface seconds after me.

"What? You two were all lovey dovey, staring into each other's eyes. You didn't even see me coming. It was an opportunity not to be missed." He laughs, holding on to his stomach under the water.

I splash him again and swim back to the ladder connected to our bungalow.

Storming inside, I go straight to the shower. I undress, leaving my bathers on the floor and step into the warm water. Mark just ruined a perfectly good moment between Chase and I, and I have to admit that I am super pissed off about it.

Part of me is wanting to be away from Chase for a little bit after the feeling of rejection earlier. I can't stop thinking about why he hasn't asked me to marry him yet. Also, I need to stay away from Mark because I am ready to detach his balls from his body for that little shit show he just pulled.

I decide to stay in the shower for over twenty minutes, enjoying the warmth spilling over my body. I snort loudly to myself. No wonder Ally was so impatient to get married. I haven't been with Chase as long as she's been with Mark, and she was so desperate to get married. I will have to chat with her about how I'm feeling, she will definitely understand where I'm coming from.

I step out and wrap a towel around my body before fixing one tightly around my wet hair. Considering my reflection in the mirror, I note that my face is a little flushed. Probably from the cocktails and champagne earlier.

Walking back into the bedroom, I notice that the rose petals have all disappeared. I feel a little uneasy knowing that the maids have been cleaning in here whilst I was in the shower.

I wander out into the lounge, rubbing the towel against my hair, gently drying it off. I look around and notice a small box sitting on the coffee table next to the lounge. *That definitely wasn't there before.* Dropping the towel I was using to dry my hair on the floor, I walk closer, picking up the box. I look over it and quickly put it back down. What if it's just a necklace or earrings?

I decide against looking in the box and turn to go and find Chase.

As I turn, I bump straight into him. He still has his shorts on, but his chest is bare. My hands lay over his smooth chest, taking him in, and my body instantly reacts to his.

I feel a pool of wetness emerge from inside me, soaking me instantly. Just the sight of him turns me on instantly. I will never grow old of this feeling.

Chase breathes in deeply and Quinn flashes through, clearly sensing my arousal.

Letting his breath out slowly, Chase leans around me and picks up the small box from the table.

I take a steading breath and hold it.

"Was this what you were hoping for earlier?" Chase enquires, looking deeply into my eyes before slowly opening the box.

CHAPTER FIFTY-SIX

THE PROPOSAL

Looking down, I watch as the box opens. It feels like it's taking years to open. But when it does, the box reveals a stunning engagement ring.

My eyes snap up to Chases and he smiles broadly down at me.

My hands fly up to my mouth to smother the small, choked sound that tries to escape.

Chase lowers himself onto one knee.

My breath halts in my throat, and I can feel tears pricking in the corners of my eyes.

Is this really happening?

"Raven," Chase breathes, the sound of my name leaving his mouth making my knees weak.

"I have loved you from the moment that I first saw you. You are my soulmate and my forever," he says clearly, his voice unwavering. His eyes bore into mine with such sincerity.

"I can't wait for you to be my wife. You inspire me each and every day. You lift me up when I am feeling down and always make me smile. I want to spend the rest of eternity with you by my side. Will you marry me?"

I choke out a sob and nod ecstatically before bending and throwing myself into Chase's arms.

Luckily, he had expected this and caught me.

"Yes, yes, yes, yes, I will," I scream in-between kissing him all over his beautiful face.

We both fall to the floor, Chase's legs unable to hold us up anymore with me thrashing around like a fish out of water.

Chase giggles and kisses my lips.

We sit up and I look down at the box Chase still holds in his hands.

He pulls the ring from the box and places it onto my left-hand ring finger.

I look down at it. It's beautiful. The main stone is centred. It's an exquisite clear diamond. Off to the sides is a line of square purple amethysts and then smaller diamonds. They go in a pattern the whole way around the band, alternating as they go.

I hold my hand up to admire my ring. I can't believe I'm engaged.

I look down and finally remember that I'm in a towel. We stand, and I again hold my hand out to admire my ring.

"I knew you were disappointed earlier when I saw your face," Chase proclaims, moving closer to me. "I was going to ask you just before Mark threw you into the water and pushed me under," he says, putting his finger under my chin and slowly guiding my face to his for a kiss.

"I'm going to kill him," I declare with an angry scowl running across my face.

Chase giggles and brings me in for a cuddle.

"I can't wait for you to be Mrs. Williams," Chase says before kissing me.

As soon as his lips meet mine, I deepen the kiss further by pressing my tongue against his lower lip. Chase opens his mouth, accepting my tongue greedily.

I push him backwards and he moves easily. If he doesn't want to move, there is no way that I will be able to move him. I know he wants what is about to happen just as much as I do.

When his legs meet the base of the couch, he lowers himself gently down, holding my waist so that I follow him. Our lips never break from our kiss.

Sitting with my legs on either side of him, I can feel his hardness pressing against my core. Still wet from the few moments ago when my hands encountered his chiselled and perfect chest, I rub myself against him. The towel is barely holding on anymore, so I pull it apart from the front and throw it to the floor.

Chase's board shorts can hardly contain his hardness, but it is making it easier for me to grind against him. Chase lets out a feral growl and his grip on my waist becomes almost painful.

I continue to grind myself against him. I break our kiss and my breath is coming out in pants. I think I'm going to come. Chase's lips move straight to my breasts, using his expert tongue to take my swollen nipple into his mouth. The feeling is euphoric. It doesn't take me long before I call out incoherently as an orgasm takes over my body.

My legs still shaking, Chase lifts his hips and pulls his shorts down between us. Grabbing his length in his hand, he pumps it up and down a couple of times. Using the other hand to hold my hips, he guides me down onto his throbbing dick.

The sensation of him filling me up is beyond words. I'm sure that no one but Chase could ever make me feel this way.

Manoeuvring my feet, I get myself into position, placing my hands on Chase's chest, so that I can bounce up and down easily. The feeling of being full of Chase's cock is earth shattering.

It's not long before I can feel my orgasm brimming around the edges, like an overflowing beer glass.

Chase feels me tightening around him and moves his hips up, meeting me pound for pound. His body slapping against my clit sends me into overdrive.

My orgasm comes quickly. I wrap my hands around Chase's neck and pull him to my mouth, kissing him hungrily. Trying to stay on this roller coaster as long as I can, I push myself firmly against Chase, taking all of him inside me.

As I come down from my high, Chase lifts me and flips me onto the couch, so that I'm lying on my back. Grasping my wrists down at my sides, he crawls up my body sexily. I watch as his arm muscles move, wanting to reach out and touch them, but my hands are unable to move under his hold.

Tilting down, Chase kisses me forcefully, pushing his tongue into my mouth ravenously. This sends volts of electricity straight to my burning core. I tilt my hips up, wanting him to be inside me again.

Sensing my need, Chase lets go of one of my wrists, grasping himself, hovering just above me, teasing me with the tip of his cock at my entrance.

I writhe under him, trying to press against him, but he moves just out of reach.

"I want you," I say breathily.

"You want this?" Chase asks, pressing his dick against my clit ever so lightly before moving away.

"Yes, please… fuck me," I pant.

At these words, Quinn flashes through and Chase rams into me harshly but pleasurably.

Chase pounds into me roughly. Reaching around, I grasp hold of Chase's firm ass, squeezing it. A low guttural moan escapes Chase's mouth as he leans forward, biting down onto my mark, causing me to flinch in both pain and pleasure.

Tasting my blood on his lips sends Quinn into a flurry. This isn't Chase fucking me anymore, this is Quinn. He is rougher…primal.

Akira is pushing me to let her in, so I do. Letting Akira take over, her and Quinn insatiably gave in to their animal instincts, making love to one another. Even though we are in our human forms, our wolves have taken over momentarily. The second Quinn released his load inside of me, he blinks, his eyes returning quickly to Chase's.

Quinn has released his control back to Chase, just as Akira has to me.

Laying in the afterglow of our love making, I look down, remembering my engagement ring.

Chase notices me looking over it and asks, "Do you like it?"

I look up from where I'm lying on his chest. "I really do, it's lovely. I always wanted a coloured stone of some sort."

Chase's face is glowing with pride. I can tell how proud of himself he is for choosing the most beautiful engagement ring. *I can't wait to be his wife.* It will definitely be a short engagement.

After another intense round of sex, and our stomachs begin to growl. Getting up, we shower together before we finally manage to make it out of the bungalow for dinner with Ally and Mark.

CHAPTER FIFTY-SEVEN

WHAT IS THAT?

Walking into the restaurant, I stand slightly on my heels, searching around to spot Ally and Mark. Apparently, they haven't arrived yet, so we take a seat at our assigned table and browse over the menu.

"What is that?" screams a familiar voice nearby.

I look up from my menu and notice Ally staring at me wide eyed, like she's just seen something fantastic. I notice her eyes are trained on my engagement ring.

I look at her and smile shyly, bringing my hand up in front of my face to admire my ring again before holding my hand out to her, so that she can take a peek.

Ally squeals loudly and almost jumps over the table to hug me. Mark gives me a wink and leans over to shake Chase's hand, mumbling a congratulations.

Taking her seat, Ally goes off on a tangent about where we will be married, what kind of dress I will wear, what kind of dress she will wear… She lets me know that she refuses to wear yellow and then begins her discussion again, asking questions this time, like what flowers I like and what I want to do with my hair.

After about five minutes, Ally notices that I haven't answered a single question she's asked me and that I have just been letting her ramble on whilst watching her. An amused smile spreads across my face. I watch her take a deep breath and reach out to grab my hand again.

"I'm sorry, Ray, I'm so flipping excited, your ring is absolutely stunning."

"Thanks, Al," I say, patting her hand softly. "We want a short engagement, so we don't have long to plan," I add and watch as her mind goes crazy again.

My eyes pan up and across the table as I can feel some eyes on me. Chase sits, staring at me. I smile and he gives me a wink before turning back to talk to Mark.

Our holiday has come to an end, and before I know it, we are in the car, driving down the main pack driveway.

Chase hasn't told his mum and dad about the proposal, so we go by their house first. Of course, they are over the moon. Alexandria hugs me to her and cries. Nicholas has to pry her off me so that we can finally head home.

I'm so tired, and even though I slept on the flight, I'm wrecked. I put it down to the time difference.

I call my dad as soon as we get home to let him know about the engagement, and he cries, telling me how much he wishes I could tell my mum. In turn, I cry also. I wish more than anything that the first person

I could have told was my mum. I haven't really thought too much about the fact that she isn't going to be there for my big day, but now that dad has pointed it out, I realise just how much of my life she is going to miss out on—all because of Ava.

Chase and I decide to be married within three months. I don't want to wait any longer. If anything, I realize just how important living my life is, because I never know when it is going to abruptly come to an end.

Ally and Alexandria help me to plan everything. Chase helps here and there, but he is very busy with all of the pack business.

I decide against a hen night and happily go and have a spa day with Ally and Alexandria instead. It is wonderful.

The night before the wedding, I send Chase off to stay at Mark's place, and Ally comes to stay with me. We make dinner together and sit together on the couch, discussing the timeline for the big day tomorrow.

I've started to feel a little nervous over the past week. My biggest fear is falling over, so Ally has promised me that she will remind my dad not to let me fall. Not that this calms me at all, but I guess it helps a little bit.

After dinner, I start feeling a little fuzzy, so I decide to grab my glass of water from the table.

"Are you okay, Ray?" Ally asks, looking concerned. "You've gone mighty pale."

Suddenly, I run. I feel so sick. Dinner mustn't have agreed with me.

I can hear Ally following behind me down the hall. As soon as I make it to the toilet, I spew up everything that I have eaten from today.

"Are you okay?" Ally calls from the doorway. "I'll get you some water," she calls before disappearing.

Returning with a glass of water, Ally finds me sitting on the edge of the bath with a towel to my face.

"What was that?" she asks, almost laughing. "It can't be dinner, I feel fine. You're not pregnant, are you?" she jokes.

My eyes snap to hers and her expression changes.

"Oh my gosh, you might be pregnant…" Ally half screams and dives on me, hugging me. "Let's check," she says, suddenly letting me go and running off again.

Not wanting to move, I assume she will eventually return.

Seeing Ally come back into the bathroom, my eyes drift to her hands. She's holding a box of pregnancy tests.

"Why do you have those?" I ask, looking up at her.

Her face changes and it looks like she's got a secret.

"Because I'm pregnant," she says, almost squealing it. "I took a test this morning."

Looking up at her, a smile beams across my face. "That's so amazing, Al. Why didn't you tell me sooner?" I say, rushing to her and hugging her.

"I wanted to wait until after your wedding," she says, hugging me back. "You need to do a test, it would be so amazing if we were pregnant at the same time," she adds, almost bouncing off the walls in excitement.

Passing me a test, I huff out air anxiously. I want to be pregnant so badly. I think it would just crush me if I wasn't.

"I'll wait in your room," Ally utters, sensing my apprehension.

I watch her leave and then rip open the test. Sitting down, I do what I need to and place the test on the bench. A wave of anxiety washes over me like a huge wave at the beach. I decide not to sit there by myself and wait. Walking out into the bedroom, I find Ally laying across my bed. She looks up at me expectantly.

"Set your phone timer for five minutes, please," I ask, sitting down on the edge of my bed.

After setting the timer, Ally moves next to me, grabbing my hand in hers. We sit in complete silence for the whole five minutes, which is so unlike us.

The sound of the timer going off makes us both jump. I'm like a statue. I literally can't move.

"Want me to check?" Ally asks, still holding my hand.

My nod is so slight that when Ally doesn't move, I think she's missed it. I look into her eyes and choke back a small sob.

"What if I'm not, Al?" I cry softly.

"I'll go see," she says, quickly getting up and moving into the bathroom.

She returns a few seconds later, holding the pregnancy test.

"Well, what does it say?"

CHAPTER FIFTY-EIGHT

OUR WEDDING

I wake the next morning, feeling rested. Today, I am marrying the most amazing man.

My hair and makeup are complete. I'm trying my best to calm myself, but my nerves are all over the place. It's almost time. I'm standing in my white silk robe, staring out of our upstairs window in the bedroom. I note that the sun is shining brightly in the distance, making everything glow and sparkle.

"Ray?" Ally calls to me from the doorway. "It's time to put on your dress."

I had gone shopping with Ally a few weeks ago to pick my wedding dress. We decided to avoid the shop that Ally had gotten her dress from, after the debacle we had last time. I was not going to go near the other dress that I fell in love with in there—Ava had ruined that for me.

I tried on about fifteen different dresses before I finally came to find one that I loved. It was totally not something that I thought I would have gone with, but as soon as I put it on, I was in love.

I decided that I didn't want just a plain old white dress anymore. I decided to try on a two piece; the bottom was a beautiful blush blue colour, and the top was white lace. I felt like an absolute princess as soon as it was on. I smile fondly as I recall how Ally cried, and from that moment, I knew it was the one.

Turning to face Ally, I note just how gorgeous she looks in her blue maid of honour dress.

I recall that day at the dress store. My memories flashing back. I had made her try on a yellow dress. You should have seen her face. It was all just for shits and giggles, but if looks could kill, people three states over would have died. It was so worth it though. I convinced her that I loved it before letting out a huge laugh. She was cross with me for a good five minutes. But I knew if I wanted it, she would have worn it for me.

"Ray?" Ally asks again, stepping towards me with a concerned look on her face.

"Hey, sorry, I was just thinking about something," I say, taking in a huge breath. "Okay, let's do this."

Ally helps me into my dress, and I feel even more beautiful now as I look at myself in the bedroom mirror. I feel like a princess.

I can tell just by looking at her that Ally is trying her absolute best not to cry. The look on her face—and her hands waving frantically—give away the fact that she doesn't want to wreck her makeup. I walk towards her and bring her to my chest, holding her in a gentle embrace.

"Thank you for being my best friend, Al," I whisper in her ear. "I love you."

She lets a little giggle bubble up from her tummy before whispering back, "I love you more."

"Oh my gosh, Raven," comes a voice from beside my bedroom

door. Ally and I both look up to see Alexandria in a burgundy lace knee-length dress. She has her hands up covering her mouth, trying to hold back a sob.

I smile warmly and take Alexandria into my arms.

"You look like an angel." She sighs, moving me back so that she can hold my face in-between her hands. "It's time. Your dad and Max are waiting at the end of the aisle for you."

I have asked both my dad and Max to walk me down the aisle. I can't wait to see Chase. As much as I'm nervous, being away from him has been agony for me. Akira has been in a mood since I sent him away yesterday. She hates being away from him.

Getting into the car, we head to the ceremony. I decided that I wanted a complete outdoor rustic-style wedding, with natural flowers and festoon lights everywhere. The weather has turned out perfectly, so we decided against needing the marquee. Everything will be out under the stars.

I hadn't even noticed that we had arrived until my door opens and my father's face appears. I note a small tear streak down his cheek when he sees me. Putting his hand out, I take it gently and get out of the car.

"You look beautiful, Raven," my dad says, holding me to his chest.

"Thank you, Dad," I say, smiling up at him. "I wish she was here," I fumble.

"She is. In here," he states, hovering his hand where my heart is.

A small, choked sound comes from my mouth before another hand touches my shoulder, causing me to turn.

I smile at him and hold my arm out for him. Max is so excited to see me. He takes my arm gently.

"Chase is one hell of a lucky man." He sighs.

They always say that people always look down the aisle to see the bride entering the ceremony, but almost no one watches the groom. My eyes are trained on Chase as I begin walking towards him.

I note the absolute look of adoration that he has on his face as I walk towards him.

I smile, and when I reach him, my whole world seems complete.

Our ceremony is peaceful, and we exchange our own written vows. Chase stands, holding my hands in his. I can feel his warmth seeping into my skin, like a calm wave on the beach.

"Raven, I have spent my whole life looking for my other half. I knew it was you from the moment we met. Real love isn't just a euphoric, spontaneous feeling—it's a deliberate choice—a plan to love each other. I plan to love you every day of our forever. I am the luckiest person alive to be standing with you today and to be facing life with you every day. You can be assured that I will protect and guard our love for the rest of my life."

I watch Chase's eyes the whole time he speaks, and small tears stream silently down my cheeks. Closing my eyes, I take a deep breath and steady myself. I open my eyes and look into Chase's eyes to speak my vows.

"Today, surrounded by all of our loved ones, I choose you to be my husband. I am proud to be your wife and to join my life with yours forevermore. I vow to support you, inspire you, and love you always. I want so badly to be able to explain the immense amount of love I have for you. It isn't butterflies and stomach knots, but more like the blurring of my soul and yours. Love is a word that is far too soft, and it could never describe the fierce, infinite and blazing passion that I have for you. You are a million of my dreams, a million of my prayers all rolled into one. You are brave. You are kind. You are cheeky. You are intelligent. Your laugh is contagious, and you can put away an entire apple pie with ice cream in one sitting like nobody else can. My love, I give you this ring. Wear it with love and joy. I choose you to be mine. I choose you to be my husband, to have and to hold from this day forward."

The thunderous sound of applause breaks the silence. I don't even recall the celebrant telling us we could kiss but Chase's lips on mine was the only thing that I wanted in this moment.

The day has gone by so quickly. They don't lie when people tell you that you literally won't remember parts of the day, and also about the fact that you never get time to eat. I'm absolutely starving.

I finally manage to get away from one of Chase's distant aunties and make my way towards the food table, when I'm stopped by someone grabbing my arm.

"It's speech time," Ally announces, pulling me.

Sighing internally, I make my way over to the awaiting microphone. I can hear my stomach gurgling loudly.

My dad, Ally and Mark all make their speeches, and of course, everyone laughs and sighs in all the right places.

Up next is Chase.

He moves into position behind the microphone, his eyes making contact with mine as I stand in the crowd, listening.

"Thank you to my new father-in-law for those kind words."

"On behalf of my new wife and I, I would like to thank you all for joining us on our special day. It means the world to us."

"This wedding couldn't have gone ahead without the love and support of our gorgeous maid of honour, Ally. Thank you for standing by my girl, none of this would have been possible without you. Thanks should also go to my best man, Mark. Thank you for making sure things ran smoothly today and for turning up at twelve-thirty, sober. There is, of course, an unwritten rule of wedding etiquette that states that nobody should look more handsome than the groom, and I'd like to thank Mark for sticking to that rule."

A rumble of laughter rings out across the room. My husband, the joker.

"Apparently, people say you don't marry someone you can live with, you marry someone that you can't live without, and, Raven, I couldn't even think about my life without you in it."

"My beautiful bride, you are the kindest, most thoughtful, selfless and supportive person I have ever met. You speak your heart and mind, you're honest and always know how to light up a room."

"Raven, you are my everything. I love you and I thank you for giving me the honour of becoming your husband."

"Cheers," Chase finishes, holding up his beer and tipping it gently towards our guests.

The whole crowd goes wild, and everyone cheers.

Chase steps away from the microphone and walks towards me. His eyes don't move from mine.

"Hello, my wife," he says, kissing me softly.

"Hello, my husband."

CHAPTER FIFTY-NINE

THE BRIDES SPEECH

Chase kisses me passionately and I hold his collar to prevent him from pulling away from me.

"Do you mind if I say a few quick words?" I ask, staring into Chase's eyes.

"Not at all, babe," Chase says, waving his hand towards the microphone.

Walking over, I tap the microphone lightly. People start to notice that I'm wanting to make a speech and they all turn back to listen to me.

"When I was just a little girl, I used to dream about my wedding day. I would think about the beautiful white dress, the gorgeous flowers, and of course, the delicious cake.

"At the same time, none of it would mean anything without my wonderful groom, our lovely friends, and our amazing families. All the material stuff is extra, but it is the people you love that make a special day like this so meaningful.

"There is a very important person missing today, but I know that she's watching down over us. Mum, I love you," I say softly, looking up at the sky.

Before I start crying, I move on. "I would like to give a special and heartfelt thank you to my beautiful maid of honour, Ally, for helping me with creating my dream wedding. Not only did you help me with the planning, you sat there through some of my bridezilla moments and did not run away screaming. Thank you for being so patient with me and for being there for me, especially today. I love you so much."

Ally waves from the crowd where she stands in Mark's arms. She blows me a kiss and I send her one right back.

"Thank you to our best man, Mark, thank you for getting my man here on time and for helping him get ready today."

Mark winks at me and raises his beer. My eyes drift to my husband. He's standing next to his parents who are just beaming with pride.

"Chase, I knew I loved you from the very first moment that I saw you. You have made me feel immeasurably happy, loved, and content, and I know this is only the beginning of our journey together as a married couple."

Chase stands, watching me intensely, his love for me almost shining out of him like a star.

"I would say that I can't wait for you to be the father of my children, but we won't have to wait as long as we thought."

Chase's eyes light up and he begins to move towards me, slowly. I can hear people start to whisper and a few shocked gasps from the crowd.

"Because I'm pregnant," I finally add.

The whole crowd is clapping and screaming wildly. My eyes don't stray from Chase, and I watch him as he literally shoves his beer into the closest person and moves towards me instantly. He picks me up and swings me around excitedly.

"Are you serious, my little bird?" he asks elatedly.

I nod quickly, a huge smile spreading across my face.

Chase's lips come to mine promptly and he kisses me longingly.

"How far? How long have you known?" he asks quickly after releasing my lips.

I remember back to when Ally exited the bathroom, holding the test in her hands.

"Well, what does it say?"

"You're…" Ally says, staring down at the stick.

Small tears start to well in the corners of my eyes. I'm not pregnant. I can feel my heart silently breaking in my chest.

"You're pregnant Raven," Ally finally says.

My eyes snap up to her from the floor, and my tears can no longer stay hidden. They stream down my face like a waterfall.

"Are you sure?" I sob, standing from the bed and moving towards Ally.

Ally turns the test around, and there, on the tiny little screen, I can see a tiny little three-plus sign.

"What does the three mean?" I ask, looking up at her confused. I know what the plus is for, clearly.

"It means you're over three weeks pregnant." Ally smiles, bringing me in for a hug. "Mine said that too."

"I'm not one hundred percent sure how far, but I am over three weeks. We will have to go to the hospital to check," I let Chase know.

He kisses me again quickly before we are swamped with people congratulating us.

I sense my dad behind me before I see him. I turn to face him and note the tears pricking at the corners of his eyes. Holding his arms out, I walk into them willingly. His embrace is both comforting and sad all at once. I can almost hear my mother's voice in my head, squealing with excitement.

"She would be so proud of you," my dad speaks softly into my hair.

Right at this moment, I can't get my words out, so I just cuddle into him a little more.

Our wedding day went by so quickly. I would have to say that it was by far the best day of my life.

For our honeymoon, we went off to Fiji for two weeks. My morning sickness put a little bit of a dampener on things, but we were just so excited to be pregnant again.

We went by the pack doctor the day after the wedding and found out that we were three and a half months pregnant. We had a little giggle when we found out because that means that I fell pregnant on our surprise holiday to Bora Bora.

I was a little shocked to find out that I was so far along and didn't have any other symptoms other than feeling tired—and now the morning sickness. It took its time to come on, not that I'm complaining, because I feel absolutely horrible.

Nine months generally goes by in the blink of an eye, but now that I'm pregnant, I feel like it's been forty years. My body is tired and I'm so over this huge boulder that's hanging off the front of me.

I'm pacing up and down the hall, willing this baby to decide on an exit plan. I'm three days overdue, but I feel like it's much longer.

Chase is in the kitchen, cooking me the hottest chilli he can. I demanded that he find a way to evacuate this baby before I rip his balls from his body.

Clearly, my pregnancy hormones have turned me into one scary bitch, but my back and pelvis just can't cope anymore.

Seeing Chase walk towards me, like a scared child towards a scary clown, I grip the bowl roughly and shovel the chilli into my mouth like a starving animal, praying that my water breaks after the first mouthful.

And… Nothing.

Angry, I place the bowl down a little too roughly, causing Chase to flinch as it bangs onto the table. I decide to head upstairs and take a shower.

The warm water running over me makes my body feel much calmer. I listen calmly to the sound of each drop falling from my body and onto the floor, swaying my hips a little to take the pressure off my swollen ankles.

Tired, I shut off the water and reach for a fluffy white towel. Drying myself, I grab a nighty and climb into bed, where Chase is already waiting for me.

Sleep seems to come easily to Chase, and soon, I hear his breathing change, knowing that he's now asleep.

Lately, my dreams have been wild and completely vivid, making it hard to sleep.

I move around for a while and finally find a comfortable spot.

Baby is kicking me aggressively, but I manage to fall into an unrestful sleep.

The bed is wet, and I wake and realize that my waters have broken. I tap Chase aggressively and he sits up and mumbles something about getting me a sandwich with tomatoes and Cheetos.

I giggle to myself before grasping my stomach as a huge contraction hits me.

"Ahhhhh."

Chase seems to realize something is up and is instantly awake.

We head over to the hospital, and after seven agonising hours of pushing, our baby arrives. I hold my hands out, waiting for my precious bundle to be handed over, when I see Ava walking away with our baby, smiling at me. I try to run after her, but my feet are stuck to the floor. I scream but no one seems to notice what's happening.

I wake, breathing harshly, my body covered in sweat.

Realizing that it was just a dream, I lay back and rub my hands over my still swollen belly.

Feeling the need to pee, yet again, I climb out of bed and waddle towards the toilet. I'm not even halfway back to bed when a huge gush of water floods the floor.

"Chase," I scream loudly.

Chase sits up, looking around, worried. His eyes meet mine and then look down at the floor.

"My water just broke," I yell excitedly.

CHAPTER SIXTY

OUR PUP

With worried eyed Chase follows my hospital bed. "I'm right here, my little bird," Chase calls to me. He's holding my hand and trying to keep up as I'm rushed down the narrow hallways of the pack hospital. The lights on the roof rush past like car headlights on a busy freeway.

Another contraction rolls over my body and I hold my breath, hoping that it will help the pain. We had stayed at home until they had become more aggressive. Chase had run me a bath, and I lay there relaxed and breathing gently whilst the first of many contractions hit my body.

When they became too hard to handle, I noticed the look on Chase's face and understood how hard it must be for him to see me in such pain. When he couldn't handle watching me anymore, he lifted me from the bath, wrapped me in a robe and carried me gently down to the car.

The nurses are all so wonderful. They are excited to be a part of the birth of their alpha's first born child. We had decided early on not to find out the sex of the baby. I liked the idea of a surprise, and so did Chase.

The pain only seems to be getting worse, and soon, I feel the need to push.

The nurses call for the doctor to come down to check over me.

The second the doctor sits down on the stool at the end of the bed, a loud growl erupts from my husband.

The doctor holds his hands up in the air defensively and gives him a stern look.

"Alpha, I have to check how far along Raven is, sir," the doctor replies cautiously.

"I'm sorry, doc, I can't help it, Quinn is going absolutely wild at the thought of what you're about to do," Chase counters, almost embarrassed.

"It's all part of the job," the doctor replies, smiling and sending me a wink.

This action, of course, sends Chase almost off the edge and I have to hold his hand tightly so that he doesn't send the doctor flying to the other side of the hospital.

Chase moves back to my side, having stepped a few paces towards the doctor. He slowly sits down on the chair next to me. His hand never leaves mine.

"I'm so sorry, Ray," Chase says, leaning forward and placing a light kiss on my forehead.

I give him one of my very best death stares. "The doctor is here to help me and you're distracting him and threatening to kill him isn't helping," I snap just before another huge contraction takes over my whole body.

Each contraction hits my body like a wave at the beach, each one causing a burning sensation to rip through my abdomen. I call out loudly and grip the sheets, praying that this will all be over soon.

"It's almost time," the doctor says, looking up at us.

I look over at Chase. "I need to sit up on my knees," I plead after the last contraction finally subsides.

Chase helps me to manoeuvre myself into a more comfortable position. I end up leaning over the back of the bed—which is sitting upright. My knees are spread slightly apart on the bed.

Chase is rubbing the pads of my feet which somehow helps with the pain I'm feeling.

"I feel like I need to push," I call out again.

The doctor checks again and lets me know that it's safe for me to begin pushing.

Moving away from the job of rubbing my feet so that the doctor can be in the right position, Chase seems suddenly lost.

He begins rubbing my back gently, and it feels so nice.

I feel like I've been pushing for hours when it's only been thirty minutes. Each contraction calls for another four tries to push, and with each one, I hold my breath and count to ten.

Unexpectedly, the doctor calls, "Stop, Raven, don't push anymore."

"What's wrong?" Chase calls, standing from the bed in a panic.

I'm too tired to move, and I lay my head on the bed and wait. These few moments of rest are what I need. My eyes close and I slow my breathing.

"The heads out now," the doctor answers.

A sigh escapes my body. Just a little more to go.

Raising my head back up from the bed, a sense of determination takes over my tired body.

The sound of a small cry pierces the silence of the room. The sound instantly resonates with my heart. My baby is here. I hear Chase let out a small sob from behind me, but I'm just too tired to move.

Cheers can be heard around the room. Our baby is finally here, the pack has been waiting for such a long time for a new baby to be born into the alpha line.

With the help of a nurse, I slowly turn over and relax against the back of the bed. My body is beyond exhausted.

Chase has our new bundle over at the weigh station, and the nurses are fussing—wiping the baby down, weighing, measuring and writing things down.

I watch him as he stands there, watching over our new bundle. I can literally sense so much love and adoration coming from him. It's leaking out of him like an overflowing pot of water.

As if he senses that I'm watching him, he looks up and our eyes meet.

"What is it?" I ask. "A boy or a girl?"

CHAPTER SIXTY-ONE

OUR LITTLE FAMILY

The nurses wrap our baby, handing the tiny bundle to Chase. He walks over to me ever so slowly, like he is carrying the most precious gem in the world and he is scared of dropping it. He gently places the baby into my arms. The new coverings are wrapped so tightly, there's no way for me to check the sex.

I start to cry, my tears streaming down my face.

"What's wrong, baby?" Chase coos, looking a little panicked.

"No one will tell me if it's a boy or girl. Is there something wrong?" I sob, looking down at the beautiful little person sleeping soundly in my arms.

"It's a beautiful baby girl," Chase says, running his hands over my hair.

I look up at him through my tears and cry even harder.

"Oh, baby, please don't cry." Chase sighs, shifting closer to me on the bed. "What's wrong?"

"I'm just so happy," I sob.

Chase's face softens and the stress-wrinkles in his forehead slowly melt away.

"Me too, my Luna," he replies, kissing my forehead and then kissing our very own beautiful baby girl.

"What's her name?" asks a nearby nurse.

I look up, not realising that we still had people in the room all around us. I'm in absolute bliss sitting here with my mate and our baby that I had totally forgotten about all of the nurses and doctors.

I smile and remember back to when we first started discussing baby names. Chase was positive that it was going to be a boy, so he had quickly decided that he wanted the baby's name to be Zavier.

The girl's name, on the other hand, we could never agree on. We had a few on a list but I never really had any connections to them.

I look up at Chase and then back down at our beautiful girl.

"You choose anything you want, baby," Chase says, reaching out to touch the baby's cheek.

I think about it for a moment. I want to include my mum in her name, somehow. I finally announce, "I would like everyone to meet Aria Rose Williams."

The first few weeks of being parents went by with sleepless nights, crying and sore nipples. I felt like a cow, and the lack of sleep was hitting me hard, but we were in heaven. Aria is a complete joy.

Returning from the kitchen, I walk down the hall quietly, peeking through Aria's bedroom door. Inside, I see Chase sitting in my rocking chair, holding onto Aria like she's the most precious thing on earth.

"I'm the luckiest man in the whole world," he coos to her. "Your mumma is the most beautiful Luna in the whole universe, and you, my princess, look exactly like your mumma."

I smile and walk as quietly as I can back to bed.

Chase soon returns to bed and lays next to me. I shift my body, placing my head on his chest.

"How did I get so lucky?" Chase breathes out a sigh of contentment.

"We are both very lucky," I reply, placing a kiss quickly on his lips. I lay back against his chest, falling into an easy sleep, listening to the rhythm of his heart.

Ally and Mark's baby arrived the day after Aria. A beautiful baby boy named Cohen. Ally and I have our fingers crossed that our babies may be mates when they first shift in sixteen years' time.

The months fly by, and soon, it's New Year's Eve. Chase and I organised a babysitter for Aria so that we could head out for the night. It feels like we haven't had a date night in months. Even if it is going to be a double date. Ally and Mark have sent Haylie and Cohen off to Mark's parents for the night and invited us around for dinner.

It's a little less crazy than what we would have normally opted for, but we are responsible parents now.

I'm a little reluctant to say goodbye to Aria, but Chase convinces me that she is going to be fine and that we will be home before I know it.

Walking into her bedroom, my eyes gaze over the tiny human that I created. She is perfect. My hand rests on the edge of her cot. Her little chest rises and lowers with each tiny breath that she takes. I can feel my heart swelling with pride. I just want to scoop her into my arms and never let her go.

Sighing, I reach down gently, running my hand over her cheek. She doesn't move but lets out a small squeak-like sound, making me smile.

"Let's go, little bird," Chase calls to me from the doorway. "The babysitter is here."

My mum-guilt hits me hard. I stifle a sob as I turn and walk away from her. We climb into the car and head over to Ally and Mark's, but I think I left my heart behind in the cot.

We arrive at Ally and Mark's place shortly after.

"Mark, we forgot the wine," I hear Ally call just as we open up the front door.

"Lucky I brought some then," I call back loudly, walking down the hall.

"Ahh, what would we do without you, Ray?" Mark says, giving me a side hug and kissing my cheek, all whilst taking the bottle of wine from me.

"One bottle?" Ally says, poking her head out of the kitchen. "Let's see how long that lasts," she adds, snickering.

Ally made an absolutely beautiful roast dinner with all of the trimmings. I'll almost have to roll home at this rate.

As predicted, the bottle of wine doesn't even last us through dinner. Ally sends the boys off to the shop to get more. I'm a little concerned that the shops won't be open, being New Year's Eve, but Ally calls ahead to check and the shop attendant says that this is their busiest day, so they aren't going to close until eleven p.m.

The trip into town takes a while, so Ally and I decide to wash up the dishes. I wash and Ally dries. We chat away as we work. We haven't been able to catch up as much as we would have liked with having a brand-new bubba each. We still talk everyday though over the phone.

Suddenly, a very scared voice breaks into my mind. "Raven, the baby," the voice calls before fading quickly.

The plate that I'm holding slips from my fingers, and hitting the floor, it shatters into small pieces.

"Ray, what's up? You're suddenly a butter fingers?" Ally jokes, touching my shoulder.

I turn quickly and rush towards the door. "Something has happened to Aria," I scream back at a very confused looking Ally.

"Call Chase, NOW!" I yell before shifting and running towards my house.

CHAPTER SIXTY-TWO

I WILL LOVE YOU FOREVER

The wind ripples over my fur as I sprint as fast as my legs can carry me towards our house. I feel as though my leg muscles will tear from the speed I'm running at.

The words, "Raven, the baby," ring in my ears, terrorising me.

Akira whines in my mind. Her anguish seeps out through my skin like sweat. I feel like I'm in a dream, where I am running but not actually getting anywhere.

The house comes into view and I skid through the door, which stands ajar. My eyes instantly land on a body lying on the floor. I can hear the steady heartbeat. Rushing forward, I shift and quickly check on the unconscious babysitter.

I slowly touch her face and she comes around.

She instantly goes into defence mode and starts swiping and slashing at me.

"It's me," I scream, watching her quickly stop and grasp onto my forearms.

"He took the baby," she sobs. "He stabbed me with a needle," she adds, moving her hand up to her neck. "I tried to save her."

I nod, not trusting my voice. Looking around, suddenly, a familiar smell hits my nose. I hadn't noticed it at first because it is so familiar to me. Even though I haven't smelt the scent for quite some time, it is one that will stick with me forever.

Cody.

I shift angrily and follow his scent. I haven't seen him since the day Ava died. So many thoughts are running through my brain. Why has he taken away my baby? Is he going to hurt her?

Pain rips through my body at the mere thought of losing Aria.

I realize after running for some time that I have now exited my territory and entered my father's pack lands.

The wind begins to sting my nose. I'm running so fast.

As I expected, the scent leads me to the lake. I shift and look around frantically.

There, under our tree, sits Cody, his back against the harsh bark. I stare at him, watching him holding my baby in his arms, rocking her gently.

He looks so at peace with her.

Unsure of his intentions, I try to decide whether to announce myself or just try my best to get in-between Cody and the water.

My only thought is that he brought her here to drown her. To our special place. To take my baby from me so that I would feel pain. He wants me to hurt because I caused him to lose his mate.

Hearing me, Cody's eyes snap up to mine. He's been crying.

I watch as his eyes move from mine back down to Aria. His hand moves up gently, using his sleeve to wipe away his tears.

322

I shift closer but don't make any large movements, so as not to startle him. Aria is sleeping peacefully in his arms.

"She's so beautiful," Cody announces, breaking the silence.

"Please don't hurt her," I beg, taking two steps closer.

Cody stands and his eyes lock with mine, noticing my panic.

"Hurt her?" he asks, looking at me as if he's wounded that I would even suggest such a thing.

I watch as he takes a step forwards, towards the water.

The only thing standing between my baby and the lake is me.

"I'm not going to hurt her," Cody says quietly, taking a step backwards.

I step forward, worried he's going to run with her.

Unexpectedly, he moves to the side, and for the first time, I notice a pram sitting next to the tree. Cody places Aria gently in the pram and puts a blanket neatly around her to keep her warm.

My shoulders slump knowing that he's now put Aria down.

Cody then turns and calmly walks towards me.

Unsure of his intentions, I take a step back.

I watch as hurt runs across Cody's face.

"You know I would never hurt you, right?" Cody asks, reaching out to touch my hand. The memory of the day we had a race back home and I fell, hurting myself, rushes to the forefront of my mind.

I almost scoff. He had promised me that so long ago, yet here we are.

"You broke my heart," I cry before covering my mouth with my hands, not meaning to say that.

"I know," he says, frowning. "I didn't want to be with Ava, I wanted to be with you."

I stay silent.

"It's always been you," he adds, stepping forward, taking my hands in his.

"I'm so sorry, can you forgive me, Raven?"

"You have just stolen my baby," I growl, snatching my hands from his.

Again, hurt spreads over his face as he takes a step back from me.

"I wanted us to be a family. I took her so we can be together."

"Can't you understand that what you did is crazy?" I reply, throwing my words at him.

Finally, realization seeps across his face and he steps back, his hand moving over his heart. His eyes search mine. The way he is looking at me feels so familiar. He walks towards me, wrapping me up in a hug.

I just stand there with my arms by my side. I take in a deep breath as he wriggles his chin into my shoulder and takes a deep breath in my hair. He is different in this moment. Almost damaged. I have heard stories about wolves who have lost their mate sometimes not being able to focus properly. Because you have lost your other half.

"Please can you forgive me?" Cody begs.

I can feel the hurt and pain in his words.

I need to do something, say something.

"Cody, I loved you so much, you were my forever, mate or not, but then you went and chose Ava over me," I pause, waiting for his reply to come, but one never does. "I love Chase. I'm with Chase now," I speak desperately.

Cody doesn't let me go; he just continues to hold me.

His arms feel so familiar and so comforting. I miss him, I miss what we used to be—'best friends forever'—that is what we promised each other.

"I'm so sorry, Raven," Cody finally speaks as he lets me go.

"I'll always love you; my mate's pull was too strong. I never loved Ava the way that I love you and I gave you up too easily. You were my whole world, Raven, and I needed to be stronger and choose you, but I didn't, and I will forever regret that decision." He breathes out loudly, placing his hand on his forehead as if he is confused.

Silence fills the small space between us.

"I will wait for you. It will always be you, Raven," Cody says, stepping back from me.

He stands for a moment, watching me. The look in his eyes makes my breath halt in my throat.

That look is how he looked at me before. Before Ava. Before my parents decided to keep us apart. My memories of the times we spent together begin to flood my mind. I loved this man. I loved him with all my heart.

Staring into his eyes, a small sob breaks through my lips. How did we end up like this?

"I loved you," I breathe. "I loved you and you broke me."

Running his hand down my cheek, he sighs. "I know." He grasps both sides of my face and gently kisses my lips.

He brings me back to his chest and I go willingly. "I will forever regret the day I found Ava. She might have been my fated mate, but you will always be the mate I would have chosen for myself."

Tilting my head up to look at him, my eyes search his face.

"The mate pull is strong, and there were so many times when I just wanted to run to you." He sighs.

"I have Chase," I breathe.

"I know." He breathes, leaning forward and kissing my forehead. "It's okay."

I love Chase with all of my being, but right now, in this moment, my feelings for Cody rush to the surface like a bubble underwater.

"I will always want this." He sighs, kissing my hair. "I will always love you."

Hearing a sound in the forest, he suddenly releases me.

Looking into my eyes, he whispers, " I love you, Raven."

He shifts and runs off through the forest, towards Alpha Sam's lands.

I breathe out quickly, not knowing what to do with his admission and with my sudden surge of feelings.

Realizing I haven't taken a breath, my lungs scream painfully. Seconds pass and I run to the pram where Aria lays peacefully, sleeping.

Behind me, a ruckus erupts from the bushes around the lake. Pack members pop out like daisies in a field. I see Chase in his wolf form, running at me so quickly I'm sure he's going to run straight through me. He shift mid-stride and collides with me, his hands grasping my shoulders, checking me over desperately.

"Where's Aria? Are you okay? What happened? Where's Cody? I'm going to tear him to shreds," Chase speaks quickly, looking around.

"He's gone," I reply, watching his face. His eyes meet mine and then glance down at our sleeping daughter.

I see my father is standing over her protectively. He looks up at me, our eyes connected. I watch as he nods slightly. He knows what happened.

I explain everything to Chase quietly. My father listens to our conversation. Chase's face contorts and I can sense anger rolling off him each time I mention Cody's name.

Chase could never understand my feelings for Cody.

We aren't meant to love anyone else but our mate. The Moon Goddess didn't make us that way.

But I did. I loved Cody with all my being.

He was meant to be my forever. I love Chase dearly but a small place in my heart will always love Cody.

"He really loves you, doesn't he?" Chase asks, clearly trying to keep the sting out of his voice.

"Yes," I breathe.

YEARS GO BY

The back-door crashes open so loudly that it causes me to jump and look up from my book.

Our—now—nineteen-year-old Aria storms past me. Making her way upstairs, she slams her bedroom door so hard that I think it's going to fly off its hinges.

I sigh, placing my head into my palms. Aria has been acting so strangely over the last few weeks.

A small sound makes me suddenly look up to see our fifteen-year-old son, Zavier, stealing an apple from the fruit bowl.

"It's nearly dinner time," I say as I stand and make my way towards him. Just as I reach him, he smirks at me and quickly runs out the back door, making it slam loudly, again.

"You look just like your dad when you do that," I call out to him, watching him disappear down the driveway.

"Who looks like me? What's up with Aria? I heard her banging my doors again," Chase asks, wandering into the kitchen and wrapping his arms around my waist.

"I'll go check." I sigh, kissing his lips longingly. Chase's hands slide from my hips as I walk away. I instantly want to move back into them, missing his warmth.

I softly pad up the stairs and prepare to serve my best mum advice. I bet anything that she's had another fight with that stupid girl Alesha. I did warn her not to go near her. Any offspring of Sarah's needs to be avoided.

I reach the door and gently turn the knob. The door creaks slightly as it swings open, and I recall just how annoying that sound was when Aria was a baby and we tried to sneak out of her room whilst she was sleeping.

Peering in, I find my baby girl lying face down on her bed, crying gently into her pillow.

I walk slowly over to her bed and sit down gently, making the bed creek slightly under me.

Aria turns over and wipes her nose on her sleeve in the most unladylike manner.

I stare at her and hold out my arms to her.

She moves willingly into my arms and begins crying into my shoulder.

"What's wrong, my girl?" I coo as I run my hands down her hair.

"I don't know what to do, Mum," Aria sobs.

"Why don't you tell me the problem and we can talk about it?" I suggest, kissing her head lovingly.

Aria sits back and looks deep into my eyes.

"You know how we have a mate?" she asks, looking away from my eyes and down at the floor.

I nod, uncertain about where this is going.

"You found your mate?" I yell, jumping up from the bed.

"No, no, Mum, sit down. I didn't find my mate."

Disappointed, I sit back down on the bed, hoping that Chase hasn't heard me.

I expect him to burst through the door any second, demanding to know who he was, so he can bury him alive.

"So, what's this about then?" I say as I wipe a stray tear from her cheek.

"I've fallen in love with someone," Aria says so fast it's like an exploding balloon going off in her bedroom.

"Who is it?" I ask, looking at her, willing her to meet my eyes.

Looking up at me, tears start to form in her eyes.

"He's not my mate, Mum, but I love him… I really love him." She bawls loudly like she's trying to make herself believe that everything's going to be okay.

Shocked, I look down at her and words fail to exit my mouth.

Aria starts crying, placing her hands over her face, my silence clearly upsetting her.

"Oh no, baby, it's okay."

"You're not mad?" she asks, looking back up at me.

I sigh and lay back on the bed. Aria curls into me and lays her head on my shoulder.

I think back to my past. I haven't seen Cody since that day by the lake. But I think of him often… he will always be my first love.

"Boy, do I have a story for you," I start, thinking back. Aria lays still against my shoulder. Her silence wills me to continue on with my story.

"I once knew a girl who fell in love with someone who wasn't her mate," I speak quietly.

"He loved her … and she loved him back…"

About the Author

Rebecca Pratt lives in Melbourne Victoria, and was married to her husband James, in 2015. Her son Spencer arrived in January 2018 and in July 2018, Rebecca was diagnosed with stage three breast cancer.

Another Wolf's Mate was a world she chose to escape the horrors of chemotherapy, multiple surgeries and radiation.

She is a primary school teacher and loves writing fiction. She has three more works in the process. Keep your eyes open for their release!

Facebook - Author Rebecca Pratt
Instagram - authorrebeccapratt
TikTok - @rebeccapratt88

www.ingramcontent.com/pod-product-compliance
Lightning Source LLC
Chambersburg PA
CBHW020327120726
47904CB00002B/314